TALES OF REAL AND DREAM WORLDS

BART STEWART

For everyone at MeadowHaven,

—Bart Stewart

Tales of Real and Dream Worlds

ISBN 0-9785817-0-9

FIRST PRINTING

Paper View Books
678 Loughton Street
Las Vegas, NV 89178

Email the author at
bartstew@aol.com

The web site for this author
premieres summer of 2006

WWW.BARTSTEWART.COM

TALES OF REAL AND DREAM WORLDS

CONTENTS

THEATER ON THE AIR

The great jack-o-lantern sat precariously on the brick chimney top. Weeks of dry-rotting that had curled his fangs into his grinning maw had also curved the top of his head forward, shifting his center of gravity and causing him to rock slightly in the late evening winds. He looked out over a darkening scene of hilly, newly harvested corn and peanut fields, scuppernong vineyards and pumpkin patches, and a simple network of unpaved roads that connected white frame houses, similar to his own. This night had high, thin cloud sheets that hung motionless, aglow with the moon and the Milky Way. It was the night before Halloween, 1938.

A strong, sustained blast of wind nudged him sharply forward, and his softened, top-heavy head folded over, the corners of his smile cracking out rottenly, wider and wider. Over and off his perch he went, landing with a horrific bang on the tin roof, before rolling off and thudding ominously, face up in the shrubbery.

Minutes passed, and the front door of the house eased open. A stout black woman with curlers in her hair and a shotgun in her hands stepped onto the porch. Remaining behind her in the doorway, a rotund white matron stood with fingertips pressed nervously to her lips, her eyes wide with apprehension as she peered out.

"If you want some of this shot, just show yourself ..." Miss Clarice Greene called out into the empty yard, the gun up and at the ready. The two women checked their surroundings thoroughly from the porch, but detected no sound or sign of movement. Neither of them noticed the grinning perpetrator in the hedge.

"All right then!" Clarice yelled, "I got two barrels of this good buckshot here for you. You want some, you just come on back!" She gave the dark yard one more long look, and stepped back inside.

Her employer, Mrs. Ivy Rutherford, had gone to the wall niche that held the family's mammoth nineteenth century Bible. Her pudgy right hand rested here, as her left hand covered her eyes and forehead and her lips fluttered through an inaudible prayer. Some minutes later, when she was finished, she turned away and went to rejoin Clarice in the kitchen.

"This terrible, terrible time of year ..." Ivy said, "Those evil, awful boys are going to be a-throwin' things at this house and tormenting us all night long, just like last year. I do not know what we're going to do if they break out a window! We absolutely cannot have any extra expenses! Lord, I wish Farrell would get home. What if they break into the shed and bust it up, or start a fire or something? You know they're coming back."

"They can sure hold some of that shot, too." Clarice stated. She dipped out two big ice cream scoops full of lard, and dropped them into an iron skillet. As it heated she took up her formidable butcher knife and went to work with a special zeal on the puny, forlorn-looking plucked fryer on the cutting board.

Ivy said, "What I am most worried about is how those hooligans might affect Ephram. He might get influenced by 'em. He's only six. He might want to be that way when he grows up."

Clarice had to wonder about this woman saying, "What I am most worried about ..." Worrying was about all she did – How could she have only one, preeminent worry? As it was, Clarice only said, "He seems to do pretty much as he pleases. I can't see that anybody's going to influence him."

From down the hall they could hear Ephram singing You Must Have Been a Beautiful Baby, a recent hit that he had memorized from the radio. They heard him clattering around in something, opening and closing the bureau he had been told to stay out of. Soon his footsteps were running down the hall toward them, and then with a prolonged swishing sound, he was sliding on the hardwood floor in the sock feet of his pajamas.

Ivy had slumped over the table with her forehead in her hand by the time he popped around the doorway, yelling out, "But Baby look atchoo nnnoowww!!"

Ivy sat up with a start, and said, "Ephram! Come here to me!" He shuffled over, in the baggy, faded blue pajamas that he had been growing into for a long time now. He made eye contact with his mother, but only briefly, as he sensed he might be in trouble.

"Why do you always have to sing such awful songs? Why can't you sing one of your Sunday school songs?" she asked. He just looked around the kitchen, letting his eyes wander among the various odd knickknacks and mysterious ornate containers.

"Ephram, what has Mama told you about sliding across that floor like that? Do you not remember that terrible splinter you got in your foot?"

Ephram thought of a response to that, if he could get it out through his sudden excitement, "Th-those splinters are not up on this end of the hall! Those are only down the hall a-ways, Mama!"

"So there are absolutely no splinters on this end of the hall, right? Not one splinter." He shook his head, and Ivy bellowed out, "You don't know where every splinter is in that hall! I want you to stop slippin' and slidin' across that floor, you hear me? And look here ... What have you got on your mouth? Let me see! Is that chocolate? ... Have you been into them chocolate pumpkins!?"

He frantically cast about for an excuse, but ended up only stammering. She met his clear, alert little eyes with her own, baggy, yellowed, and dull with anger and exasperation. Finally, he said, meekly, "I thought we should test one."

She never could sustain any anger with him, no matter how he misbehaved. Where he was concerned, vexation escaped from her like air from a worn out tire - no pressure ever developed. She knew she was this way, and Ivy also knew that he understood it and took advantage of it.

Ephram had not been her first child. That little boy had perished before Ephram was born, in this very house, on the very bed where both children had been born. Ephram was a virtual look-alike of his lost brother, except that child had been frailer, not as healthy over all. And how this house had rang with his cries before he slipped away. The sound had been nearly identical to Ephram's the time he slid his pajama covered foot onto the wooden snag.

Ivy said, "I know one thing. You are going to sit right there and eat every bit of that supper tonight. I mean every bite of them collards and peas, too. Lordy! I wish your father would get home!"

"Yes ma'am," he said, humbly, and stood silently by for a moment. He then stepped softly into the center of the kitchen, and when both women had returned to their private thoughts, he whipped out the sparkler pistol he had hidden under his pajamas. The women jumped as he yelled out, "I gotcha!" and the gun went vrrrrr! vrrrrrr!

Clarice hollered, "All right! That's a whuppin'!"

He dashed down the hall, as she went stomping off after him. Ivy returned her forehead to her hand, and sat gazing at her reflection in the dark panes of the kitchen window.

Some time later she was in much the same position, as the three of them were seated for dinner. Clarice offered the grace, and Ephram said, "Ain't we waitin' for Daddy?"

Ivy said, "We are not sitting up all night waiting for your Daddy, no. You need to eat that supper and be getting on to bed here pretty soon ... I want to see that whole plate clean, too."

She had a slight cracking to her voice as she spoke, as if she might cry. She would cry, sometimes, and Ephram would be quiet and well behaved for its duration.

There was no talking during this solemn meal, except once when Ivy pointed out some bits of edible matter left on Ephram's chicken bone. She returned to looking at the window, and thinking about how she would handle it when her husband, Farrell, finally made it home. He was late enough right now that she would have to say something to him about it. She was duty-bound to do that much.

Clarice also watched the window while she ate. Still no headlights, not even on the far distant main road. She had to decide where she would be spending the night tonight -- here, or at the residence she kept with her aunt in the little black neighborhood a mile away. The paved roads between the two communities were long and circuitous, but the well-worn footpath through the woods was a straight shot. On nights with enough moon she went that way, if she felt like going home. In all the years she had walked the footpath, no one had ever bothered her. But she had her derringer in her pocketbook just in case, and often daydreamed of dispatching some cretin with it.

It occurred to her that if Mr. Rutherford was much longer in getting home she would have to stay and help Ivy, who would be in a heartbroken state. Clarice decided then that she would stay anyway, as the Rutherfords had a fine radio, and after they had their fight would most likely sit and listen to it a while tonight.

Neither woman looked at Ephram or appreciated the expression of martyrdom he wore as he struggled against the vomit reflex to eat his collards. At least they had some trace of hamhock flavor. Not so the peas. Those dark, waxy, detestable little green balls were utterly contaminated with a taste from the plant kingdom. Sweet tea, along with heavy hits of butter and salt, made the vegetables just barely edible. With a heavy heart, he saw that he had several forkloads left to go.

He tried to concentrate on the reward that waited at the end of it all: the red frosted cupcake that sat in plain view on a saucer on the counter. It was topped off with the wooden Mickey Mouse-head cake decoration that was always saved and washed to be placed on top of Ephram's dessert. Always. If he was really lucky his father would come home pretty quick and say he could stay up and listen to some radio.

Suddenly, headlights streaked into sight on the road. The three diners watched silently as the car approached. It was only when the faltering sound of the engine reached them that they could be sure it was the Nash. It came in off the road at a sluggish pace and made a wide arc toward its usual parking place in the yard next to an oak tree. The arc was a bit too wide tonight, though, and the left side of the vehicle wedged audibly against the tree.

He sat with his hands on the wheel, knowing they had seen him crunch the car, knowing they knew he had been drinking, and knowing too that another wall-shaking row with his wife could well be waiting for him when he walked in. He just sat still with the engine running. He sat for a minute more before turning the headlamps off.

Farrell sure did not feel like getting in to it with that woman tonight. After drinking homemade wine with his co-workers, he had somehow skipped the feel-good part and gone directly to the hangover. Maybe this meant he would wake up in the morning feeling high, he thought to himself, with a grim smile.

He knew that any real fight would be initiated by him and be poorly resisted by her. But she would make the fight unavoidable, with a ceaseless bemoaning of some triviality; her vocal gloom was the background sound of their home.

Rarely did they make love anymore, even though she was still physically appealing enough to him. Apparently he, or sex itself, was repellent to her. Whenever the moment came that he was ready to make love, her usual downcast mood deepened, and it would be obvious that she had no such desire. She spoke sometimes of the woman's Christian duty to serve her husband and bring forth children into the world, and how in her case the duty had been long since fulfilled. He had been ordained as a Baptist minister and was aware of a Biblical basis for only just so much of her sanctimonious airs. It was something else they fought about.

The fighting had been getting worse in recent weeks, and he sensed their troubles were coming to a head. Would tonight be the big blow up? Their marriage was wrecked and had been for years. They were staying together for the kid.

To Farrell it seemed inevitable they should start thinking about separation, although the idea was like poison to him in many ways. He looked at their simple one story frame house, and the mostly harvested one acre garden behind it. He was living week to week and just skirting foreclosure as it was. The house would have to be sold.

This house was never meant to be more than a temporary set up. It was funny to him how such a plain looking structure could be so emotionally evocative, as if there were something special about its very coordinates in space. It was the eight years' encrustation of memories that affected him now, looking at the old place in the moonlight.

The magnolia tree by the road with the low branch had been his place for a private cry the day he lost his church. The cause had not been scandal or fire, but all the worse from his viewpoint, simple lack of interest. He had put too much emphasis on his message, and not enough on location. This area already had enough churches to accommodate all who wished to attend. His attempt at a new start-up had never drawn more than a very few people. What a personally dark day that had been for him when he finally saw that his best effort was not going to be met with success.

He had been sitting with a friend from the Bible College in this very car, parked right here, but a little further from the oak, when he was told that the extended Baptist family had located a job for him. It was clean, safe office work, too, with a local tobacco warehousing firm. It was about as menial as clean work got. But he considered it temporary when he took it, just something until he could get another store front and get to work at building a congregation again. And how long ago had that been? How many years of being thankful for having some kind of a job?

He had been at work on the day his first son was mortally injured playing in the neighbor's field across the road. Only five years old, the boy had been kicked by a stallion. The acreage was now weedy and had been long up for sale. The people at work had granted him half a day off that following day, and then the full day of the funeral.

Neither he nor Ivy were the same afterwards, but Ivy had been the most changed by it. In his case, he simply never had time to come to terms with it. No sooner was the kid in the ground than it was back to shipping and receiving, bills of lading, logging of evaluations, railroad and auction schedules, and the wolf at the door. Maybe in a way it had been for the best. Maybe if he had been home all day with it like Ivy he would not have held up so well either. As it was, he was confronted with it only in the evenings, when he sought to relax in the porch swing that directly faced the spot of the tragedy. The swing was soon taken down, and now swung from a sturdy bough on the other side of the oak from where he was now parked.

Ivy's second pregnancy had followed the death by scant months, and by that oppressive summer of 1932 a listlessness had set in on her that never fully lifted. He would come home to find no housework done, Ivy sitting in the stifling house, fanning herself and poring over the Bible. Their serious quarreling began in those days.

It had seemed then that as their private lives were breaking down, the world around them was on a similar course. Hobos and drifters, like an army on the march, filed down that road daily, begging for work or hand-outs. He was in constant fear that one of them would attack Ivy while he was at work. It came as a blessing in disguise then, the day that Clarice had appeared on the road.

He would never forget her gaunt, haggard look that day. She was barefoot and wore a homemade garment that looked like it had been made from a bed sheet. She trudged along the road past the Rutherfords as they sat on their porch snapping green beans. She carefully avoided looking at them as she made her way down the baking red dirt track. But as she neared the far edge of their yard, something stopped her. She put a hand on her hip, turned toward them, and in a voice both weary and irritated called out, "Y'all got any washin' need done?"

He had answered her as he did all the nomads on the road, "Got no work."

But Ivy had astonished him by yelling out, "Oh yes we do!" And she was up and out at the roadside for an on-the-spot negotiation with the woman. That first day had been some long overdue cleaning and straightening of the house in exchange for a dinner, a dollar, and a couple of dresses Ivy could no longer squeeze into. But within the week Clarice had an arrangement of room and board and four dollars a week for her services. It had meant considerable scaling back of their budget, but the necessity of it became clear soon enough.

The place became livable with some housework getting done. And Farrell felt more secure knowing Ivy was not alone all day. The arrangement had a discernable effect on Ivy's disposition that he appreciated, although the two women often had a conspiratorial air that could be rather maddening to him. By the time in the fall of that year that he came home to find she had midwifed at Ephram's birth, Clarice had cemented a place for herself in their home.

Their home, he thought to himself, such that it is. He shoved open the massive car door, climbed out, and had a long stretch. He would be able to think better, and feel a little better, with some food in him. He crossed their patchy, unkempt yard and opened the front door. He could hear Ivy yell out, "Your daddy's home, Ephram!" and then the sound of the boy's chair sliding away from the table, and little shoeless feet running across the kitchen floor toward the hall.

Father and son exchanged their customary greeting hug, wordlessly on this particular night. Mr. Rutherford bent over, rather than squatting down, and the blood vessels in his head began knocking and pounding. He found himself pushing up from the boy's shoulders to return to an upright stance.

With his usual exuberance, Ephram announced, "We're having fried chicken again, Daddy! I have just about finished mine! I-I could go and find some music for you on the radio!"

Just for the amusement of watching his reaction, Farrell asked the boy if he was sure he knew how to work it, and Ephram became almost indignant. The two walked hand in hand back to the kitchen, Ephram offering every assurance that he could "do" the radio.

"Good evenin', Reverend." Clarice said, stacking plates in the sink.

"Ladies ..." he replied, "Ahhh! Good to be home! We were going over some new procedures at work. Dull stuff, Eph! You get a better job than Daddy's when you grow up."

"Yes sir," Ephram said, then informed his mother, "Daddy says I can find some music on the radio for us tonight."

Ivy busied herself fixing a plate of re-warmed food. Looking at Farrell, she addressed the boy, "Just so you're not up too late. You don't want to get bags under your eyes." Turning to her son, she added, "There ain't nothing going on in this house, or on that radio worth stayin' up for, young man."

She approached her husband with the bright red glass plate that held his dinner. She said, "How you feeling?" as she set it in front of him. Then she silently sniffed him, sniffed again loud enough for him to hear, and turned away, muttering something in a singsong tone of strained patience.

She was startled to hear his gravelly voice behind her, "What did you just say?"

Ivy rattled together some plates and saucers and didn't answer him, and he said, sharply, "Did you just say something about 'worm of the still' ...?"

She made no reply, and Clarice said, "Ephram, let's put your cupcake on a tray, and you can eat it in front of the radio. Come on now."

Ephram said loudly, "Yeah, 'cause I won't get no crumbs on the floor." He looked from one parent to the other, then quietly got up and followed the maid out of the kitchen. He heard the sound of his father bolting to his feet, his chair raking backward and the table jolting forward. A livid cry boiled out, "I am not going to hear that self-righteous sass in my house!" The whiny reply his mother made faded as he plodded down the hall.

Ephram lay on a throw rug in the parlor, and listened to his father's voice boom and rage from the kitchen. The words were not always distinct to him, but most of the statements ended with the words "my house." Ephram took out his tin Buck Rogers Rocket Police Patrol Ship from under the radio and swept it in long arcs before him on its little black rubber wheels.

"Ain't you gonna have none of this cupcake?" Clarice asked, and handed him the treat on an enormous tin tray. He took it, and joylessly went to work peeling off its paper holder, and removing the time-worn toy head.

Clarice noticed the cast of his eyes, how they were set to shoot over to the doorway if the voices became harsher. She was monitoring the argument as well, but had so far decided that this altercation did not rate as a bad one. Even so, when she heard an open palm slamming down suddenly on a counter top, she said, "Hey, I thought you were going to do us some radio here."

His mouth was now full of bland, crumbling cake. Slowly he got to his feet. Neither he nor Clarice mentioned that they had forgotten to bring the cup of milk he always had with his dessert. He faced the hulking radio, the most ornate object in his life, and with a degree of reverence he reached out to turn the great round On/Off knob. It went "Tock," and the radio slowly came to life with a wavering whistle that ascended out of the hearing range, followed by a muddy hum that remained more or less constant. The dark eye in the center of the radio's face began glowing brighter and brighter until it looked red hot.

A bizarre voice sang out, "Hooooeeeee!! Pig 'N Whistle!!" But Ephram understood that this was not an authentic radio person. The Pig 'N Whistle was a place he had seen. It was in town. This man talking about its specials was a real person who had somehow gotten himself a spot in the world of the radio. With great consternation, Ephram wondered how he had done it. He thought, too, that if he could ever be on the radio he would surely talk about something besides the Pig 'N Whistle. Among other odd sounds drifting through the room came sobbing, as Mrs. Rutherford ran down the hall to her bedroom and slammed the door.

One radio talker led to another, and Clarice looked up from her knitting and said, "Ephram! Shoot! Find some music!" He obediently went to work on it, wondering, as he turned the dial, if the resulting chaotic screeches meant that the radio was being hurt in some way. He came to a clear station, and though the piano music was more sedate than she had hoped for, Clarice nodded for him to leave it there.

Ephram went to the doorway and called out into the hall, "I found some music here for us!" There was only silence, and he returned to his cupcake and rocket ship.

Some minutes later, Clarice looked up from the holly leaf design she was knitting into a scarf, and saw that Farrell was leaning in the doorway, hands in his pockets, smiling down at his son who had not yet seen him there.

"He's done real good tonight, Reverend," she said, "He's found us a good show."

The boy looked up at his rumpled, slouching daddy, and the whiskery, smiling face that said, "He knows what to do with that ol' radio." Farrell took his seat in his decades-old easy chair, and patted his knee for the boy to come over, which he did, at once.

"You gonna be a radio man when you grow up?" he asked his son, as he often did.

Ephram's voice quavered, "Yes sir."

This was amusing and satisfying, and he hugged the boy and sat him on his knee. "So, do you figure we have a fine program on for tonight?"

"Yes, probably," said Ephram, "... But they keep buttin' in on the music, don't they, Clarice?"

Clarice said, "Somebody keeps comin' on talkin' about they seen explosions on the planet Mars!" She looked up from her needlework, and said, "Now why is anybody goin' to care about that?"

Farrell had a laugh, to blow off some of the tension from earlier on. He said, "I cannot imagine, Miss Greene. I reckon that is far enough away that it won't do us any damage, what do you think, Eph?" The boy giggled, and Farrell bounced him on his knee. He went on, "I guess if worse comes to worse we'll have to get Flash Gordon to take care of it." Ephram giggled all the more, and his dad started in tickling him until he was squealing and kicking.

Then, suddenly, Farrell pulled the boy in close, and held him tightly for a long moment. When he relented, he said,

"Go and bring Daddy's pipe and pouch from off of the bureau. Go on." He slumped back in the chair, and Ephram went tearing off to the next room.

On the radio a follow-up bulletin was announced, in which the Government Meteorological Bureau requested that the nation's large observatories keep a watch for any further disturbances on the surface of the planet Mars.

With the soft rattle of the bedroom doorknob, Ivy's eyes popped open. She lay on her side in the dark room, fully dressed with her shoes still on, right on top of the quilt of the featherbed where she had thrown herself upon entering the room.

The door eased open, and the dark silhouette of a male figure was visible, but only at about one third scale of the one she had expected to see standing there. Ephram padded softly into the room, not speaking.

He noticed at once the linty stuffiness of the air, and that the heavy blue drapes were drawn to shut out the moonlight.

Only faint illumination from the hallway intruded here, so that he found himself relying mostly on the resounding click-clack of the alarm clock to guide him to his target. He sensed that his mother was awake, but he went on in silence.

As dim as it was, he could make out several objects on the bureau because they were shiny -- two sets of polished bronze baby booties on separate marble bases, a glazed ceramic burro with its saddlebags crammed with bobby pins, and several small bottles of odd shapes. Ephram picked up and examined those that caught his interest. One smelled like Mama at church. Another smelled like Daddy's hair.

Another had a glass butterfly on top. All along the base of the mirror at the rear were the glinting glass framed photos of people who were now in Heaven.

A dim ring of amber light suddenly appeared around Ephram. He looked over to the bed, where her miniature flashlight floated in the darkness, shining at him.

"I'm fetching Daddy's pipe." he said.

After a momentary silence she spoke in a voice that was soft, but low-pitched and strained, "Well, you know where it is. You could just about find it by smell ... Lord knows I can smell it from here."

"I like how it smells!" Ephram said. He soon retrieved it and the pouch from their saucer on the bureau. Then he turned to look again at the bright dot of light over the bed. Clowning came naturally to him, so he popped the pipe into his mouth and struck a pompous pose. Then he made an exaggerated scowling face, and wagged his finger in mock recrimination, until a low, weary laugh came softly from the bed.

"Take that awful thing out of your mouth," she said.

He did, and was on his way out of the room with it when she called his name. He drew near the side of the bed, and she reached out and took his hand.

"You're not going to smoke when you grow up, are you?" she asked him. He shook his head. The flashlight beam had been lowered to shine on their clasped hands. Ivy said, "You're always going to be a good boy, and make Mama proud?" He nodded, and she seemed at a loss for what to say next.

"Come here and give Mama a hug." For a brief moment, they held each other.

Ephram said, "I better go give Daddy his pipe."

"All right," Ivy said, "Can you give Mama your witness before you go?"

Ephram thought a bit, and said, "Lord is my Shepherd ... Shall not ... Won't ..."

Ivy said, "No, it's 'For God so loved the world' ..."

"I had better get the pipe along to Daddy, Mama." he said.

With a heavy sigh, she gave in to him again. But she took his hand, and said, "All right, then. You want Mama to go with you?"

He said, "Yes ma'am." Ivy turned off the flashlight, and rose from the bed. She smoothed her simple dress of navy blue with white dots. Hand in hand, she and her son made their way to the parlor.

Ephram put the pipe back in his mouth and executed a comic strut as they made their entrance. He was ready for some attention, maybe a sing-along that he could lead. But no sooner had they crossed the threshold then he found there was now a very different atmosphere in the room from the one he had left. His father was right up next to the radio, sitting on the tiny three legged wooden stool that was Ephram's. Clarice's knitting was slung aside in the basket on the floor, and she sat on the edge of the sofa. Seeing Ivy, she motioned urgently for her to come and sit down. On the radio, chaotic crowd noises and police sirens set the backdrop for the terse, authoritative voice of an announcer -- an absolutely authentic radio person.

Clarice was making rapid gestures with her hands as she informed Ivy, "... There is a huge, blazing, flaming object that has fallen out of the sky at a farm up in New Jerrasey. It is ... huge. That's the newsman on the scene now."

Farrell went, "Shhhh!" and held up his hand for quiet as the radio reporter described in a rapid fire cadence a scene of hundreds of cars parked behind him. Police were trying to rope off the road leading up to the farm, but it was no use. The crowds had broken through. Automobile headlights were throwing a broad spot on the crater where the object lay half buried.

Ivy said, with only slight alarm, "Well isn't it an aeroplane crashed? That's what it sounds like to me. Wouldn't they be able to tell that it was a plane crash?"

Seeming to seethe with disgust, Farrell snarled, "Of course they could tell if it was a plane crash, so that ain't what it is! Now be quiet!" The radio voice asked if the audience at home could hear the curious humming sound that seemed to be coming from inside the object. He said he would try to move his microphone closer.

Ivy spoke up again, "Maybe it's the carriage from a blimp. They can fall off, I bet."

Farrell yelled out, "Shuddup!!" He tamped the air with his open palm for silence, and turned the volume up to nearly blasting. His reddened eyes were fixed beyond the radio to a gray corner of the floor.

The radio newsman asked a certain professor if he thought the thing was a meteor.

This professor explained in a mellifluous voice that its metallic casing was extra-terrestrial, which he explained meant not of this world. Meteorites generally become pockmarked as they enter the atmosphere, he said, but this thing was smooth, and ... cylindrical.

"Hmmph!" went Farrell.

The reporter cried out suddenly. Something was happening -- the end of the cylinder had begun to turn! It was rotating like a screw! The crowd in New Jersey yelled out in amazement and apprehension, as the audience in the Rutherford parlor sat bolt upright. Ivy lifted Ephram from where he sat and placed him on her lap, as a heavy metallic clank rang from the radio. Men were heard to cry that the top was off.

"Stand back there!"

Not sure what it was all about, Ephram's face was a grimace as his mother's powerful arms compressed him against her soft body. He could sense trembling starting up in her and grow more pronounced as the radio newsman went on.

In the faltering tone of a man coming undone with petrifying fear, he said that this was the most terrifying sight he had ever witnessed. Then he gasped, and screamed out that there was something actually crawling out of the cylinder. Something, or someone. He could see shining in the blackness of the cylinder's opening, two glowing spots. Could they be ... eyes? It might be some kind of a face.

The crowd in the radio suddenly released an awe-stricken shout.

Clarice fumbled with her crucifix necklace with a shaking hand, as the Rutherfords mumbled separate appeals to the Lord. From the mysterious New Jersey farmyard, the radio voice exclaimed that now indeed something was slithering out of the shadowy metal cylinder. Like great gray snakes, one after another emerged. They were tentacles! The main body came next - as big as any four men! This unearthly thing was glistening with slime, and for the poor news reporter was simply impossible to describe.

This field correspondent said that he could barely force himself to keep looking at the thing. But then he went on to give a fairly detailed description of beady snake-like eyes, and throbbing, wiggling lips of a cavernous mouth, dripping froth.

Ivy's bulging eyes rolled down to look at Ephram. He smiled up at her, and whispered, "It's a monckster."

Clarice found she was having trouble breathing. She settled back on the couch in a temporary faint, as the fevered reportage went on,

" ... The thing's rising up! The crowd falls back. They've seen enough."

Farrell was on his feet at the window this time, looking out into the night. Turning back to the little room, he met his wife's anguished eyes. He said, dismissively, " 'Thought I heard something out there."

Ivy's doughy face buckled into weeping, and she wailed, "What is it about, Farrell!? What is goin' on?"

He did not face her but offered only his profile, downcast, and scanned the floor. He said, "Right now I don't know, sugar beet. Let's be quiet and hear a little more, and I'll think." He faced away from her, hunching back down on the wooden stool.

Ivy noticed the large dark perspiration stain that had formed across the back of his white work shirt. She imagined the expression of intense concentration that must be on his face now as he monitored the broadcast.

The radio offered some slight reassurance to its stupefied listeners, as it was announced that a large contingent of troops had arrived at the scene. It was astounding to Ivy how fast all these developments were taking place, but she decided it must only seem that way to her, due to the sluggish pace of events in her own life.

The officer in charge sounded upbeat and confident, considering the great unknown he was facing. He said it should be a good outing for the troops, and advanced them in formation toward the cylinder, and its occupant.

The military maneuver had not gotten very far before the panicky radio voice said that a hellish shape was rising from the pit. A bright light had flared up! Then, a jet of flame blasted forth, right at the advancing troops! It enveloped the entire column!

Bone chilling shrieks pealed from the radio, and Farrell, now a mass of gooseflesh, hastened to the sofa to take wife and child in arms. Ephram perceived at once that both parents were trembling violently. His father's face was bloodless, a pale shade of gray. When his mother began sobbing, he joined in sympathetically, though still with no idea what was afoot. Farrell only rocked his family gently back and forth as he stared blank-faced at the radio and its hot red dot. The sofa frame began to squeak as Clarice, wide awake again, was rocking and praying out loud.

The radio was louder, and the situation it relayed was a rapidly deteriorating one for the heroic New Jerseyites. The entire farm and surrounding fields and woodlands were a sea of fire. Automobiles were exploding by the score. Ivy stopped weeping for a moment when her breath was literally taken away by the wholesale numbers of human beings who had just been vaporized before the news reporter's open microphone.

The broadcaster, with the manhood of a Pershing, kept right on reporting from the scene even as he described a tidal wave of flame curling in towards him, mere yards away. There was a loud crash, and then there followed something never before heard on the Rutherford's radio -- dead silence.

Ivy bleated out, "Farrell! What are we going to do? Are we ..." Their eyes met, and Farrell's face was the one he wore when looking at the hobos, and the itinerant tramps and trash that had to be kept away. That face was as horrifying to her now, in its own way, as the thing on the radio. It cut off Ivy's words. Farrell turned away, and sat down again on the three-legged stool.

It was announced that a high-level official was set to address the nation. As he came on, Farrell's open hand shot into the air for silence, though there was certainly no other sound to be heard in the room.

A grim representative of the national government came on then, saying he had a grave announcement to make --

"However inconceivable it may seem to be, the evidence of science is in, and the conclusion has been reached. Those hideous creatures who fell to earth in New Jersey tonight are ... the first shock troops of an invading army of the planet Mars!"

Farrell lurched to his feet, half stumbling backwards over the stool. "Get your coats on!!" he screamed.

Anything else the official had to say was lost to a sudden, tumultuous suiting-up for travel in the Rutherford home. From the hall Farrell roared out, "Where the hell is my shotgun!?"

Clarice retrieved it from the pantry, and soon he was out in the front yard with it, scanning the skies.

The brisk wind washing across him helped clear his head. He had never in his life been so terrorized. Not in the war, not in the riot - not ever. When those soldiers were incinerated by the giant monstrosity with the V-shaped orifice and the plate-sized eyes, his foundation of reality fell away.

Now he sprinted for the car, his most rational thought being the need to get further away from the nearby city of Raleigh. When the Martians hit this area, Raleigh would be the first to go. He jumped into the Nash, fired it up, and worked it in drive and reverse a couple of times to free it from its jam against the tree. Then, throwing a cloud of dust, he made for the road in front of the house, only stopping when a high-pitched shout reached him through the open passenger's window.

Here they came, running up the drive, Ivy lugging something big and bulky in front of her, Clarice with Ephram under one arm like a sack of rice, and a canvas tote bag slung over her other shoulder. They piled in and he took off in earnest, hurtling down the unlit dirt road at speeds the Nash had not made in years. It was some time before anyone ventured to speak, although Farrell mumbled to himself from the start.

As they reached paved roads, Farrell heard his wife's voice from the seat beside him,

"Where is it we are going, darlin'?"

"Gettin' away from town. Town's ain't gonna be safe. We'll get out in the country, up to the foothills. I know some farmers out that way." he said, shakily, staring straight ahead.

Ivy said, "Are you going to see if Clarice wants to go to her auntie's?" though that was the last thing Ivy wanted. She thought it would be unlikely to happen now, with the distance that had been laid down between the car and home.

Farrell barked out, "You want to go back to Miz Greene's, Clarice?"

From where she sat in the backseat with Ephram on her lap, Clarice replied, "I'll be arright. Just go on where you're goin'." But with the initial shock now subsiding, she too was confronted by the terrific uncertainty of this situation. She thought of the faces of her family. She wondered not so much when she would see them again, but how she would even get a message to them that she was okay. And was she okay? With Ephram's sleepy head pressing onto her chest, an undercurrent of despair rose in her. Leafless trees flashing past the window looked all the more gnarled and spectral in the distortion of her tears.

Ivy's hands played across the Crucifixion scene impressed into the leather cover of the enormous family Bible on her lap. The lack of a radio in the car, and the dim prospects of any conversation with her husband meant she would be alone with her thoughts and the sound of the engine for a while.

Farrell's mind was agog with images of ghastly Martian giants, lumbering across the landscape, mowing down division after division of fine young men with hellish and unfathomable weaponry. American cities occupied, the United States under invasion! If he had heard it anywhere else but a radio news bulletin he would not have believed it.

He cautioned himself to keep his mind free of panic, lest he not be able to function. The gas gauge abruptly became the focal point of his world.

"Need gas ..." he said out loud, "Not but a quarter tank!"

Terrifying visions of being stranded on this bleak roadway came to Ivy, and soon her lips pressed together, her eyes batted in tears, and she began a quiet jag of weeping.

Farrell was reasonably sure he knew where he was on this particular stretch of road, not that he came out this way much anymore. If he had already passed by a certain unmarked crossroad that was out here, that would not be good, in terms of finding gas. He started speaking his thoughts aloud:

"Now, there <u>should</u> be a junction up here a ways, and down left a couple of miles there was a store that had a gas pump ... At this hour they would be closed. But as I recall they had a boy that lived back of the place ... That's going to be our best shot, that store. Otherwise, we'd be looking at almost the whole way to the state highway, and Morton's place."

The crossroad he had in mind came into view before him. He veered off and sped down the worn-out asphalt strip, jostling here and there over welts pushed up by tree roots. Towering trees grew quite near the roadside. Crosshatching their boughs above, there was virtually no moonlight here, making it uncommonly dark. It was a considerable relief to see the faint light of the general store's parking lot.

A single bulb mounted on a pole, with a tin cone for a rain guard, offered the palest glow around Glover's Country Store, as the Coca Cola sign read. The place was closed. The remembered gas pump was there, nearly ten feet high with the glass reservoir and Mobil globe on top. A shiny padlock on the nozzle caught Farrell's eye. He clambered out of the Nash to inspect it.

He had the sinking feeling now that there was nobody in back of the store, or anywhere around here. A quick check of the rear of the building confirmed this, and he was back to inspecting the locked pump. The hasp was as thick as his little finger. There would be no prying or sawing this one.

"Why did they have to lock it?" he cried out, "I would have left the money! God!" He slumped momentarily against the pump.

Ivy rolled her window down and yelled, "Can't you see if there is a neighbor or somebody around who can help? What if we run out of gas?"

He looked at her blankly. Had he ever seen one iota of support or encouragement from any of them? How long had it been since she had looked at him with a remotely pleasant expression, much less a smile? He glared at her, and said, "Ivy, tonight may be the genuine end of the world. I know you're ready, 'cause there can't be anybody who has rehearsed it more." He shoved off from the pump and returned unhurriedly to the driver's seat.

The engine of the Nash came to life, revved good and hard, and powered the vehicle in a tight arc back the way it had come. In the backseat Clarice, who rarely rode in automobiles, was trying to control the increasing queasiness in her stomach. Ephram awoke on the seat next to her, refreshed and recovered from the insecure feelings that had led him to go to sleep. His head and folded arms appeared between Farrell and Ivy on back of the front seat.

"I am glad we're taking this little trip tonight," Ephram said, blithely.

His mother instantly said, "I think you better sit back and be still. Your daddy is trying to think." But her voice was soft and subdued and he didn't hear, or pretended not to hear.

Suddenly he pointed straight ahead out the windshield into the darkness and yelled out, "Hey! There went a shooting star!"

The Nash weaved and wobbled crazily in its lane. As it straightened out again, a low-slung roadster tore past with its horn blaring and disappeared from view within the minute.

Farrell wheeled around and snapped, "Sit your butt down and be quiet! Right now!"

He turned back to the road, talking to himself in a deep, obsessed timbre, "Got to gas up ... Got to make it to Morton's and gas up!" From the backseat Ephram said, plaintively, "We're going to need to stop pretty soon." And twenty three dark, dismal miles dragged by.

Farther along on the approach to State Highway 49 stood Morton's Roadhouse 'N Gryphon Gas, a one story cinderblock structure that sprawled out over a considerable area. Its paint scheme was green, white, and flaking, with swirling Art Nouveau advertising designs from the 1920s remaining in places. There was a single automotive service bay on the end, big enough for a mid-sized truck. Two expansive plate glass windows revealed an ice cream counter, coffee urn and hot dog warmer, with a separate section for traveler's sundries and various items from paperback books and cosmetics to punchboards and framed pictures of Jesus and Roosevelt. This evening the establishment featured the venerable Morton himself, seated out front next to the gas pumps on a cane chair, as the Nash pulled up.

Morton insightfully welcomed them with, "Restrooms are around back and unlocked ... Colored facility on the far end, miss."

Farrell introduced himself as the other three trotted away. "I don't know if you remember me, Mr. Morton," he said, "I am Farrell Rutherford. I was with the Jensen's revival, a few summers ago. And I believe we have met other times over the years."

"Reverend Rutherford, sure, sure I remember," he said, "It's gettin' to where I can recall the people who don't much come around better than those who do!" His warm smile of recognition faded suddenly, and his slight shake of Parkinson's increased as he said in a low, whispering voice, "Reverend, what do you make of all this tonight?"

"You heard it, then?"

Morton said, "Well, my wife called up here and told me to tune in WBT quick as I could, and yeah I heard some of it. My radio needs a tube, but we listened for a while ... an' that damned boy I had helpin' me here, he took off! Quit, I guess. And no sooner was he gone and me here by myself, than a column of cars like you would not believe starts pouring in here, wanting gas and everything else. I bet I've done two days business in the past two hours. I'm usually closed up and headed home by this time, but I thought I should stay open while they come. I think it might be about over now, though."

The two were silent for a moment, resting their elbows on respective sides of a rack of oil cans. Their body language assumed the hunched-over aspect that men have when facing grave trouble.

Morton said, "Farrell, my wife is about scared offa her nut. She kept callin', tellin' me to close up and come home. I finally told her to just turn it off and get to bed. What's funny is that some of the folks who passed through here tonight seemed to think it wasn't real! They didn't believe their own radios!"

Farrell said, "Disbelief is the great plague of our times."

Morton stared down into the gray water of the squeegee bucket. He said, "I'm old, Reveren'! I cain't handle this! I tell you true, I don't want to believe it!"

"It's not a matter of wanting or not wanting it, Mr. Morton. It is the news that we have to deal with."

"So ... You think it is true?" Morton said.

"I think it is incredible, but true, that we are under siege by an army from the planet Mars." Farrell said, soberly.

Morton staggered, and said, "Mah-h sweet Jesus! Ha' mercy ... Ohh-h ..."

"Just keep your wits about you, Morton. Don't give in to panic." Farrell said, "Just think out what you're going to do, and then I would get to doing it. Tonight."

"So, what're y'all goin' to do?" Morton asked.

Farrell said, "I am thinking of heading up to the foothills west of here, maybe on into the mountains. I know people up around Taylorsville and Wilkesboro." And he added confidentially, "I also know of a big cave up that way, with a spring not far from it. I can't say any more about that."

"Oh. I understand." Morton said.

"Anyway, if Ivy and them don't drive me nuts first, that's the plan." Farrell said, "I will be needing to gas up, too."

"Oh, you will ..." Morton said, and he seemed bothered by this. He had to think about it.

Farrell said, "You're not going to tell me you are out of gas, are you?"

"Well, I don't know exactly." Morton said, "Gryphon was supposed to come yesterday, and I ain't seen 'em yet. And we just had that big rush, like I said. Anyway, I know Ethyl is dry, Farrell. As far as Regular, I really don't know. I ain't had a chance to put the stick down there and check this evening. But I hate to tell you, I wouldn't be surprised if it was about gone too, now."

Farrell looked quite despondent, and old man Morton said, "There's only one way to tell." He started spinning the crank on the side of the pump, and gradually the precious, pinkish fluid began rising in the glass reservoir on top. Farrell nervously counted to himself as the level rose above numbered gallon marks.

He had never seen a gas pump run dry before. It bubbled a little and then stopped. "Not quite eight gallon." Morton sadly said. Farrell needed a lot more than that, but as he thought about it, he decided that with what little he already had, he should surely be able to make it to another station out on 49 somewhere.

Farrell reached into his deep front trouser pocket, and produced his flat leather billfold. After a quick check inside it, he said, "Was sort of hoping we could set up a tab on this. Of course, under present circumstances ..."

As the Rutherford family reappeared from around the corner of the building, Morton said, "You put that wallet away. No, put it away. In fact, here, take this nozzle ..." He handed over the nozzle and strode off to his store.

Farrell stuck the nozzle in the car, and as he watched the gas draining slowly down, he whispered to Ivy, "He ain't charging me for this."

Morton came back with a pair of hot dogs in either hand, neatly wrapped up in paper napkins. The four travelers received their snacks in an orderly fashion, with Ephram being first. It was just then that Farrell noticed that the boy was still wearing only the blue, footed pajamas under his too-small coat.

"God bless you, sir." Farrell said, as he gripped the old fellow's shoulder with his free hand.

The others spoke their thanks as well, and Mr. Morton became misty-eyed. He said, "I am about as old as I can get! I don't reckon I shall see any of you again in this world, what with all the ... troubles. I just wanted to send you off as well as I can, and, just ... God go with you!"

Tears spilled down his jowly cheeks, and he kissed Ephram's forehead, and blubbered, "God watch over you, little one!"

As they climbed back into the car only Ephram was not choking back tears. The child seemed mildly baffled by the old man, but pleased with the hot dog.

Farrell closed his door, cranked down the window, and said, "Go home to your wife, Morton. Tell her we will remember you in our prayers." They drove away with a honking of the horn, and everyone waving. With a tremulous hand, the old man waved them goodbye.

They were not far out of the parking lot when Farrell said, "Save those hot dogs! Don't eat them now. Here, Ivy, wrap them up in that newspaper!" Ivy collected the hot dogs and began a frenzied effort to enclose them in layer after layer of newsprint.

The Nash rolled on down to the highway junction. Farrell looked forward to making good time on this better stretch of road. He swung onto the westbound lane and began a steady acceleration, intending to hit sixty, the car's top speed.

Suddenly, the headlights reflected on the bumper of a vehicle on the side of the road up ahead. Next, a man became visible standing beside it, facing them as they approached. He wore a kind of trench coat, and his hands rested on his hips. It looked almost like a military stance, and seemed so odd, alone on the dark roadside as he was. Farrell slowed down out of curiosity.

As they drew near him, the man casually raised his hand in a gesture of halt, like a policeman at a roadblock. Farrell came to an immediate stop, causing them all to pitch forward in their seats. The man walked calmly to their car. Farrell said,

"Roll down your window, Ivy!"

As she did, they got their first good look at the stranger, a surprisingly young fellow, with a narrow mustache and close-cropped, shining black hair. He looked in, and looked them over, and was so long in speaking as to seem impertinent.

"She's thrown a rod, I'd say." he remarked, and for just a second, Farrell thought he was talking about Ivy. The man went on, "I was just passing that junction and something went pow." He smiled. "Anyway, now she's dead." He gestured to the Studebaker on the shoulder.

Farrell leaned forward and said, "There is a service station not far down that road you just crossed. It won't be open now, but in the morning you could get some help there. They work on cars."

The young man laughed, in a cold way the Rutherfords were not accustomed to hearing. "Maybe an archeological team in some future age can do something with it." he said, "I daresay that vehicle will be sitting right where it is, for a very, very long time."

His eyes fell on Ivy, and she winced. His strange statement suddenly made sense to her. The human race was on the run, scrambling for its very survival. An unserviceable car might very well sit where it died until it rusted and rotted away. He smiled down on her, and it eased the tension enough that she smiled back.

"My name is Preston Wooldridge." he said.

"Farrell Rutherford!" Farrell called out, "Look, I don't know your destination, but I'm just getting out into the countryside and away from town. I am figuring the towns and cities are going to be the areas hardest hit."

"Your assumption may be well founded," said Preston Wooldridge, "I'm a student at NC State, and the word on campus is that a cylinder has fallen just north of Raleigh."

"I knew it." Farrell said to Ivy, "If we had stayed in that house we would not have lived to see the sunrise."

"That's a distinct possibility." Wooldridge said, in his cool, unruffled manner, "Even if there are no Martian craft in Raleigh right now, you may rely on the fact that there will be within a day or two. All the state capitals will be hit. The capitals and the major cities will be the first to go."

To hear this articulate, intelligent young stranger speak of the Martian invasion brought a new wave of anguish on Ivy. The long night of fear and discomfort was catching up with her, and she sprawled to one side on her seat, and exhaustedly said, "Give us strength ... Oh-h Lord! Let us pray for strength..." She was astonished to hear Wooldridge half chuckling, apparently at what she said.

He then said, "The mountains are where you want to be. Their mechanical locomotion won't do as well on that terrain."

"What locomotion are you speaking of?" Farrell asked.

"You didn't hear that part of the broadcast?" Wooldridge said, "The cylinder reared up on precision controlled robot legs, and went marching off! Crushing anything in its path!" An intense expression came upon his piercing features as he pictured it. He added, "Then you must not have heard. New York City has ... fallen."

Farrell gasped audibly. Clarice too. Ivy groaned in despair. Millions of their fellow citizens had been summarily slaughtered this evening. Farrell just shook his head, speechless. He remembered he was burning gas, and shut off the engine.

Preston patted his hand against the top of the passenger side door, his prominent school ring tapping against the metal, and he said earnestly, "We here cannot do anything about that! We can only preserve ourselves, and that we must do!"

Farrell nodded slowly in agreement. Ivy and the stranger looked over at the sagging features of his gray, whiskered face.

Preston Wooldridge added, in a strong voice, "Those with an opportunity to survive, and a strong mind with a will to survive ... shall survive."

Clarice muttered, "Amen. This too shall pass."

Preston said, "You have some advantage in having a running car ... Running! Ha! Running is going to be as important for humans from now on as it was in Piltdown times."

When he said Piltdown a tiny fleck of his spit touched down under Ivy's ear, and she recoiled, internally. He was leaning in at them as he spoke. With all the color drained out of his image in the moonlight he looked to Ivy like a character from a black and white movie, come to life in three dimensions, and pulling out from a dark screen into the real world.

"You spoke of my destination," he said, "My destination is the same as yours -- away from towns, away from Martians, and away from death..." He paused, and again remained silent for a long time, with the cold wind whipping into the car's open window. "I could be of some benefit to you, I'm sure." he said, "If we only pitched in together for a little while ..."

Ivy looked intently at her husband's impassive face. Now Ephram appeared again on back of the front seat and studied his father. He then turned for a closer look at the stranger, who seemed to notice him for the first time.

Preston looked back to Farrell, and said, "This spot right here would be as good as any, but it is still not quite far enough from Raleigh. The Blue Ridge Mountains would be ideal."

"I know what you mean," Farrell said, "Well ... I guess we could haul you a while."

"How are you set for gas?" Preston asked, "We could pull some hoses out from under my hood and probably siphon a good bit from my tank. Come on, give me a hand."

Farrell perked up noticeably at this. As he was getting out of the car, taking care about the shotgun, he noticed the look on Ivy's face. He said, casually, "He seems like a nice fellow. Might be a big help when we get where we're goin'." He then reached across and patted her hand. She nodded and looked away.

Preston had the hood of his Studebaker up and hoses snapping loose when Farrell walked over. For lack of a flashlight, he held them up for inspection against the glow of the moon. He had a small roll of electrician's tape which he used to join the hoses. To lengthen the siphon further he spiraled the tape off from one end. Farrell noted to himself that he would not have thought of any of this.

As gasoline trickled into a coffee can, Preston stretched and scanned the starry skies. "Yessiree," be said, "One day we're all worked up about the Sudetenland, and then the ol' worm takes a turn. Kind of puts stuff in perspective, eh?"

"I reckon." Farrell said, flatly.

His words fogging in the cold, Preston said, "What's the old line? Every day, in every way, it's getting better and better? Ah, ha ha!"

He bent the end of the hose and had Farrell hold it. He pinched the rim of the coffee can into a spout, and carried the first few cups of fuel to be transferred.

Preston spoke as he worked, "Your family there. They're looking to you for the backbone in this crisis, right?"

"I guess so," Farrell said, "And by the way, they have heard a-plenty tonight on the radio. I would really appreciate it if you wouldn't say anything that might get them more upset than they already are."

Preston said, "Believe me, nothing I'm going to say will get them upset. The first charred skeletons we come upon might get them upset. The first Martian we encounter will upset them, I would imagine. But I would not worry about me upsetting them, Mr. Rutherford."

The siphon ran dry finally, and the Studebaker was stripped of its few remaining portable assets - a spare tire, a blanket, a few tools and the windshield wiper blades. On returning to the Nash, Farrell was surprised to see that Ivy had moved to the backseat with Clarice and Ephram. Without making mention of it, he got behind the wheel, and Preston said, "'Guess I'm riding shotgun!"

The engine of the Nash sputtered to life, and as he nervously watched the needle of the gas gauge creep forward, Farrell made some quick introductions.

Preston said, "It is an honor to meet all of you. I would just remind you again to be brave tonight. Getting upset won't do you any good."

Ephram's elbows hooked across the center of the front seat and he made a close examination of the strange person. Ivy at first reached forward to retrieve the boy, but something stopped her, and she settled back. When the newcomer wouldn't speak to him, Ephram said, "You don't have to worry about me gettin' upset. I ain't like that, am I, Mama?"

Preston glanced over his shoulder as the car rolled forward, and said to the kid, "You're not afraid?"

"Awww no!" Ephram said loudly, as if offended, "Why should I be?"

Preston said with great gentleness, "Why, because of what you heard on the radio tonight?"

Ephram rolled his eyes and made a dismissive gesture with one hand. He said, "Listen, there's no radio show that scares me."

Clarice spoke up to say to Preston, "It's probably better to let him go on thinking that way for now."

Ephram said excitedly, "I like shows with monsters a lot, but I tell you what, I like those singin' shows the best!"

"Really!" Preston said, "That's outstanding!"

"And I'll tell you something else," Ephram went on, "I am one excellent singer!"

"That's enough, Ephram" his father said, "Sit back with Mama."

Ephram said, "I can sing Flat Foot Floogie with a Floy Floy!" And at that, his mother grabbed him solidly and slung him onto the seat next to her, saying, "Oh no you don't! You are not ever going to sing that again! Maybe a little later on you can sing a nice hymn for our new friend. Later on."

Ivy spoke again, "Mr. Wooldridge, I would appreciate it if you would give us your estimation of just what all is going on tonight. All we really know is what we heard on the radio earlier."

In a voice from the heart, Preston replied, "I will certainly give you my best appraisal of the situation, Mrs. Rutherford. I did hear somewhat more of the news than you all did. I should warn you up front, though, that this news is about as bad as it gets. You asked, and I will answer, but you have to promise me that you will be strong!" He looked back at her expression, of something less than great strength, and continued on:

"Apparently, an immensely superior race of life forms exists on our neighbor planet, Mars. Long aware of the natural resources on our world, they logically organized an army to invade Earth. Unfortunately, they chose to do so during our lifetimes, although they had to have been aware of this world for eons. All that we have observed about them so far would indicate that they are most likely millions of years more advanced than we are.

"We may never know the reason for their timing, but some facts are obvious. They are as superior to us physically as they are mentally. You may have heard that prior to the first cylinder fall in New Jersey, explosions were observed on Mars. These would have been colossal cannons, blasting the cylinders to our world. The living Martian soldiers in each cylinder would have to survive both the initial concussion <u>and</u> the uncushioned impact on our planet. They must be completely godlike alongside of us. In a way, I can't wait to see one.

"What we know for certain is that these creatures could wipe us from this planet with no special weaponry whatsoever. But in fact they are armed with war machines ... beyond our wildest nightmares!

"It was no ordinary flame-thrower that killed those soldiers tonight," he said, "But I think I understand the rudiments of what it must be."

Farrell shot an angry look at Ivy when she asked, "What!?"

Preston replied in a low-pitched murmur, "... An Atom Ray."

After several more miles of driving in unrelieved darkness, Ivy suddenly screamed out, "Well, what are we going to do!? Go traipse around on some freezing mountain!? How are we going to get by!?"

"We're going to be strong!" Preston cried, "We're going to survive like our ancestors did in the wild. The first step is not to crackup or cave in. Look here, do you realize I have not had any decent sleep in about three days? I was aching for a night's sleep when the news of the invasion came over. I am still aching for sleep, but how would it look to the people I have thrown in with for me to climb into their car and nod off?"

Farrell said, "She'll be all right. Let her alone. Go to sleep if you want to."

Ivy wailed, "I am not sleeping on no freezin' mountaintop tonight, Farrell!"

Preston exclaimed, "You're not going to have to, Ivy! Cripes!"

Clarice interjected, "Tell that man about her, Reverend! ... She has female trouble!"

Farrell barked out, "All right! All of you shuddup! You!" he said, prodding Preston on his shoulder, "You have any money on you? There's a gas station coming up, and we're bad in need." He tapped a fingernail on the window of the gas gauge. Preston looked at it, and blurted out, "Jeeeesus Christ!"

Clarice said, "Call on Him whom ye serve!"

Preston took a deep breath, let it out, and said, "Okay, okay. First tank is on me. You must have been about empty when we did the siphon."

The bright white, well-lit service station came into view in the distance, lifting spirits in the Nash. But as they drew near the art deco Gulf pumps they saw a hand painted cardboard sign which read,

"No Gas."

"Oh come on!" Preston cried, "This isn't legal! They're hoarding!"

A pair of men in bibbed overalls stood up from behind the pumps as the Rutherford car drew near. Rifles in hand, they shook their heads and waved Farrell off.

Preston rolled down his window, and said, "You're hoarding! If you've got gas you gotta sell it! This is a national emergency!"

The men raised their guns in unison and took aim at the Nash.

Preston shouted, "You ... This is ... Go! Go!! GO!! Floor it!! Duck your heads!!"

Ivy and Clarice screamed long and loud, and threw themselves across Ephram on the backseat as the car whirled out of the parking lot and down the road.

They were a mile away before the first attempt was made to take stock. All three backseat riders were wailing, and Preston confirmed that it appeared no one was hit, at least not in the lungs. Farrell wanted to know if shots had really been fired. Preston said he didn't know, but that the men had definitely leveled guns at them.

Farrell saw that the college man was intensely upset by what had just happened, or perhaps by the cumulative effect of things. At any rate, he seemed to be fuming in fury. He was growling out language that Farrell hoped wasn't carrying to the back seat.

When the adrenalin from this latest incident receded Farrell found in its place an immense weariness. He was now hours past his normal bedtime, and some hours into the pillage of civilization by superhuman monsters. The sounds of the women weeping filled his head, shortly followed by an odd, rumbling noise.

"That's the edge of the road there, Rutherford!" Preston snarled, "The shoulder! My side!"

Farrell corrected the course, and then softly called his son's name. Ephram appeared with a sniffle from the back seat.

"Can you sing Daddy a tune, pumpkin? Sing Daisy for me, son."

Ephram wiped his eyes, cleared his throat, and dutifully began it in a slow tempo in his trilling voice,

"Daisy, Daisy, Give me your answer true ... I'm half crazy, all for the love of you ..."

By the time he finished it, the women had stopped their crying, and Preston was quietly looking out his window. Ephram usually had applause at the end of the songs he sang at home in the parlor. There was none this time. But he felt better as he took his seat again. He held up the tin rocket ship against the window and let it fly along with them, against the moon.

Farrell spoke in what he hoped was a soothing voice, "There's another service station on up the road a ways. We'll be doing okay, once we get there."

This was putting a brave face on it. The old term "bone tired" floated into his mind, as he felt like his nerves and flesh had frayed out and bones alone were driving the car. He began nodding a little as miles slipped by with no gas station in sight. The only sound other than the engine was the purling conversation of the ladies in the backseat.

Ivy cleared her throat, and spoke, "Clarice has had an idea that I think we need to consider." She paused as if marshaling the thought in her mind. "This horrible creature that came from out of the cylinder," she said, "... What if it is, in fact, the beast of the Revelations?"

Preston, who had seemed to be asleep, slowly shook his head. Farrell glanced back at her, seeming to say with his eyes that this was a debate best left for another time. Conversation ended, and more dark miles went by.

When a white and gold spot of light became visible on the horizon, Farrell's spirits got a boost. He recognized the colors. Nudging Wooldridge awake, he pointed ahead, and said,

"HiHo station."

Preston squinted at it, and then at the gas gauge, and slapped the back of his fist into his open hand.

It was farther away than it appeared, so that by the time they closed in on it, everyone was wide awake and looking it over. Preston counted out quarters in one hand.

Farrell pulled up to a pump. The place was brightly lit, and men were visible sitting in the station's small office. The Nash had crossed the bell hose, Preston clearly heard it ping. But a minute passed and no one came out. It was then that Ivy's shaking hand came across the seat to point at little padlocks on the pump nozzles.

Preston snapped, "Just wait here! Keep the engine running." He was out and striding toward the station house. With the windows rolled up tight against the cold, they could not hear the discussion that began between Preston and the burly fellow who had stepped out from the station's doorway.

Whatever was being said, it was not going well for Preston, who was becoming wildly animated, his hands flapping at his sides with fingers splayed wide open. No sound penetrated the noise of the engine, but Preston's hair began to fly around in disarray as his head jerked about in an apparent screaming fit.

Ivy gasped aloud as Preston pulled a revolver from his trench coat.

A man with a shotgun materialized from the far end of the station house, and the man in the doorway produced an enormous .45 automatic. The two of them started backing Preston toward the Nash. He was not averting his gun from these chaps, even as he backed down.

Farrell's hand rose and made its way to the gear shift. He was just gripping it when Preston turned and ran, bouncing hard off of a gas pump. He dove into the car, roaring out, "Move it! Move it!" This time the crack of a gunshot was clearly heard over the squealing tires and thundering engine.

"Is anybody hurt?" Farrell yelled, as he straightened the car on the road. Hosannas of thanksgiving poured out of the back seat, indicating that all were intact there. As for Wooldridge, he seemed to be back in an incommunicative rage but physically unharmed. All Farrell could get out of him for some time was the word "hoarders" and assorted blasphemies. The blackness of the pine forest settled in around them.

Some miles down the road, with the needle of the gas gauge resting motionless beneath the big red E, the strains of Nearer My God to Thee resonated in the Nash from the trio in the backseat. Preston was sitting nearly in a fetal position, and Farrell was waiting for the minute at which the car would quietly roll to a stop.

At a particularly disharmonious crescendo, Preston screamed out, "I am trying to think! Knock it off!"

Ivy let out a mortified gasp. She said, "Young man, we are seeking the intercession of the Lord. I think you need to wake up to the reality of this situation."

"I need to wake up!?" Preston cried out, "Ma'am, we are going to be walking pretty soon, and that is when reality is going to pay its first visit to you! We need a plan, and I will need to hear myself think to come up with one!"

Clarice said, "You need to hear some of His Word!"

An exasperated cry rose out of Preston. He then said, "I want to know why there's not one word in that Word about life on Mars! That's what I want to know!"

The squabble ended abruptly as they felt the car stop. The engine had not died, however. Farrell had applied the brakes. He turned slightly, looking at each one in turn. They were wondering if he might blow up at them when he said, calmly,

"Do you see where we are right now?" They noticed the car was on a bridge, over water.

"It's a lake." Farrell said, smiling gently, "It's Badin Lake. And do you see that little, tiny row of lights, wa-a-ay over there? That is a fish camp. I have eaten there many times. Remember Peek's Fish Camp, Ivy?"

She did, with great fondness, and Ephram called out that he remembered the place too.

"You've never been there, Ephram," Farrell said, "But there is no doubt in my mind that that is where we are. Haven't been there in years, but that's it." He eased the car forward again, and after crossing the lake, he turned onto a muddy dirt road.

Farrell said, "We should make it on the reserve tank. We won't be going any farther. But here's what is so beautiful. They had a gas pump there at one time. They used it for boats. I know these people! If it is the same couple running the place, this could be the answer right here."

They pitched and swayed down the rutted dirt track, with low hanging tree limbs raking across the roof. Preston was deep in thought. Some minutes later he said, "You say these people won't hold out on you. But we have hit hoarders twice now. I say, tuck that shotgun under your coat. You and I go in first, and check things out. If everything's copasetic, we gas up and go, or pass the night and get a fresh start tomorrow. But if these people have gas and supplies and won't come across, I say we have to take it at gunpoint." Farrell thought for a moment, and then grimly and silently nodded his agreement.

Preston had imagined a more modest fish camp than what he now saw up ahead. No mere shack, this was an expansive two story house with a covered picnic area and a prominent pier extending far out into the dark lake. Preston suggested they stop the car about a hundred yards away and kill the headlights. The road sloped downward from here.

"We can roll her down from here, if the place checks out," he said. "And if it doesn't, we shall be camping right here."

Farrell said, "I'm sure things will go all right. The Peeks were always good people. We're just going to be a little more cautious going in, this time." He got out of the car, and gingerly slipped the shotgun under his long coat.

"We go in real calm and businesslike," Preston said to Farrell as they started out, "Don't even mention the invasion unless they do. We're just taking a little hunting trip, say, and we are low on gas."

"Right," said Farrell, "Sounds good." Then he added, "And, listen, Preston, for however much longer you're with us. I would appreciate it if you would go a little easier on my family back there. We're all in close quarters and, anyway, let's just try not to antagonize the situation."

Preston bristled visibly at this. He stopped walking and said, "Okay! But let us remember that I am not the <u>cause</u> of the present situation. I merely wanted to spell out the realities of it for you all. Frankly, sir, I was holding back!"

"Well, just don't make a bad situation worse, right? It has been a tough few months for us. So, a little patience and discretion ..."

"This situation we are in can only get worse, Farrell. Are you awake to that?" Preston said, testily, "I think you could all use a good dose of unsweetened reality."

The men were clearly visible to the three in the car as they stood there wrangling. Now and again, Farrell would look over at the dark old Nash.

Preston said, "As more and more city dwellers start pouring into the countryside and mountains the competition for slim pickings will get totally ferocious. Then, in a few weeks, it is going to start getting cold, Farrell. I don't mean brisk, like this ... You know what I mean."

Farrell began, weakly, "You are probably right, I have not thought through all the implications, Preston. I really haven't been able to take the time. But, we will just have to do the best we can out there."

"Farrell, have you ever thought about parting with them?" Preston asked, offhandedly, as he began walking down the track again.

Thrown for just a second, Farrell said, "It is not something I have ever really thought ... through."

"There might be other places they could stay. Even if it is just until you get established somewhere," Preston said, "Well, even right here." He waved a hand across the grounds of Peek's Fish Camp. "If it turns out you are still on good terms with these people here, maybe they would take them in."

"Haven't thought about it." Farrell said.

"I could see some advantages to setting up around here myself." Preston said, "The only problem is, it is too exposed. Those Blue Ridge Mountain caves and gullies are the place to be for long term survival. That terrain is defensible from other people. As I said, there are going to be other people on the scene out there, which isn't all bad, by any means. There will be women, count on that.

He went on, "The issue for you now is not companionship, but dependency ... versus the ability to pull one's own weight."

Farrell hugged the shotgun against his gaunt body as he trudged on with this student. He figured that it must be apparent to Preston that he and Ivy's marriage was on strained terms.

"I guess I haven't thought about what to do." Farrell said.

Their footsteps crunched across the gravel parking lot, just in front of the entrance to the house-turned-restaurant. Preston stopped again. With a sudden deadly seriousness, he said,

"I have been hesitating to say this, Farrell. But I might not get a better opportunity than now, and I'm going to clear the air a little, as much as this might hurt ..."

Farrell said okay, and was listening and waiting. But Preston hesitated as the front door of the place swung open. An elderly couple dressed in their Sunday finest stepped out and began painstakingly to negotiate the front steps. As they strolled past Farrell and Preston the old folks smiled and nodded, and the gentleman said,

"Best hushpuppies in the state, right here!"

Momentarily baffled, Preston regrouped his thoughts, and spoke, "It's like this, Farrell. It is very much in doubt as to whether you and I will survive for any period of time. But, your family is just not going to make it, realistically, in the hard new world we are entering. Your maid would be the most resilient of them, but frankly I'll be surprised if any of them are alive in six weeks."

Farrell shook his head, wide-eyed and stunned, "I don't want to hear this, Preston."

"I know, I know," Wooldridge said, "But figure it out! If the Martians don't get them, starvation and cold likely will. And there will be roving bands of desperate people. Unchecked disease. The odds of any one of us lasting a year are ..."

Farrell cradled his forehead in his hand.

Preston went on, "Remember too that when the Martians begin depopulating the outlying areas they will likely use poisonous gas. If you have any compassion for your family you won't want them to die like that. Do you know what gas does to a human body? Were you in the war? I just want you to bear in mind ... a shot to the brain stem is essentially painless."

Now Farrell was mortified through and through. He pressed his hands over his mouth, but a faint wailing sound escaped between his fingers. Preston walked on to the front steps, and Farrell cried out, "Maybe no Martians will come down this far! Maybe they'll just stay up north!"

Preston paused, mildly irritated, and said, "They have not come this far to invade New Jersey, Farrell. They are here to conquer the world. You, sir, need to have it in your mind what you are going to do when your moment of truth hits. It is your call. They are your ... passengers."

The interior of Peek's was homey and unpretentious. An aroma of fried fish prevailed. Mounted large mouth bass adorned pine paneled walls. The hardwood floor was wavy from untold decades of dining and partying.

A teenage girl played sentimental piano music on a wind-up Victrola. She took note of the two visitors, and yelled through a back window, "Mama!" Few diners were in evidence, but it was late. Men with beer cans sat at two tables across the room. A busboy was clearing up messes elsewhere.

A swinging kitchen door flew open, and a dowdy lady in an apron and hairnet entered the public space. She cried out, "Good evenin'! The kitchen is closed, I am sorry to say! We got beer and popcorn!" Her greeting smile faded as Farrell approached her in a shambling gait. Close examination of his face made her draw up in alarm.

He stood before her and said falteringly, "Hello, Miz Peek. I don't know if you remember me. I'm Farrell Rutherford. I saw you last when we came through with Reverend Jensen's revival a few years back."

She noticed his eyes were cobwebbed in red, and had dark gray bags under them. She smiled again and said that it had certainly been a long time.

"Lordy, I appreciate you remembering me." Farrell said, "It is the funniest thing! My friend Preston and I were going up to the mountains to take in a little hunting. And we have just about run slam out of gas. I guess I underestimated our need. Anyway, I was wondering if you still have that ol' gas pump out back."

"Uh, yes we do," Mrs. Peek said, "I'll have to get Terrence to unlock it and run it for you ... You mean you drove past the HiHo and all the way back in here for our boat pump?"

Preston made a grumbling sound when she said HiHo, and she looked at him.

"Yeah!" Farrell said, with an unconvincing chuckle, "We didn't notice it until we were across the lake. Just talking and not paying attention, you know. Anyway, we thought we'd take a chance on you, and we're sure glad you can help us."

"Ummm, okay." she said, "Let me get my husband. You can just pull around back."

"Thank you, but we will need just a minute," Farrell said, "The car is up at the top of the hill." When she looked suspiciously at him, he said, "We weren't going to drive the whole way in if you didn't have any gas for us."

She gave him a sidelong glance, and walked back the way she came. Preston stood in close by, and whispered,

"They don't know."

Wooldridge had a bit more pep in his step, walking back up the road to get the Nash. He said, "Try to get some ammunition from them before we go. We need .38 bullets and shells for your scattergun." He looked around the bucolic lakeside setting and observed, "Nice place. Nice people. 'Might be just the ones to look after your folks 'til we get a permanent settlement put together."

When the Nash rolled around to the rear of the building near the gas pump a man was standing there impatiently, as if he were tired of waiting on them. When Farrell pulled up and greeted him, Mr. Peek also looked like a man whose wife had just told him to check out the crackpot who wants to buy gas.

With the nozzle inserted and gasoline flowing, Peek said, "Taking your wife and kid ... and your maid... on this hunting trip, Farrell?"

"Oh, they're just along for the ride." Farrell said, "Sightseeing and so on. Say, about that hunting, would you be able to sell us some ammunition, like .38 bullets and some shotgun shells?"

Peek looked at him and at the furtive, trench coated figure in the front seat. He shook his head slowly, side to side.

As Preston paid him, Peek surprised them with a small box of cold fried chicken for the road, apparently with the child in mind. "We would have just thrown it away," he said, "Y'all have fun on your trip."

With a gas tank brimming full, a small sense of comfort came over the travelers as they made their way back to the main road. When they reached it and turned onto pavement again, Preston announced, "We are set for gas and grub, and at this time I am going to ask everyone to be as quiet as you will, and let me catch a little sleep."

Farrell smiled and said he would probably pull over at the next spot that felt right. A strange second wind, or third or fourth, had entered him, and he didn't want to waste it on resting.

The car plied along the country road past lakes and ponds and clusters of sleeping cows huddled together against the chill. Farm houses with dark windows passed in and out of view. The sheet clouds had left the skies, replaced in the moon glow by those of amorphous shapes for Farrell to interpret. The peace of the rural night came finally to the car's interior. Ivy and Clarice snoozed quietly in the backseat. Ephram flew his space ship, and drew flowers and stickmen in the condensation on the back window. Gradually, he got tired of that, and looked around for another diversion.

Quietly, he explored the limited world of the backseat of the Nash. He slipped over to the passenger side door, where there was a small gap between the front seat and the frame of the car. Sure enough, Preston's trench coat was sagging down into this space, with the weight of the revolver in his pocket. Ephram had only to reach in and take it.

His uncle had one a lot like this, as did the Lone Ranger. From the two of them, he knew something of its workings. It had certain moving parts other than the trigger, which he knew not to pull. He flicked the safety switch up and down several times.

He understood about the hammer, which would cock the pistol if he pulled it out too far. This he just wiggled a little. More fun was the little lever that caused the chambered cylinder to fall open on its hinge.

And what an interesting piece of work the cylinder was! He spun it again and again. The exterior grooves were intriguing, with their rounded ends. He noticed how snug his finger fit into the interior holes, where bullets would go. This gun had no bullets, as he verified, holding the six holes and the barrel up to the moonlight. He quietly closed and opened the cylinder many times. Then he gave in to a bit of movie fantasy, a certain move that required a real revolver, not a toy one.

He stood up, and, as Tom Mix, pretended to load six slugs into the cylinder. With a devil-may-care twist of the wrist, he slung the cylinder back into the gun, with a resounding <u>cl-clack</u>.

Preston's eyes went from closed to bulging. His hand flashed down against his empty right coat pocket, and he was up and screaming, "Where's my gun!" and, "Give me that gun you little rat shit!" He tore the pistol from Ephram's hand, as Clarice shrieked and the Nash lurched wildly in and out of its lane.

Wooldridge roughly snatched the pistol out of the kid's hand, and that had Ivy yelling out, in a strong, powerful voice,

"Don't you put your hand to our son! Don't never raise a hand at our son!!"

Preston hollered back at her, "You tell your precious son to keep his mits off of ..."

"I don't care! You don't be striking our son!" the mother roared out.

"Amen!!" bellowed the maid. The car had come to a stop, and the boy sat, wide-eyed between the two women. He looked nervously at Preston but also noticed how Clarice had her hand resting on the derringer in her open purse.

Preston said to Farrell, "I think you better have a word with your boy." His pistol was held down, but he kept it in hand.

Again, Ivy cried, "You better never lay a hand on our child! I know that!"

Farrell's haggard face turned toward the backseat, and then to Wooldridge. Then he said, "Get out."

Preston flinched, visibly, and tightened his grip on the pistol. "You gotta be kidding me, mister." he said, gravely.

Farrell said nothing, but shifted the shotgun a little that had lain at his left side. Now its barrel pointed up around the rear view mirror. The two men eyed each other, and the women held their breaths.

Ephram's voice warbled out, "He ain't got no bullets in there, Daddy. I looked."

Farrell lowered the shotgun, and snarled, "Get out! Get out of here!"

Preston swallowed hard, and opened the door behind him.

"Now back up!" Farrell yelled at him, "Back up some more!" He then glanced to the backseat and said, "Ivy, you and Eph move up front, but leave the back door open."

As the two of them climbed out and scrambled into the front, Farrell gingerly handed the shotgun over the seat. "Hold that on him." he said to Clarice.

The front door closed, as Preston heard Farrell saying to Ivy, "We'll all pull our weight. We'll make it, somehow."

The last Preston saw of them was Clarice looking at him down her nose and the double barrel of the shotgun. The Nash sped away, as the back door slammed shut.

Preston stood on the dark roadside in a hollow astonishment. No headlights were visible in either direction. No mailbox or driveway or other sign of human habitation was anywhere in sight. He walked a while until he reached the crest of a hill. From there he confirmed what he expected to see. Pine trees in the moon glow stretched out before him, without end.

He stood waiting for a while, on the off chance that another vehicle might pass by. Surely they would stop and pick up someone so utterly marooned. As it happened, though, no one ever came. He had no watch and no idea how long it would be until dawn.

Finally giving in to what he saw as his only option, he walked until he reached a relatively open place, and made his way into the woods. He was nearly fainting from lack of sleep. At least here would be some cover from the wind.

It happened that he had a folded up Help Wanted section of newspaper in his breast pocket. Wadding it up, the sheets made for a crucial layer of insulation under his coat. With this, and no other comfort, he settled in beneath the trees to take what sleep he could. He drifted off in grim fears of what the next day would hold for him and the rest of humanity.

Sound sleep came to him in the cool, mossy hollow -- almost hibernation. When he snapped into wakefulness the next day he felt physically revived. He stood and stretched and shook out the newspaper wads from his coat.

The road was visible from here, but finding his path back out of the woods proved to be the first problem of the day. There seemed to be more briars and underbrush now than last night. He inched along wondering how he had come in so far.

Tall pines were cutting off much of the daylight, or so he thought at first. But based on the angle of the sun, relative to the westbound highway, he finally decided that it was not morning at all, but early evening, and that he had spent the entire day asleep in this forest.

A sharp sound struck him then, coming from deep in the woods -- A loud metallic clap. Automatically he ducked down upon hearing it. Now he stood again, staring into the dense pines. Something other than trees was out there. A new sound hit him then, the whirr and rumble of someone starting a car. He followed the direction of the sound, and moved along through the trees.

There was a dry, muddy creek bed, and then he started laboriously climbing up a steep slope. On reaching the top, he saw a wooden guard rail, and just beyond that, a paved street. A sidewalk began at the end of the rail, leading up to a residential neighborhood with white and pink houses and cars parked along the street. And somehow, somewhere, someone was playing a piano!

He stood and thought about that for a moment, and was startled when the piano sound stopped abruptly. He stepped across the guard rail, and carefully made his approach to the row of homes. It was very quiet now, and he sensed things were not as they seemed. No human being was visible anywhere, but then with a shift in the wind, he was dumbfounded by a passing odor of -- pumpkin pie?

He continued his half-staggering progress up the sidewalk, to where the street took a sharp bend. There, coming around the curve in the twilight was a sight so mind bending that every muscle in his body seized up.

They were just over three feet tall, the two of them, walking side by side down the center of the street toward him, stiff-legged and robotic. Their humanoid forms were covered from the neck down with a kind of silvery foil. Shiny metal domes topped their heads. Their faces were a vivid, lime green.

He backed up against a picket fence and froze as they goose-stepped in unison to the sidewalk. They passed him, and continued on, and in the fading light he saw that they carried paper bags. They were little kids.

He slumped on the fence until it was creaking. As he stood uncertainly on his own again, he saw a rotund country gentleman walking toward him in overalls, smoking a briarwood pipe. He could have been part of any illustration of American holidays, so homey and rustic was his countenance.

The old fellow didn't stop in his stroll. But as he neared Preston, he took the pipe from his teeth, nodded politely, and said in a gentle, grandfatherly manner,

"There went a little trick-or-treat for ya."

THE END

THE STATUARY CATS

"So beautiful to see so many of our wonderful ladies of the area here today. Jill Rawlings of the Carolina Traveler is here again today. Always so fine to see you, Jill. And Millicent. Hi, Milli ... And to all of you touring the estate for the first time, welcome.

I grew up surrounded by masterpieces of art, as well as just ... pieces of art. It was only in my late teens that I began to take some interest in what my forebears have established here at Black Pines. Since my teens were not so long ago, I hope you will forgive my occasional lapse into ignorance about our collection. You see, I spent most of my life out on our lake, fishing! It's true. I have logged many years searching for those little creatures, hidden just below the surface. Oh well. I thought before we got preoccupied with the art we might have some of this fine Cabernet I picked up on the West Coast. We might as well, right?"

Gentle, approving, feminine voices filled the air around the finely dressed young man, as so often they did. Women always greatly outnumbered men on the invitation list for these private showings of his family's formidable art collection. With fine wine being served to this gathering of art writers in the main hall of his family estate house, Teddy Harnes settled back in a throne-like overstuffed armchair and steadily inhaled the bouquet from the glass he held to his nose. Aspiring journalist Milli knelt by his side, gushing platitudes.

In his lavishly embroidered jacket, he looked a bit like the 18th century dandy who gazed out from the wall in a nearby oil painting. With his long wavy blonde hair and dark mustache, he was reminiscent of a face on a playing card. The Jack of Hearts come to life for a little wine tasting with the local damsels. The year was 1967, and Teddy and his younger sibling Lisette would represent the highpoint of fashion for five hundred miles in any direction.

A massive television camera was wheeled in to bring a glimpse of the Harnes art hoard to North Carolina's educational TV. It was not their first broadcast from the Black Pines Estate, and familiarity meant the producer and cameraman needed very little time to get the lighting just right. They knew they could count on the academics and art gadflies to drift by and offer up interviews to fill out the program.

Ted remained seated, sizing up the people in the scattered crowd around him. Some nominal rivals in the art collecting world were present; those with the most unctuous smiles were the most envious of his holdings. A few of his outside friends and clinging vines from the local music scene had shown up. Some rich old clods he had to invite sat on the settee. His sister Lisette was talking to some strange mousey girl in a bargain store dress. Apart from that, he was rankled to see that a guy he didn't know was openly flirting with one of the finer women in the room.

Then there was the Rubenesque Mrs. Eddens, with her pure white angora cat on a leash. A family friend from the old days, she knew their art as well as he and Lisette, but there was no way to have an exhibition without the presence of her and kitty. She took a whopping goblet of wine and drifted off on her own, not waiting for the official tour.

Ted spoke up, directing his voice to the retreating form of Mrs. Eddens, "We certainly won't hold anyone to the guided tour! You are welcome to make your own way around if you wish!"

She neither broke her stride nor acknowledged him in any way, which tickled Millicent intensely. As Mrs. Eddens disappeared down the hall, he went on, "Just confine yourselves to the first and second floor of this wing, please. I think the rest of it is locked off. Right, Liz?"

His sister was still talking to that frail young woman, the one who looked so uncomfortable and out of place. Lisette suddenly stepped away from her and said, "That's right, love. And if everyone will come this way, I will begin the guided tour in the tapestry hall. Remember to be back here at two, when we'll have a nice lunch for you. Afterwards, I'll open up the strong room, and we'll view the Vermeers."

She gave an exaggerated wink to no one in particular, which went over big with the assembled art fans. The unknown waif came back, insisting on handing Lisette a large manilla envelope even as she was trying to assemble guests for the tour. Finally Lisette took the package from the awkward lady, and folded it so it would fit in her handbag. The whole maneuver was just odd enough that it caught Ted's notice.

Newcomers took the guided tour. Old friends of the Harnes family made their own way around the two floors of grand galleries, laden with 18th and 19th century oil paintings, colossal tapestries, and ancient bronze and stone statuary. Eclectic was the word for this sprawl. There was very little in the way of a central theme. Unkind writers had called it an accumulation, not a collection at all. Antique musical instruments with forgotten names were on display, and framed autographs of long gone authors turned up among other unexpected items.

Mrs. Eddens was unconcerned about getting cat fur on her gown, or on anything else, and carried her long-haired pet in her arms as she made her way up the grand staircase to the second floor. She knew the layout well. She had known not only the parents of Teddy and Lisette but also Miles Harnes, the grandfather, in his final days. It was Miles who had established their vast fortune through currency trading and land speculating after World War I. She paused at the top of the stairs and looked across the hall to the sunlit room of French doors that had been his office.

The door stood half open. Down the hall the familiar galleries were spilling over with the voices of guests. She peered inside the old office. No one there. This space was not usually part of the art tour, she knew. Its artifacts were of more sentimental than aesthetic value. These were the trophies and personal effects of Miles Harnes, including souvenirs of his extensive travels during the 19th century. There should be some interesting items here, and some of no small value.

 Elaborately carved Maori canoe paddles were crossed on the back wall. The massive stuffed head of a broad-lipped white rhinoceros jutted out above them. One wall was mostly made up of draped French doors. Mrs. Eddens stepped inside, stroking her cat's chin until he closed his eyes and purred.

Magnificent old Moroccan rugs covered a marble tiled floor. There was an ornate oak desk, seemingly quite old, that dominated the far end of the room. Display cases covered the walls on three sides around the desk, their shelves crammed with curiosities.

The items on display were pleasing to the eye, but Mrs. Eddens had no idea what many of them were supposed to be. The fading, typed labels placed in front of the various objects were not always comprehensible. There were some odd juxtapositions here, too. A display of Japanese netsuke sat next to what looked like old machine parts. The label said only, "Gearing from the Morgana."

A leaf of incunabulum sat in its frame. Proclamations from governments of certain defunct nations stood waiting to be read. The silver plated skull of an infant had a label written by hand, in ideographs she had never seen before.

She passed along, left to right, and came to where the glass door of a case was standing partially open. She raised her left index finger, touched her long red fingernail onto the glass, and pushed it closed. Its magnetic catch clicked shut and Mrs. Eddens saw what was stored inside.

A pair of nearly identical seated cat figures, each nearly three feet in height, dominated the display case. She gasped slightly on seeing them. They were carved from some kind of black stone, possibly onyx, and seemed to be lightly glazed. The eyes were done in a different stone, a cloudy quartz. There was an old label for them, too…

"Statuary Cats. Ancient. Variations on Bast? Acquired Ankara, Turkey, 1902."

They were reminiscent of the Egyptian cat deity, Bast. But Mrs. Eddens' familiarity with art was enough to know that images of Bast usually featured a ceremonial pendant around the neck, and would likely have more decorative features in the Egyptian style. These figures were not even placed on pedestals, or bases of any kind. They were merely sitting side by side on the shelf. They had a certain regal, imperious effect, with their heads held high and ears swept back. They were distinctive. The longer she regarded them, the more evocative they seemed.

From his place snuggled at her breasts, Mrs. Eddens' cat abruptly stopped purring.

His green eyes popped open wide, and his head made an instantaneous pivot to face the artworks. She glanced down to see his head moving slowly down and back, as he began recoiling. His white fur flared out, and now he was a squirming, growling armful of energy.

"Stop that!" she cried out.

Her cries turned to shrieks as the animal dug its claws into the bare skin of her upper chest, and powered itself over her shoulder and off to the floor. The leather leash was still wrapped around Mrs. Eddens' wrist. He nearly pulled her over from her high heels as he struggled to run away. Then he was on his back, chewing at the leash in a frenzy.

Halfway up the staircase outside, Ted Harnes and a young woman were stopped cold by the screams. They watched, wine glasses in hand, as the white angora shot out of the office, skidded on the hard wood floor, and hit solidly into the wall at the top of the staircase. Trailing his leash behind him, apparently dazed, he staggered past them down the steps. A sound of muffled sobbing grew louder, and Mrs. Eddens appeared at the banister. Ted's eyes fell onto her upper chest and shoulder, which trickled thin streams of blood.

Several hours later, Lisette Harnes had finally bathed the stresses of the day out of her system. She lay across her bed, wrapped in a terrycloth robe. A television had been blaring in her expansive bedroom, but she shut it off, and now the silence was such that she could feel the blood circulation of her inner ears. She was not sleepy, and considered setting up the film projector and watching one of her movies. But the silence was better, so she lay still for a while instead.

Later she noticed the corner of a manilla envelope sticking up from her handbag.

This might be a good way to cap off the day, she thought. The lady who foisted it on her had certainly been eccentric enough. Most likely this would be some fairly funny reading. "Researches of Mindy Linton," it said on the flap in tiny handwritten letters. Mindy was the same age as her, and lived in town, but their common ground ended with that. It was only because of the persistent calls and nuisance appearances at the front door that Lisette had agreed at last to meet with this woman, who had been so reticent about explaining her business up front. She invited Mindy to the art show, spoke to her briefly, took her material, and still could not be sure what was the point of the matter with this whispering, self-effacing little soul.

She opened the envelope, and spread out typed sheets and photocopies of photographs across her bed. It all seemed fairly well organized, not a scatterbrained effort. Lisette began reading. It didn't take long to see that numerous paragraphs dealt with the Harnes family, primarily her father and grandfather, and their art collection. The papers contained pretty detailed information on their personal histories. She skipped ahead. There were cryptic pages of what seemed to be science material photocopied from college biology textbooks, with diagrams that left her baffled.

Grainy copies of photographs showed State art museums in Europe and Russia. Shots of individuals she did not recognize followed, and numerous pages were taken up with photographs of carved stone animal figures. Some of these were clearly views of the seated cat statues in her late grandfather's office, downstairs!

Lisette returned to page one and began reading carefully. Fifty three pages of single spaced text melted away in just under an hour, after which she had to get up and pour herself a large glass of wine. She went back to flipping through the photos for a moment, sipping her wine, deep in thought. She then shoved all the papers into the envelope, placed it in her desk drawer, and took the key and locked it.

In bathrobe and bedroom slippers, wine glass in hand, she left her room and made her way down the hall to a closet where a large storm flashlight was kept. Checking that it was powered, she proceeded in silence down the carpeted staircase to the second floor.

The old Miles Harnes office suite was cold tonight; the heating vents were kept closed in this rarely used room. Lisette turned on what lights were available, and went to the desk. She sat her wine down and turned her attention to the center display case. The Statuary Cats sat side by side on their shelf, staring straight ahead in stony majesty. She regarded them silently for a long moment. There had always been something about them.

She considered calling a housekeeper to hold the cats while she examined them. They were sure to be heavy. But as late as it was, it would mean rousing someone. And she would tell them -- what? She herself was not entirely sure what she was looking for.

A door of glass was held closed with a magnet. She pulled it open and leaned in for a close inspection of the stonework first of one cat then the other.

Great detail was visible throughout. Muscle definition was clear to see. All over the glazed surface faint etchings represented fur. The black stone had a vague swirling pattern in it, which the ancient artist had apparently followed to set the pattern of the fur. Bearing in mind what she had read in the Mindy Linton papers, Lisette squatted down and tilted one of the figures. She aimed her flashlight at its underside and saw that this area was not smooth and flat as she had assumed it would be. Each of the cat statues had carved representations of genitals. Lisette was amused to see that they were a male and female.

It was so strange to learn something new about items that had been sitting around her home for her entire life. She rose and took a long pull from her wine and thought it over. Turning back, she lifted out one of the weighty stone figures. It was not as cold as she expected. Hefting the thing up and down in her arms, she guessed it weighed fifty pounds. She turned it upside down and looked at the remarkable attention the artist had given to a side of the object that no one was ever intended to see. Who could know what religious trip had motivated that, she thought.

She turned the statue upright again, cradling it in her arms like a baby while she passed the flashlight beam over its various features. The nostrils and ear openings penetrated deep inside the head, out of sight. And those eyes ...

Where did the artist find stone like that? Curving striations made for a whirlpool effect in the quartz, if it was quartz. The eyes were fascinating. She had never examined them this closely before, and had never guessed that these old souvenirs, as they were called, could have such stark beauty. She held the beam near to the brilliant eyes.

Exquisite.

She drew in closer, and then pulled back with a start. It looked as if a bug had gotten into the figure, in back of the quartz eyes, and had moved suddenly. Something had moved in there. She looked again more closely, and squinted in the dazzling reflection of the light on the stone until she had to pull back, blinking.

It was then that she saw its mouth was open.

The lips had parted, as though they were flesh. The mouth had opened. Black fangs pointed downward from behind the upper lip. Lisette froze at the sight and took in half a gasp. She felt her fingertips sinking into the back of the cat, which was now pliable, no longer as stone.

Its jaws shot open wide and a long hissing breath streamed out against her face. As she wavered, its arms whipped around her neck, and it pulled itself toward her with irresistible strength. The compact, fanged jaws slammed shut on her nose and lip.

She roared in terror and agony and struggled to pry off the unreal creature. But it bit down again and again, and ripped at the back of her neck with its black claws. The cat was viciousness incarnate. It could not be dislodged. Lisette collapsed. Seconds later, she moved no more.

On the shelf of the display case the other cat sat immobile, staring straight ahead. Then, slowly, it relaxed. It shifted its jet black head downward and gazed with gleaming eyes at the scene on the rug below. After a moment or two, it leapt deftly down and sidled up next to its mate to feed.

A lone harpist played softly as two hundred people filed in and took seats at the outdoor funeral for Lisette Harnes. The grounds behind the Black Pines estate house were bordered by willows and dogwoods and consisted of nearly as much acreage as what separated the front side from the road. The air was cool today, but the angle of the sun made for a harsh and oppressive light from a cloudless, vivid blue sky.

Inside the wrought iron fence of the family burial plot, well removed from the rows of mourners, Ted Harnes sat next to his frail, encumbered father, who had been driven up from his home on the coast. He would have to get back to that sea air as soon as possible, for psychological as much as respiratory reasons. Ted shifted his gaze from the ground long enough to look him over and wonder if the old fellow was going to survive the stress of this day at all. Ted's mother and four grandparents were in this ground before him. And now, Lisette.

Sobbing from a nearby section of family servants caught his attention for a moment. They might well weep, he thought to himself. They knew the killer must be sitting amongst them in their row. Every valet, housekeeper, butler, and gardener was under suspicion by the police. Ted himself might have been, but he had been out on the town with friends that entire night, and thus had an alibi. These people had been in their beds asleep, or so they all said.

Not that there was the slimmest rationale for anyone to have hated Lisette. The whole thing was unimaginable. Through his bottomless heartache, all he could grasp intellectually was that one of their trusted servants was leading a double life as a monstrous psychopath.

Well, by God, that person would be found, he swore. But so far the police had been surprised by a number of factors that made no sense. Not least being the absence of any trace of blood anywhere outside of the immediate murder scene. Ted had been processing this and some other uncanny facts for the past five days, to the point he thought he might lose his own sanity.

When a news helicopter came clattering overhead, he stood up and let off some steam. He summoned an usher, pointed up at the thing, and let go a verbal barrage. Only the usher heard exactly what he said, but by the way the old fellow took off running to the house, all the guests understood it was about getting a phone call made regarding that chopper. Ted returned to his seat and placed his hand over that of his father.

Too many speakers spoke, and then, after the lowering of the flower-heaped casket, Ted and his father endured an endless receiving line.

Mrs. Eddens spoke at great length to Ted, assuring him that an eternal bond existed between their two bloodlines. Teary-eyed people who Ted barely knew turned up to squeeze him to their bosoms. When it reached the point that he feared for his father's life in the crush, he yelled out orders to some of the servants. They circled around him, and politely held off the guests. Wheeling the old man in his chair before him, Ted grimly led a procession back toward the family home.

In the weird light of that freakish day, the securing ring of servants parted suddenly, and a dubious looking young woman in wrap-around sunglasses gained access to Harnes.

"I knew your sister," she said to him bluntly, as they walked along, "I will be talking to the police this week about what happened. First I think you should hear what I have to say. It can wait until tomorrow, after you have settled things here."

Ted looked at her, in an almost helpless silence. It was the oddball lady Lisette had spoken to the day of the art show. He was somewhat shocked that she had gotten this close to him, whoever she was, and he only stared and said nothing to her.

"I won't ask admittance to your home. I will meet you at the gazebo there."

She gestured across the lawn to a little rise where there stood a picnic table sheltered under an elegant round roof.

"Twelve noon, please." she said, and broke away from him. He watched as she retreated across to the car park, climbed into a rusty Volkswagen Beetle, and rolled away.

The Beetle was back at precisely twelve o'clock the next day, and parked in the same spot. Ted watched from a first floor bay window as she climbed out and retrieved a large portfolio bag from the back seat. He tossed back the last of a Bloody Mary, pulled on a denim jacket, and strode with a darkening expression out the front door.

They were in view of each other but made no greeting, not even when reaching the high roofed gazebo after a walk of some distance.

"My name is Mindy Linton," she said then, "I should only require ten or fifteen minutes of your time, Mr. Harnes, if you will let me speak."

Ted leaned up against one of the support columns and folded his arms. He made a shrugging gesture, and said, "You say you have information about Lisette. My afternoon is yours."

"It's only that I have tried to talk to you before, over the years, without much success. Maybe you don't remember. You are a hard one to get to see. Lisette was more open to talking with me. Anyway, I should start at the beginning. And I should tell you up front that for some time now I have been working on a book about your family."

He did not look especially pleased at hearing that, and his suddenly glowering countenance threw her a little. She nervously said,

"The book is about ... what I am coming to, directly. But I should start at the beginning."

"By all means," Ted said.

Mindy Linton said, "I first visited your home twelve years ago. I was a Girl Scout at the time. Your mother had invited a big group of scouts with artistic interests to visit and view the artworks. She was a very sweet person. She let us roam around everywhere. You were there, too. Maybe you don't remember."

Ted shook his head.

"Anyway, that's when it all started, Mr. Harnes," Her voice began rising, as she continued, "I want you to know that there is something in your art collection, on the second floor of that house, which has been the preoccupation of my life since I first set foot in there. For half of my life, I'm saying! It is what my book is going to be about. It is why I am here again today. It is something that has cost me, enormously, in money and time researching it over these twelve years. And it is directly related to what happened to your sister last week. So, I am going to hold you to your word that you will hear me out today, and let me speak my piece!"

Ted glanced at his watch and said, "I wouldn't dream of stopping you."

Mindy slapped her canvas portfolio on the picnic table, and pulled out a large sheet of sketch paper.

"This is an ink drawing I made that day twelve years ago, in the old Miles Harnes office suite on the second floor. I was immediately attracted to the cats. I started sketching them right away." She placed the sheet on the table, forcing Ted to sit down to have a look. It was just an ink study of one of the stone cats, adequately capturing the proportions and details.

"Very nice." he said, flatly.

"Thank you. Well, later that day, when I was home, I was comparing my drawing to a photograph of the cats in this book they gave me ..."

She pulled out a dog-eared copy of a decades-old Harnes Art Inventory, which fell open to a full page photo of the two Statuary Cats. She positioned it next to her childhood sketch, and waited for any reaction. But none came.

She said, "It didn't hit me right away, either. But look at the feet."

Ted immediately saw what she was talking about, but did not see any great significance in it. The legs and feet were positioned slightly differently in the drawing than in the photo.

"Okay." he said, "One foot is a little forward of the other in your drawing."

"That's just it," she said, "It's not only in my drawing. I could not see how I would draw the feet askew if they were perfectly straight. I was always very meticulous as an artist. I wrote to your mother and pestered her for another photograph of the statues. She finally sent me one. And, here, you can see it ... I think you can see quite clearly. The right foot on the right cat is exactly as I sketched it, about a half an inch forward of the left foot! Noticeably different from how it is in this 1928 photograph!"

She triumphantly placed the recent photo next to the older one, and her ink drawing.

"I was more puzzled than anything." she said, "I wrote back to your mother to ask if you had any other Statuary Cats sitting around. She wrote back one more time and said those were the only ones in the collection. Of course, it has to be the same cat in each photo; you can tell by the little etchings of fur. They are as distinctive as fingerprints."

Ted looked at the pictures in silence for a long moment.

"It's an illusion." he said at length, "It's a trick of the camera angle."

But as he said it he could see that the angles of the photographs were fairly similar. It was mildly intriguing. He could not immediately understand how there could be this variation in the positions of a stone figure. But the mystery only held his attention in the most fleeting way. He shrugged, and shook his head. Mindy quickly spoke up.

"I was sidetracked with school at the time. But I never forgot about the Statuary Cats. I was able to visit here once again before I graduated from high school. I broke away from a tour group to dash in and look at them for a few seconds. They looked exactly the same as when I sketched them years earlier ..."

She drew herself up, bracing for any reaction before she continued.

"Five years ago, when I was a freshman at UNC, just before your mother died, I was able to get myself hired for summer work on your housekeeping staff. Only twice in those three months was I able to slip inside the old office. I was able to view the figures for only a minute. But in that time I could see that the positioning of both cats was slightly different, measurably different, from how they appeared the time before."

He looked up from the picture and met her eyes. She held the eye contact and said, "There is so much more I could tell you. But at the root of it all is an unavoidable fact about those two figures. Ted, from time to time, on very rare occasions ... they move."

She could not tell what he was thinking. His eyebrows went up a little, and then they went back down. She pressed on with her point, urgency rising in her voice.

"I have evidence to back up what I am saying, sir. You are looking at some of it, but there is more. How much do you really know about them? They are not part of the regular art collection. How much time have you ever given to studying those cat figures?" she asked.

"I know enough about them to know that they are nothing all that special." Ted said, "Granted, I have never seen them get up and do anything. I guess that would be noteworthy." He shook his head, and said, "I'm not sure what to say about your ... belief, Miss Linton."

"You haven't done any special study of the cats." she said, "I have."

Ted said, "The Statuary Cats are old. That is their main attribute. But antiquity alone is nothing exciting. There are tons of old knock-offs of Egyptian artifacts. Very little of such stuff is important, Mindy. The cats were carved by some ancient unfortunate with a thing for Egyptian deities, and my grandfather received them as gifts, or bought them or stole them around the turn of the century. That's about all there is to say about them. I would not keep half of what's in that office if it were not for a clause in the old man's will that says we are to leave that one room just as it is, as sort of a shrine to him."

"Are you aware that there are others just like them in other collections around the world?" she asked.

"Yeah. That's mentioned in the Harnes Art Inventory." Ted said, "They were made by an ancient school or cult, and there are hundreds of them floating around. As it says, they were undoubtedly religious fetish objects, modeled after Bast. There is no shortage of such junk on the antiquarian art scene, Mindy."

She returned to her portfolio and pulled out more photographs.

"After your mother died I lost my access to your house. I shifted gears and began researching the other examples of this kind of statuary art around the world." She held out a photo. "This is a private museum in Amalfi, Italy. They have a pair of the cats. Did you know that they are virtually always found in pairs?"

Ted sat in silence and glared at her.

"I spoke to the secretary of the museum on the phone. She told me about the antiquity of the cats, and how it is unknown where they were made. Then she said that she wished the museum would deaccession them, because she felt so ill at ease around them. I got her talking about that, in spite of the transatlantic charges, and she told me that a janitor had once been murdered in the museum, right in front of the display of the Statuary Cats!"

Ted loudly cleared his throat and said, "Cursed artworks, then. At last I am getting your drift. Well, I can't say I am with you on it ..."

Mindy placed a grainy black and white photograph in front of him. It was a police photo of the upper portion of a man's cadaver. Little chunks of his throat and face were missing. An eye was missing. A man attacked by piranha fish would not have looked worse.

Mindy said, "I flew to Italy and researched this murder for ten days. That was all the time I could afford to give it. It remains unsolved, as far as the police there are concerned. I am going to see what the medical examiner working on Lisette's murder thinks of this picture."

She did not ask, "What do you think of it, Ted?" There was no need. He was suddenly drained of all color. This photograph was a minor personal earthquake for him, having viewed his sister's remains. The marks were not identical, but there was no escaping the similarity. He wanted to look away, but instead found himself drawn in, studying the shape of each little wound on the dead Italian. Could there really be something relevant here?

Having successfully played her ace, Mindy relaxed a bit, but kept talking.

"You spoke of cursed artworks." she said, "That was never my theory. But ironically, I came to a conclusion on all this after I had been reading up on just that very subject. There's not much written information about the Statuary Cats themselves, but there is an endless pile of books about cursed artworks, and haunted artworks, and statues that come to life. You may be surprised at what a huge vein of folklore that is."

She mercifully covered the police photograph with another image, a photocopy of an old woodcut book illustration showing a medieval peasant being menaced by a huge black cat with glowing eyes. The caption said, "Devilment in Hereford."

"It is astounding the correlations I have found between the Statuary Cats and old stories from folklore and mythology. I have located over fifty stories involving statues suddenly springing to life. Always they are in pairs, jet black, and just about waist high. They are usually cats, but not always. Some describe hounds, falcons, and dragons. Shape shifter myths are almost universal, you know. You'll find them in mythology all over the world, including the tribal cultures."

"Shape shifters." Ted said, wearily.

"In essence, shape shifters." Mindy said, "But not of a supernatural origin. There was such consistency in those fifty stories of moving statues that I mentioned, and such wide variation in the other mythical monsters I read about. I think only those very consistent myths were based in reality. Well, I told you I had arrived at a theory on all this. Being convinced that the statues move, I have a conjecture of what they are."

Mindy gestured with open palms, as if parting a fog, "Imagine an unknown phylum of biological life. That is, a kind of animal, as different from all others as insects are to mammals. This would be a kind of creature entirely unknown to science, and for good reasons. They are extremely rare, for one thing. For another, their survival strategy is one that prevents recognition of their being alive at all!"

The eerie woodcut illustration began to bother Ted now. He reached under the pile of papers and pulled out the bottom sheet. It was the ink drawing of the Statuary Cat. This he placed on top.

Mindy said, "I envision a life form that survives by exerting control over its body down to the molecular level. It can alter its body chemistry at will, into that of a solid. In this ossified state it can remain in suspended animation for extended periods of time, possibly riding out whole centuries. Shaping its appearance after that of another animal would pose no problem to such a creature. It would awaken at times and look around, and de-ossify to feed and reproduce when it saw an opportunity. This would be the perfect life form, and certainly the perfect predator. There would be zero warning of its attack, and zero chance to fight it or flee from it ..."

Ted was still giving her time to speak, so she went on, "In my book I am going to state my case for the existence of these animals. I think humans would be their ideal prey. Imagine how a prehistoric human would have reacted to finding a pair of stone animals in the forest. He would likely have carried them straight back to his village, or brought the villagers out to the stone animals. Maybe sacrifice a virgin to them from time to time.

These creatures may be the root of the human trait of worshiping idols. Then, when civilization came along and people started collecting artworks, well, the future was set for these predators."

Ted finally said, "You're telling me that my sister was not murdered, but was killed by wild animals, unknown to science."

"If I'm right, and I know I am right, she was one of thousands of their human victims, down through the ages." She leaned forward, imploring him to believe, "Can you imagine it, the same scene repeated time after time, in modern homes and ancient, candle-lit bedrooms? Unsuspecting people, all comfortable and relaxed, suddenly witness the movement of objects that had been sitting for years as decorations on a shelf? Most of them probably died of coronary arrest from the shock."

Ted mumbled, "An animal that can turn to stone."

"And back again, at will." Mindy said, "In my book I call it an Ossifier."

A light breeze lifted the old ink drawing of the cat, and made it undulate on the table. Ted muttered to himself, "An Ossifier."

"And I think you have a couple of them in your house." Mindy said.

The two fell silent for a moment. They began looking off across the rolling lawn to the stone facade of the four story mansion. Both focused on the same second floor balcony, with its row of French doors.

She saw he had finally digested all she had told him when he looked up at her and broke into a broad smile. Just the break in the tension had her smiling back at him.

"Mindy, Mindy, Mindy..." he said, "You are different. That is for sure." He reached out and patted her hand. "Mad, mad, Mindy. You go ahead and write your book. I don't mind. I guess the big question for now is -- What do you want of me? What can Teddy do so that there need be no further meetings with our own Mindy Linton?"

She kept a smile in her voice and said, "First you must secure the cats in a strong box. A safe would be ideal. I am guessing you have one big enough to hold them? Good. Then put them in it, and leave them in it! That is the main thing I ask. Later, they can be studied in the proper surroundings, if we can work that out with you. I guess that's all I have for now."

As she spoke, something occurred to him in a flash. What was really the most believable scenario for Lisette's death? An "Ossifier?" A long-time family servant suddenly turning homicidal? Or, an attack from a very strange and eccentric woman who suddenly shows up out of the ether, expressing a deep interest in the family and its art?

"Mindy!" he said, "I am so glad we could have this talk." He shook her hand. She was tiny, too small to have overpowered Lisette. Unless it had been a sneak attack.

"It just so happens that there is an old safe on the second floor. I am going to put the cats in it right now, just to put your mind at ease. In fact, since we have been denying you a chance to see them all these years, why don't you come with me? They are too heavy for one person to lug them both. You could carry one of them down the hall with me."

"I don't know if I should." she said.

"Well, why not? Won't they be hibernating for the next hundred years?" Ted said.

"Probably so. I don't know."

"Are you nervous about being in the room where Lisette was killed?" Ted asked.

"No."

"It is all perfectly clean and tidy now." Ted said, "You would never guess what happened in there. Come on, I need you to help me. I gave the staff the day off for mourning."

He kept insisting until she went along. With Teddy making glib chatter it seemed to take only a short time to traverse the lawn, enter the house, and climb the stairs to the second floor. But on entering Miles Harnes' office there came an oppressive sensation of time decelerating. The light was dim. Specks of dust hung motionless, twinkling in sunbeams at the French doors. Ted stopped talking, and the silence became leaden and disturbing.

The rhinoceros stared down at them. The Moroccan rugs were gone. Marble floor tiles gleamed from a thorough buffing. The display cases looked much as she remembered them from the last time she had been here. And there in their regal dignity ...

The beasts.

Ted casually walked over and pulled open the glass door of their case. He gingerly lifted out one of the Statuary Cats and looked it over. Sitting down on the oak desk top, he placed the cat next to him on the corner and put his arm around it.

"It may blow your mind to know that I used to play with these when I was a boy." he said, "Sure! Grandpa didn't mind. Of course he was a little old and out of it by then, so maybe that's why. They seem to have survived me, and the centuries, rather well. They're in better shape than I remembered. Well, come on! Don't be stand-offish. I doubt you will get a chance to see them this closely again! You're not uncomfortable being in here, are you, Mindy?"

"No." she said, "Well, maybe just a little. It's kind of dark. Is that a flashlight?"

Ted reached across the desk and picked it up.

"That's right." he said, "So, they left it in here. They have cleaned it quite nicely, I see. This flashlight was found in here, next to Lisette's body. It was drenched in her blood."

He flipped the switch back and forth a couple of times without result.

"I guess they took the batteries out."

"She was in here, inspecting the cats with that light." Mindy said, in a pained voice, "She had read my essays, and she came down here right away to look them over. I guess that part of it is only hitting me just now! It's like I am somewhat responsible ..."

"Are you?" Ted said, drumming his fingers on the side of the cat. "Responsible? That's a heavy word, Mindy. Especially in light of what happened. I mean, it was the cats that killed her. Right? And yet you have this sense of responsibility."

"Just a feeling," she said, "There is that feeling of partial responsibility. Well, we should be locking them away now. Let's get them into that safe."

"How late did you stay the night of the art show, Mindy?" Ted asked.

"How late? I don't know. There were still crowds of people here when I left."

"Where were you that night? Say, late that night?" he asked.

"Sleeping." she said, still not following his meaning, "Tell me, was there much blood on the cats when they found her?"

"Mindy, there was blood on the cats, blood on the shelves, blood on the rugs ... much, much blood ... all over this area." he said grimly, "And I am going to make sure that whoever was responsible gets busted for it, and gets what's coming to them. Just so you know."

"I can imagine how you must feel." she said softly, "Well, let's get them put away."

Ted was looking at her in a cold way that ought to have made it plain he was not happy with her presence in this situation, but she was still oblivious to it. She was more interested in the stone cat at his side. She had always felt a mild hypnotic effect when she had been in this room, in the presence of the cat figures.

Ted said, "I don't want to rush you out, after all the times we have denied you a chance to see them. I am sorry it's so dim in here." He stood up, and beckoned to her, "Come on! I'm right here with you. Come look at them!"

She drew closer to the desk, and looked into the crystal eyes of the figure. Ted opened a desk drawer, plucked something out and moved over to Mindy's side.

"There have been a lot of cigars smoked in this room." he said, and held up an antique cigarette lighter, "Let's see if there is any fluid in this thing."

After a couple of strikes an inch wide flame appeared on the old silver lighter, and the face of the cat was bathed in wavering yellow light.

"That's better." he said, "There's your kitty, Mindy. I have to tell you, it doesn't look like much more than carved stone to me."

He turned to look closely at Mindy, examining her narrow, pallid face in the same flickering light, searching for any signs of emotional abnormality that might be showing.

She whispered, "It is no work of human hands."

Obsession was plainly evident in her squinting eyes. One of them was having a bit of a nervous tic just now. As her eyes lost their squint and opened wider her pupils contracted in the harsh light of the close flame. She had that look of inner turmoil, of psychological instability. Her eyes were widening further and moving rapidly in a tight pattern.

"Mindy ..." he said.

Her mouth flew open and she took in a sharp gasp. He turned to see the left arm of the cat had risen up, away from its body. In an instant it drew up higher, and then slashed across frontally, striking the back of his hand like a small baseball bat. The cigarette lighter shot to the wall and clattered on the marble floor.

Ted and Mindy took three slow steps backward, as the cat remained seated on the desk. Its eyes no longer looked like quartz, but instead seemed clear, and liquid. It sat motionless, facing them. The office door was several long steps away behind them.

Apart from severe trembling, the two young people did not move. The frozen moment dragged on to an excruciating length. If it had not been for the egg-sized bruise swelling up on the back of his right hand Ted might have been able to tell himself he had imagined the snap of movement from the cat. Apart from its eyes, it looked much the same now as it had looked all of his life, just sitting there, facing forward. And then, as Ted was about to speak, a black, snake-like tail curled into view from behind the cat and slapped down heavily against the side of the desk.

The tail curled upward again and came down on the other side, onto the desk top. It made a sharp knocking sound, and it looked as if the last quarter length of it was still solidified. It was as if the cat was working out the last petrified segment of its body. When the tail curled upward again, it seemed entirely flexible, and alive.

The creature leapt onto the floor and stepped forward. Ted and Mindy held each other in a tight clinch and reflexively staggered back. The cat looked steadily up at them, rolled back its lips to bare its fangs, and released a long, dry hiss. It moved closer, then diverted left and went past them. It ended up by the office door, where it lay down and stretched out.

Casually it rolled over on its back and stretched some more, as if it had just awakened from a long refreshing nap.

Under his breath Ted said, "It's blocking our way out."

A light thumping sound threw their attention back to the display case. The other black cat had leapt down to the floor. It sauntered toward them, stopped, and sniffed the air. For a long, agonizing moment it stood there, regarding them with its glassy eyes. The ghastly images of Lisette and the police photo from Italy whirled through Ted's mind. Then the big cat shuffled on toward its mate.

The creature by the door was pacing in a slow, tight circle. It leaned in to rub its shoulder against the door each time it passed by, and the door was gradually being pushed closed. Intentionally or not, it was closing the door.

"They're going to kill us." Mindy sobbed softly.

Though Ted's mind was seized in the most withering fear of his life, he cast about for a solution. There were objects in the room that might serve as weapons against the animals, but fighting them had to be the last resort. Their strength seemed out of proportion to their size. His right hand felt like it was broken. They were pacing around near the door, and it seemed only a matter of time before they turned on him and Mindy. Their otherworldly strangeness made it all the more grotesque to contemplate death and becoming their food.

Just then the weirdness escalated to another level. The cats had been pacing around together, one behind the other. Now the lead cat slowed down and stopped. Her mate playfully batted her tail a couple of times. Then, he was up on her. Growling and panting, the two horrors mated. After a long minute they were finished, and were rolling together, play fighting. They seemed to rub noses for a moment. Mindy was becoming faint by this time.

Ted was going to slap her face but feared to make any sound. He shook her and said, "Brace up. We're getting out of here."

When he saw she was listening, he said, "The French doors are locked. I'm busting through. You follow me out. Get over the banister and drop to the ground. Just follow me."

"Drop? How far?"

"Hey, it's about ten feet! Do you want to stay in here? Just follow me."

He took a final look at the cat creatures playing on the floor across the room, and then in three long strides he had reached the closest of the glass doors and crashed right through.

He stumbled onto the iron railing that enclosed a small decorative balcony outside and pulled himself over it for a second story drop to the ground. Lurching forward, he was just in time to miss being hit by Mindy, who landed immediately after him on the same spot. He glanced upward to see two black heads with pointed ears appear through the railing, looking down at him from above.

"Come on!" he screamed.

She stumbled along after him, her knee and ankle suddenly throbbing from the fall. He was bleeding in places from smashing through the glass. Adrenalin drove them forward as they saw the black cats moving out across the grounds in a flanking maneuver to their left. The floral wreath on Lisette Harnes' grave was plainly visible in the family plot in the distance, as one of the cats crept rapidly along in a low crouch - the classic stalking pattern.

Ted reached the corner of the house, lunged around it, and made a break for his black Corvette convertible parked not far away. He dug into his pants pocket as he ran, retrieving his key ring, which was fully crammed with keys.

He jumped in over the door and searched for the ignition key. Then a cat was all over him. Its claws ripped into his scalp as needle sharp teeth penetrated the collar of his denim jacket. He turned into a punching, screaming, fighting fiend and threw the cat out of the car. He jammed the key into the ignition and the cat was back on him again, snarling and slashing away at him. He fired up the engine as Mindy vaulted into the back seat followed by the other cat.

With both hands Ted threw off the cat, and slammed the gear into reverse. The Corvette shrieked off the paved driveway and out onto the lawn where Ted executed a hard turn that pointed it toward the road. This had the added benefit of ejecting the cat off of Mindy, who was herself slammed hard into the side panel of the car but remained inside. The car fish-tailed across the lawn and reclaimed the long rolling driveway, bottoming out a couple of times before reaching the road. Mindy held on, but dared to rise up and look back behind them. The two big cats were running along in pursuit for a moment. Then they slowed and turned back.

The return of Ted Harnes and Mindy Linton to the Black Pines Estate took place after a passage of several hours, and involved a procession of four police cruisers with blue lights flashing. When they pulled up to the front door, no one immediately got out. There was radio communication between the squad cars for a minute. Then, all the doors opened at once.

Teddy emerged with extensive head and shoulder bandaging, carrying a shotgun he had stopped to buy at a K-Mart on the way back. He carefully looked through the shrubbery before entering the house. Mindy limped along on a crutch, staying amongst the group of police officers who followed Ted.

At first there were some harsh words for the butler and house keeper he met on the first floor. But in a discussion refereed by the police, he soon satisfied himself that there had been no good reason for any of them to have been close enough to the office to have rendered assistance. Unfortunately none of them had been outside when Ted and Mindy peeled out in the Corvette. None of them had seen any unusual animals.

With the Deputy Police Chief among several officers in tow, Ted strode up the grand staircase to the second floor. He kicked open the door of his grandfather's office and stepped inside. To him, it was like re-entering the bad dream all over again. Because, as he suspected, there sat the two Statuary Cats, side by side in their display case, gazing out into eternity. They were solid, inanimate, lifeless stone.

"Oh no you don't!" Ted bellowed at them, as loud as he possibly could, "You're finished! It's over!" The room reverberated as he continued on that way for several seconds. The officers' faces reflected astonishment, and pure sadness at the apparent psychological collapse of someone who had been an important citizen in the locale until now. The heir to the Harnes Estate was screaming denunciations at a pair of stone statues. When Ted raised his shotgun at the cat figures the Deputy Chief stepped in and grabbed the barrel.

"We're going to do some calming down before we go shooting up the place." he said, "Yeah, I insist, Mr. Harnes."

He took the gun away and handed it off to one of his men.

Ted looked to Mindy, and said, "That's all right. We're going to do this the way you wanted, Mindy. I'll need a couple of your men to help me for a moment, Chief. There is a safe down the hall. I want to wheel it in here."

The Deputy Chief nodded his consent, and two officers accompanied Ted to the door. But before he stepped out he said, "If you see any movement in either of those cats, shoot them both. And I mean let them have it."

A police sergeant who remained in the room turned to Mindy Linton and said, "I hear that you are backing up his story about the statues, ma'am? Is that true?"

She said, "I was here for every bit of it, sir. What he said is true. Those are two extremely dangerous wild animals right there. They are what tore Lisette Harnes to death."

Ted and the two cops returned, pushing a large antique safe on wheels. He squatted down and began working the combination, twice looking over his shoulder at the Statuary Cats. He turned the latch and pulled open the heavy steel door.

"All right. You. Pick up that first one there and bring it over. If you feel anything unusual, throw it down and back off. Okay, let's go."

Suddenly nervous, the officer transferred first one and then the other of the stone figures into the safe. Ted slammed the door, threw the latch and spun the dial. He then slumped across the top of the strong box. Mindy released a long sigh of relief.

"It's all right now," Mindy said. "Now, they will be studied. All the facts will come to light. We can't expect you to understand now, but soon it will all be resolved."

"I hated telling you a story that I knew you wouldn't believe," Ted said, "But I wanted you to know the truth. Now we will get the right people to work analyzing them, like Mindy said, and you will have all the facts. I'm sorry if I have caused you any trouble today."

The Deputy Chief said, "It's no trouble to me, Mr. Harnes. It's just that I hope you understand that nobody but nobody is going to believe something like that without seeing it. You don't have an atom of real evidence."

"What do you call this!?" Ted cried, pointing at the slashes on his denim jacket.

"Mr. Harnes, by your own admission you threw yourself through a glass door!" the Deputy Chief said. "I can see blood streaks on some of these shards that are still in the frame."

"How about the fact that there are two of us making this claim?" Mindy asked.

"That's stronger than one person making a fantastic claim." the Deputy Chief said, "That's about all I can say about it for right now."

"And for right now that is fine with me!" Ted said, "First thing in the morning my attorneys start making arrangements for the state crime lab to do a thorough examination of these two creatures. It is as good as done. Sir, I thank you for your assistance and that of your men." He turned to Mindy and shook her hand, "Thank you for all your hard work, Mindy. We will be in touch soon. Get some rest now."

Attorneys were indeed mobilized at the opening of their offices the following morning. Ted's family political connections were invoked in a series of phone calls to the state capitol, and by that afternoon a prominent North Carolina State Bureau of Investigation van had pulled up to the front of the Harnes mansion. Ted supervised as the safe was rolled out of the house and loaded for transport. He had typed a letter which he sent along taped onto the top of the safe.

By the next morning forensic technicians were puzzling over the letter in a basement lab at the Bureau's main facility in Raleigh. In the letter, the combination to the safe was followed by a statement typed in all caps and red ribbon which implored them to have armed guards standing by when the door was opened. Armed officers were not hard to find at this facility, so it was easy enough to honor this plea. The safe was opened, and two stone statues were lifted out of it.

Ted's letter described in a rambling way his experiences of that day, and something of Mindy Linton's theories on the Statuary Cats. It was apparent that whoever wrote this had just been through a wrenching experience, possibly one that had temporarily unhinged his mind. The lab was being asked to determine it these statues were anything other than carved stone.

The Bureau's technological resources were cutting edge for 1967, but the lab technicians still needed a directive that made sense. They were unsure about just what they were supposed to be looking for. Their director had said only to read the letter and examine the items. Such vagueness was outside of standard procedure, and the technicians were sharp enough to surmise that some political pressure was being applied to the Bureau in this case. It would not be the first time.

X rays seemed a logical place to start, so they conducted a long series of them.

The cat figures under x-ray were revealed as a wispy swirl of solid material, similar to the faint swirling pattern on the exteriors. There were no bones, organs, or anything to hint that there had ever been an animal inside. The stone was solid, and apparently a composite. There were no hollows except for entryways at the ears and nostrils, which penetrated some distance into the head before narrowing to a close. The eyes were not just balls of quartz, but featured slender extensions on the inner side that went back several centimeters into the head.

The team took a rubbing from the cats, tested the material chemically, and studied it under a microscope. The sample contained silicon, carbon, calcium, sodium chloride, ferrous oxide, and manganese. No radiation or magnetism. No unusual properties. The team was able to detect minute traces of human blood on the figures, but this was understood.

From these few facts, a voluminous report was prepared and sent to the parties concerned. Carbon dating might be possible but would require the removal of a significant chip. An address was requested for the return of the figures.

Angrily dismissing these results, Ted Harnes next had his team of attorneys arrange shipment of the statues to the FBI's National Crime Lab in Quantico, Virginia. Here they were received, in their antique safe, but investigation did not immediately proceed. Ted's people had enough clout to get an agreement from the FBI to study the figures, but no specific timetable was offered. The job was not high priority for the FBI, particularly after they reviewed those lab findings from North Carolina.

Months passed.

Ted's father died suddenly, leaving him sole ownership of the Harnes Estate. He had not slept a single night there since his sister died, and had lost all of his former love for the place. The horrific memories overshadowed all else. Ted set in motion the complete liquidation of all of his family assets, and relocated to a private island in the Caribbean. Shortly thereafter, he began what would become a lifelong exploration of the bars of Europe.

Mindy Linton found a small press that took a chance on her book, The Strangest of Life. It had all the impact of a marble tossed in the sea. Mindy never wrote another one. Eventually she married and found modest success as a portrait painter. She also began receiving a monthly stipend check from the Harnes estate, with no explanation from the accounting firm that sent them, other than they would be coming to her monthly for the rest of her life.

When the FBI's National Crime Lab finally decided they had studied the cat figures long enough to satisfy the request of a certain North Carolina Congressman, they contacted the attorneys representing Harnes to ask where to return the items. Ted's instructions had been for the statues to be destroyed after the investigation. But the statement from the attorneys to the lab was phrased, "Dispose of the statues."

This instruction percolated through the layers of the lab's administration, and for months nothing happened. When space limitations forced a decision to be made, the items were shifted over to General Services Administration with a document describing them as artworks of ancient but uncertain origin. A new president was elected not long after that, bringing with him some shuffling and reorganizing of the federal bureaucracies. Then it happened again, with the president after that one.

Today the Statuary Cats sit side by side, heads held high, on the top shelf of Rack 12 in Storage Room D-41 of the Antiquities Museum of the Smithsonian Institution, Washington DC.

THE END

SILENCE OF
THE STATUARY CATS

"All right then, where are they? ... Did they just get up and walk away?"

In the depths of the storage facility for the Smithsonian Institution's Antiquities Museum, a red-faced rage had come over Tuft, the new weekend manager. What was supposed to have been a tranquil job, gentle on his nerves, had proven to be one wrangle after another for him. Now, halfway into this Saturday, two artifacts were missing, probably due to theft.

He assembled the skeleton staff that had been working in the building that day, two maintenance men and the paunchy, elderly security guard. Figurines and trinkets from various bygone civilizations sat on metal shelving all around them, making the vacant spot seem all the more conspicuous. Tuft pointed a damning finger at the empty shelf section.

"Those cat sculptures were sitting right here this morning when I came in. Not four hours ago I saw them. Now, where are they?"

The faces of the maintenance workers were as bereft as the shelf. The security guard wore an expression that said he understood he only had to hear just so much of that tone of voice from this man on this job, and he that he had almost reached the cut off point. The weekend manager carried on,

"Okay! We were the only ones in the building today. That can be verified. So I want to know about this right now ... Where are they?"

Nobody knew.

The security guard spoke up, pointing out that the two statues in question were each nearly three feet high and solid stone. They would be just heavy enough to make them difficult to carry out. Most likely they were still here in the facility somewhere. Maybe they had been moved for some reason other than theft. When Tuft challenged him to come up with a good explanation, he could not. But he had more to say,

"Why is there nothing else missing, aside from those carved cats? Isn't this Mayan comb made of solid gold? Why did nothing else get grabbed?"

When Tuft muttered in a threatening tone that he was bringing the police in right now, the guard suggested making a call first to Mr. Burton, the Director of Security. This proved to be an astute move, because when the director was reached at his home he insisted he alone would deal with the police.

When Burton heard Tuft reading the description of the missing items, he was perplexed by their low estimated dollar value. "Less than ten thousand dollars" often meant considerably less than ten thousand dollars, in the language of the museum's inventory. It struck Burton that these were not artifacts that would have any black market value. He mulled it over for a long moment, and then said the whole thing could wait until he came to work Monday morning. He hung up.

But he came in that afternoon anyway and called Tuft in to his office.

"'Decided I wanted to go ahead and get started on this incident of the missing artifacts," he said, "My assistants won't be here 'til Monday. No point calling them in. You can help me. Pull up the inventory file on these missing pieces. What are they? Sculptures, you say? ... Statuary Cats. Get their support packet or whatever material we have on them. Then lock up and have everybody who worked today wait outside this office. I'll be talking to them."

He spoke with the employees individually. Tuft had wanted to be present for this, but he was sent out of the room to wait indignantly for his own questioning. The interviews were brief, nothing like what the FBI would be doing. But before he finished Burton felt there was only a remote chance that any of these men would be engaged in such a theft. Time to haul out the surveillance footage, which would likely resolve everything. He gave Tuft instructions for retrieving it and setting it up for a screening.

It turned out the missing statues were in a section very poorly covered by cameras. In his grumbling way of speaking, Tuft reminded Burton of that when he brought the tape cassettes to the office. Tuft didn't seem to like being drafted into this helper position so Burton sought to pacify him by sharing some of his thoughts with him.

"I know that particular section is not well monitored," he said, "and there is a reason for that, which takes us right to the heart of the matter. That section is the lowest priority, lowest valued stuff in the entire system. Whoever stole these items did so just because he liked the looks of them. Somebody has committed a federal crime to obtain something with no black market value. I find that damned puzzling."

The storage section in question was covered by one old twentieth century camera that recorded a still image every ten seconds. Had they waited until Monday the relevant footage would have been lost to a recycling of the tape. Now it was all set up and playing on the screen in the director's office.

The same static shot of the storage racks clicked by over and over in grainy black and white. The side view of a passing maintenance man winked in and out of the frame. The two black cat figures were just visible in their space on the shelf, sitting at a three quarter angle. Their lower half was concealed by a clay pot, but the two black heads with pointed ears were clearly visible.

Minutes clicked by -- and then, there was only one.

The director stopped the video. One cat head was still present on the monitor.

Tuft blurted out, "So ... in the ten seconds that elapsed before this shot was snapped, someone slipped in and snatched the other figure!"

The director jotted down the time, then sat back and thought about it for a minute. He started the tape again. After a passage of three minutes the other cat vanished from the screen. No human appeared anywhere in the footage except for the cleaning man who had walked by some forty minutes before.

Tuft said, "I am wondering what you're going to put in your report."

Burton responded only by sending him out to bring back a number of other surveillance cassettes from elsewhere in the facility. They would spend a solid hour and a half looking at these without seeing anyone or anything suspicious.

"I think now is a good time for me to wish you goodnight, Mr. Tuft. I will finish up here and get ready for the FBI." Burton said, "They will be contacting you for another round of questions, I'm sure."

Tuft stood and placed a heavy cardboard box on the Director's desk.

"Then I will leave you with the support packet for the Statuary Cats, as you requested," he said, "For such a low-dollar exhibit, this box is completely crammed. Goodnight, and good luck."

Director Burton made himself a mug of Earl Grey tea and settled in at his desk. Apart from a strange absence of people on the surveillance tapes he had only one interesting tidbit for his report. It had come out during his interview with one of the maintenance workers. Today instead of just sweeping the floors they had also mopped them with ammonia. One of the guys had raised the bay door of the loading dock about ten inches to air the place out.

The cleaning man said he had replaced the padlock on the bay door after cracking it open, so there was no chance anyone could have opened it any higher. And he was certain it was not open high enough for any person to slip in. He swore it was open approximately ten inches.

If the door had been up a little higher, it might have been possible that the artifacts had been slipped out, whether any person got through or not. It suggested an accomplice had to be outside on the loading dock. That kind of an effort to steal such unimportant pieces did not make much sense, unless there were some facts about these cat carvings that had not made it into the inventory.

On Monday he would have his assistants plow through this support packet, which was a box containing any material on an exhibit not scanned into the computer. Lifting the lid, he saw Mr. Tuft wasn't kidding about it being crammed. Maybe there was some clue to a higher valuation somewhere inside. For now, he only wanted to pluck out the photographs that should be in it.

The box held a sprawl of folders, papers, and disks. Some Smithsonian materials were on top, bearing a dated stamp from twenty two years ago. Burton shook his head. How long had these things been sitting around in storage?

He read softly to himself, "Statuary Cats ... ancient ...origins unknown. Likely religious fetish objects. Possible variations on Egyptian Cat Goddess, Bast."

He found a stack of glossies. Nice close up photos. These artifacts made for an intriguing sight all right. The clear quartz eyes were especially interesting. Somebody had gone a little nuts taking extreme close up pictures of them.

Numerous documents from different sources were in here. Apparently these low priced heirlooms had been the subject of some wide ranging studies and lab tests, some of them dating back to 1967. It was odd. Chemical analysis, x rays, microscopic examinations - it went on and on. Then there were photocopies of newspaper articles from somewhere in North Carolina, also from that distant year.

Burton was shocked to read that the cat sculptures had been associated with a murder case back then.

He poured through the newsprint to learn of a wealthy young woman, found slashed to death. Her brother and some friend of his had seriously tried to make the claim that the stone cat figures had sprung to life and mauled her! Officials working the case had dismissed their hysterical tale of moving statues as being a joint delusion between two traumatized young people.

A joint delusion. "Must have been one potent joint," Burton thought to himself. He decided that one was funny enough to remember and tell the guys when they came in to work on Monday.

One of the clippings said the friend of the brother had written a book in which she set forth a theory of a kind of animal, unknown to science, which could petrify its flesh like stone and "de-ossify" back into living tissue at will. Under the last of the newspaper clippings, sat a copy of that very paperback! A hand-written letter from the author was tucked inside, asking that her book and the newspaper clippings remain with the Statuary Cats exhibit. Someone at the Smithsonian had obliged her on it, all those years ago!

He thumbed through the yellowing pulp pages of the paperback for a few minutes. As expected, this was distilled weirdness. The writer envisioned a genuine shape-shifter, a life form that had total control of its body chemistry, to the point that it could enter a rock-like state and then return to supple flesh at will. Such an animal might survive for eons. The author, Mindy Linton, claimed that the two sculptures, which had now gone missing, were in reality just such creatures, and that ages ago they had shifted their appearance to resemble cats.

Bemused by it all, he let his eyes flash across several paragraphs of the eccentric writing. "Ossifiers" dwelt in these pages. Little black statues, always in pairs, they would stir and move and turn predatory after decades of gathering dust on a shelf.

He read the obligatory ancient tribal legends of stone idols consuming meat, and assorted tales of haunted sculptures in medieval castles. Included was the uncanny testimony of an 18th century French librarian whose doorstop grabbed at him, and chased him out of the building. Unsolved 20th century murder cases were presented, with some fairly appalling morgue photographs.

Burton shook his head with the disgust of insulted intelligence and plopped the book back in the box again. Then an idea struck him. Even though this book was likely a single edition printing from decades in the past, it could have a bearing on the theft. Maybe the book had a true believer. Maybe somebody out there believed in this book, and coveted the Statuary Cats. Some New Age zany probably got in here somehow and swiped them for his prayer altar. They were thought to have been carved as religious idols, after all. A mystical motivation for the theft made more sense than somebody hoping to get big money for them.

He recalled that early in his career an old detective told him, "When a case makes no sense at all, think of it in terms of sex or religion."

He made some notes on this, and wrote instructions for his assistants to have the complete text of the Linton paperback and the newspaper clippings scanned into the system. Burton would also have the complete files on this theft sent to the top three international databases on stolen art. And he wanted a copy for his own private "odd cases" collection. Only then did he place a call to a personal friend at the FBI.

Investigative work on the missing cat sculptures filled out the rest of the day inside the storage facility. Outside, after sunset, the wind picked up and swayed the boughs of centuries-old oaks on the grounds of the Smithsonian Institution. As evening passed into night, a yellow full moon made its arc across the sky. The spacious grounds were deserted. Only the oaks moved, with their millions of leaves hissing softly as the gusts blew through.

In pre-dawn darkness, halfway up an especially magnificent tree, a well-fed Eastern Gray Squirrel emerged from his nest in a hollow. He had sensed that the first glow of the sun would soon appear over the roof of the storage facility, though right now it was still dark as midnight. Sudden high winds raked through his fur, and he held tight to the tree bark with his slender claws.

When the wind stilled he sat up on his back haunches in the moonlight. Like a little cartoon man he stood upright and looked around, urgently. An expression of concern came to his rodent face as he sniffed the cool night air.

Instantly, like a preying mantis grabbing a fly, two clawed paws shot out of the foliage and snapped together on the squirrel's midsection. Wriggling and bleeding, he was deftly lifted up and held before two glassy round eyes that reflected moon glow.

These were eyes without pupils or irises. They were translucent balls, nothing more. Every other feature of the face was that of a cat.

Lips drew up and back to reveal curved, pointed black fangs. The jaws parted, came down over the squirrel's head, and closed. The movement was as effortless as one biting off the end of a candy bar. There was a quick shot of blood and the rodent was lifeless meat, now pinned onto the tree limb under the cat's paw. Strong winds rolled in again, stripping leaves off the oak and making the cat growl in irritation at being jostled.

At the far end of the bough, dense leaves parted with the emergence of a second, identical black cat. His claws, like carpet knives, dug into the bark with each careful step as he approached his mate in a low crouch. He repeatedly sniffed for a hint of the prey as he drew near. This provoked his counterpart to lean forward, bear her formidable teeth, and release a long rasping hiss that speckled the limb with squirrel blood and her own inky black saliva.

It was a display that would have dissuaded any other life form, but the two mates hissed at each other often, and the male only inched closer. Ultimately he touched his black tongue to the blood on the branch. The female snatched up her kill in her jaws and began climbing to the tree's highest limbs. Her mate followed along behind.

After some grumbling, the two sat facing each other, sharing the snack on a spindly branch with a view of much of the Smithsonian complex. They consumed all but the fluffy tail, which they watched spiral down through the oak. Tenderly they licked the gore from each other's muzzles and snuggled together on the swaying treetop. Soon the first light of sunrise was reflected in their perfect eyes.

When dawn was well established, but before the mist had burned away from the grounds, occasional joggers and walkers began to appear.

Among them, a noisy and brightly colored trio of visitors made their way through the fog. A wide-hipped woman in a hot pink jogging suit with yellow leg warmers was pushing a sky blue, three-wheeled child carriage. A shining golden retriever on a retractable leash led the way. The baby carriage held a child just old enough to loudly announce every sight he saw. He had learned the word dandelions, and repeatedly proclaimed their presence at the top of his lungs.

The Golden Lab came to a sudden stop beside one of the oaks. The young mother, slightly winded, did not mind waiting while her dog sniffed intently around the tree's knobby roots. A squirrel tail lay in plain view on the ground. Tentatively the dog examined it. The child, too big for his carriage, leaned forward and cried out that it was a squirrel's "coat."

He whined, "Can I have it, Mama?" pointing down at it, and knowing he could not have it.

The woman was suddenly more interested in the behavior of the dog. He had sniffed the squirrel tail and now was standing motionless, staring down at it. He seemed paralyzed, and tremulous.

"What's the matter, boy?"

The dog stepped back and whimpered. He looked all around, whining softly. Suddenly he took off, striding away from the oak. His leash unreeled to its maximum, and when it latched, he pulled her along. The woman barely had time to turn the stroller in the right direction. She called out for him to stop and stay. But he pushed on at a pace just short of running. He would not let up. Only once did he look back to meet her eyes. She stopped yelling at him then, and followed along with the child. He was heading in the direction of the parking lot and their mini-van. She thought to herself that more obedience lessons might be in his future. Or maybe she would just trust him this time since he had never behaved this way before. In any case, their morning stroll was over.

Minutes later, with no one around the tree, the two black cats made their way down to the lowest bough and casually dropped to the ground. Side by side they moved gracefully out across the park through fading fog. Acres of partially wooded terrain stretched out around them with bike trails and foot paths snaking through. The cats kept to a straight course, as though they had a definite destination.

At one point, a woman's piercing voice rang out with, "Oh my God! Look at the size of those cats!"

An alarmed male voice followed, "What are they?"

The powerful creatures continued across the park, slipping under dense shrubbery and passing along for some distance beneath it. They came to a rest, cuddled side by side in a cool, dark, earthy-smelling patch of old leaves. Through the bush they could watch sparrows flitting and fussing in a grassy area before them.

It was a flat lawn, likely meant for croquet or badminton. The birds scattered when a yellow tennis ball rolled their way. A massive German shepherd came bounding along after it. He retrieved the ball and trotted back. After a minute, the cats watched a repeat of the process.

Several times the tennis ball went zipping by with the broad chested black and tan dog in pursuit. Maybe the cats grew tired of seeing this, or maybe they had rested here long enough. They moved out onto the lawn as a pair.

The ball crossed their path a few feet in front of them; they took no notice of it. When the shepherd barreled out of the fog in their direction they looked at him and turned to face him. This had an effect like a long rug being pulled backward under the dog. His front end dipped lower than his hindquarters and his paws splayed out in every direction as he went from a full sprint to a dead stop.

His mouth was clenched shut but his eyes were as wide as they could go. With his fur standing straight up off of his body, he looked as if he had been electrocuted. The stand off ended as soon as it began, with the German shepherd tearing away back toward his master. He did not stop when he reached the bewildered-looking fellow in jogging shorts, but kept on running.

The young man stood with a box of dog biscuits in his hand, looking first at his retreating shepherd, and then turning to view the creatures staring back at him across the lawn in the mist. Two pairs of eyes burned steadily at him, holding him as if frozen in an apprehensive trance. They broke away then, moving off simultaneously the way they had been going before. They passed under more bushes and emerged onto a city sidewalk. Soon a grimy, deserted commercial area was unfolding around the trotting cats.

They made their way with purpose down a street of closed businesses, hugging close to storefronts and security gratings as they passed. Pigeons and other small animals vanished. A white plastic bag rolling in the wind caught their attention for a moment, and then they continued on in the muted light of the overcast day.

Across the street on the next block, a bearded homeless man pushing a grocery cart stopped at the sight of them. His expression went from blank to aghast as he watched their approach. He paused, then stepped into the street and spontaneously launched into a frenzied, screaming tirade of religious denunciations.

"Hell spawn! The Lord God rebukes thee!" he shrieked, "Beasts of Satan! Thy wickedness shall be bound!"

The cats regarded him for an instant and kept moving.

"Demons! Thou shalt be cast into the pit! The outer darkness!"

He hauled a Bible out of his flannel shirt and held it up as he reached back into his cart for a glass bottle. The cats had reached a point directly across the street from him.

"Devils!" he cried, and hurled the bottle at them.

It smashed on the curb throwing fragments everywhere. The cats hesitated for the briefest tick of time, and curved their path out onto the street where they came to a stop facing the scruffy man at a distance.

Gasping sharply, he was confronted by a new reality. He found himself looking around, as if for another person or a car, or at least an open doorway. There were none of these. But there was a narrow alley, and now he bolted for it.

The faint pattering of small padded feet on asphalt was audible to him above the sound of his own running feet and wheezing breath. He did not dare to look back, but poured it on, running faster than he had since his teens. He knew they were behind him, perhaps by mere seconds.

Dashing up the broken pavement of the alley he caught sight of what might save him. A vacant lot was just ahead with a cyclone fence around it. Awash in adrenalin, he tore forward, leapt onto the fence, scrambled up and fell over to the other side.

He lay on the dirt and beheld stark images straight out of his most fevered hallucinations. They were inches from his face; only the metal strands of the fencing held them off. They were silent, but their dark mouths hung open and long, sharp black teeth were in plain view.

One of them jammed a paw under the fence at him, dragged its claws across his shoulder and tore his shirt. He rolled away weeping.

The other monstrous cat threw open its mouth and flared its eyes as if screaming at him. But only silence followed.

The mated pair then turned as one and walked back down the alley. The man remained on the ground holding his shoulder, and watched them walk away.

At the street they made a left turn and sauntered past his grocery cart down the sidewalk. A car shot through the intersection ahead. Across the street a man in dark glasses moved slowly along sweeping a white cane back and forth before him. He paused for a moment, listening.

At a tree by a three-story brick building the cats climbed up, transferred onto the roof, and continued on their way along the ledge.

There was a series of buildings of this same height, so they were able to traverse all the way to the corner, where they stopped and sat together, looking out onto the world.

They took interest in the activity going on in the park which spread out from the opposite corner. Even at this distance, birds, squirrels, and tiny chipmunks were easily discernable in their flawless vision. The quick, small movements they made held the cats transfixed. Other creatures passed in and out of view through the cover of leafy trees. Dogs on leashes trotted around chaotically. Mature humans and children accompanied the dogs, and wandered about on their own. All of these life forms were good, suitable food for the cats, and as they sat observing their motions from high above, a sense of superiority and ownership came upon the two predators.

Vehicles sped by on the street, but non-food held no interest. Motorized vehicles were a recent experience in the millenniums-long lives of the cats. But their fascination with them had faded during the time of the Model T.

Hunting and feeding fantasies often filled the consciousness of the two creatures, and so it was now as they surveyed the park. They were also aware of the need to find a base. They knew they would soon need to find a place where it would be safe to sit, ossified, for however many days or years or decades suited them. But living through ages of time at the absolute top of the food chain imparted a unique sense of confidence to this pair. They did not have to bother themselves. What they needed would materialize for them. In this case, it took about an hour and a half.

People began setting up tables in an empty parking lot on one of the corners. A large banner was stretched out between two poles. Its flapping motion held the cats' attention for a few seconds. Hand painted lettering on the banner read,

"Kiwanis Club Flea Market! White Elephants! Knick Knacks! Stuff! Things!"

Mini vans and station wagons pulled in and balloons and flags rose as the sale came together. Items for sale soon began to appear on the tables. Old stereos, books and computers were set out on display. And then, something came into view that shifted the cats' focus away from the park..

There were figurines. Horses. Elephants. Eagles. Dragons. There were statuettes, in all sizes and materials. A sense of exultation swept over the two creatures on the ledge.

They went from intense staring at the flea market statuary to snuggling their heads together, and rubbing their faces against each other's bodies. They did some play fighting and took turns petrifying into a granite hard state, and back again, over and over. When playtime had gone on long enough, their attention turned to getting down from the third story roof and over to the tables of the tag sale.

It was early yet. Customers were outnumbered by the matronly sales staff. The volunteer sales ladies drank coffee from a communal urn. They also savored the sense of roughing it, being out here sacrificing their Sunday for the greater good of their standing in their social club. They shared chit chat when no customers were near their tables, whispering their impressions of the bleary early morning crowd.

Sitting at a table, an elderly sales lady suddenly let out a yell, and claimed that a dog or something had just brushed by her leg. She awkwardly bent down for a look under the tablecloth. Nothing there.

One of the girls at the coffee urn nodded in the direction of the old woman, and said it had surely been a while since her leg had been grabbed by anything, and they all giggled.

Early afternoon saw a crowded, bustling marketplace. Not enough parking spaces had been provided, and people skirmished and wailed over them.

At a table of hand-carved figurines imported from some far away sweat shop, business today was snappy indeed. The rotund proprietress waited until her table top was nearly sold out before she restocked it. This limited the number of times she had to kneel down and reach underneath into the boxes of items she was selling.

Having just made a sale of several carved marble dragons to a chatty couple and sending them on their way, she saw her table top was looking bare. She let out a sigh, plopped her kneeling pillow on the paved ground, and shifted her weight down onto her knees. She bent over, threw back the tablecloth, and there before her sat two visions from a dream world.

Seated amidst her bric-a-brac were two enormous carved stone cats. They faced her directly. She knelt, still holding up the tablecloth with one hand. For her it was a moment of fundamental shock. For starters, who could have put them here without her noticing?

When she recovered to the point of moving again, she reached in with both hands and grasped one of the figures at its shoulders. It was a cool, glazed black stone, covered with etchings that looked like fur. She pulled it toward her and struggled to heft its weight. She lost her balance and sat down hard on the pavement, the heavy cat statue pitching forward onto her breasts.

The statue had a look of antiquity, yet its condition was beyond excellent. The crystalline eyes in particular were flawless. She passed a fingertip across the statue's bulging eyes, and found them perfectly smooth, perfectly round. Swirling fissures in the clear eyes went back deep into the head, out of sight.

The volunteer sales woman was usually a great talker, but she was dumbstruck as she got to her feet and wrestled the pair of carved cats up onto her table. She stood examining them in silence as the market crowd circulated around her.

She made no reply to the query from a neighboring volunteer, "What ya got there, hon?"

Idle browsers began to take notice, too. At least one man asked, "How much?"

When she did not respond the fellow walked away in a huff. This one-sided encounter attracted the attention of someone who stood at a distance but observed incisively. His attention was soon fixed entirely on the cats, and the woman examining them. She was someone unfamiliar with what she was selling.

He positioned himself in front of her at the table, aggressively cutting off another man who had arrived there seconds before. In his expensive looking suit and precisely coiffed hair, his presence was imposing, even intimidating. He had a dark olive skin tone, and apparently no compunctions about using his piercing eyes to maximum effect on dowdy sales clerks with whom he intended to negotiate prices. He seemed to be someone who was older than he appeared. He took out his wallet and flipped it around playfully in his long slender hand. The open side with the visible layers of currency faced the clerk.

He said, "I am thinking these items did not come from the crafts club of the ladies auxiliary." He smiled.

The sales woman was still unnerved by the two inanimate objects on her table. Now with this third pair of staring eyes trained on her, she slipped a little and said,

"I don't know where they came from."

He turned one of the stone figures to face him. The round feline face struck an immediate chord. Here was a splendid representation of one of the classics of nature – the observant, patient, predatory cat.

"Extreme realism," he said softly to himself, "Uncluttered ... There's a quality of timelessness. It has the air of antiquity, however old it may be."

He prattled on to the clerk as he inspected both pieces,

"Flea markets are chaotic places, of course. Items get shifted around, delivered to the wrong booth. But with this market we're in luck because all the proceeds are going into the same ... kitty. Am I right?"

"Oh, yes!" she said, "It's all to benefit Kiwanis."

"So, no commissions involved? That's good." he said, "Well, there are some items at this market that caught my eye, but nothing like these. They are ... very nice. So, I need to know what you are asking for them."

The clerk said, "Their tags seem to have come off."

"Yes," he said, "I didn't see any."

He picked up the heavy statue and carefully turned it upside down. The saleswoman leaned in to help steady it, and they were both presented with its prominent stone testicles, and its nub of a penis.

The gentleman could not help laughing; the sales woman drew back. He turned it upright on the table again.

"No price tag." said the prospective customer.

He proceeded to draw up what he said would be a fair price based on multiplying the price of one of the marble dragons by the difference in the size of the cat figures.

"... So, let's round it up to four hundred dollars." he said.

"For the pair?" she asked.

He smiled tightly and plucked a credit card from his wallet and placed it in her hand. She dutifully ran it through.

"I'm afraid I don't have a box to fit them." she said as he signed the slip.

He picked up one cat and transferred it to his left arm, then slid his fingers under the other and boosted it up to his right arm. He used a thumb to lift the flap on his jacket pocket. She tucked the credit card and receipt inside.

"Thank you, Mr. Costino." she said.

He smiled, winked, and walked away toward the parking area. People stepped aside from his path as he neared them.

Some time later he was slipping down a tree-lined avenue in an old Georgetown neighborhood in his Jaguar convertible. The Statuary Cats sat side by side on the leather seat next to him, a seat belt and shoulder strap holding them securely in place. A copy of Architectural Digest stood between them to prevent them scratching against each other. Mr. Costino placed a call on his phone,

"Hey you! I'm about to turn into the driveway. Come out and meet me, and bring Frankie and a camera!"

He wheeled into the brick driveway of a two story Georgetown home, this one painted a much brighter shade of yellow than any other on the street. The driveway went straight back into a garage, but also forked off into a circle at the front of the house. He chose to park up front where the sunlight was better. He hurriedly scooped up the figures in his arms as he heard the side door unlocking and crashing open through weatherstripping.

His wife and teenage son made their way to the car as he leaned against a fender, not unlike a teenager himself. He was beaming, with a heavy black stone cat sitting cradled in each arm.

"Looky what I got!" he called out.

Jerri and Frankie stood staring for a few silent seconds, then she raised the camera and snapped the shot.

"They're amazing, Dad!" said the boy.

Raul Costino passed one of the figures off to his son, saying, joyously, "Slope head at the yard sale didn't know what she had!"

His wife asked, "Do you know what you have?"

Placed at opposite sides of a bookcase in a great, airy living room, the new decorative accessories entered the Costino home within the week of the annual Halloween bash. The Costino family was the smallest on the street in terms of numbers, but they always threw the best parties. Was it an unconscious effort to make up for the fact that theirs was an only child? The neighbors could only guess and gossip, and go to the parties. These affairs were not to be missed, especially those held on New Year's Eve, Saint Patrick's Day, Raul Costino's birthday, and Halloween.

Numerous jack-o-lanterns glowed from strategic locations in the grand living room. Tonight the framed proclamations of political groups (for which Raul Costino had consulted) shared the walls with puerile Halloween decorations made by Frankie and "Sneddy," as well as the cutesy hangings bought by Jerri at a party supply store. On the glass-topped coffee table, baskets were heaped with submarine sandwiches and orange sugar cookies. Vintage Karloff and Lugosi unreeled on the video screen. The Costino's impressive sound system played twentieth century Halloween novelty songs, until the high school crowd that was accumulating in the room cried out for something else, anything else.

The music had been mother Jerri Costino's idea, and she let it play on for a while. She could easily control what played, since the sound system was housed in a cage-like box of ornamental burglar bars. Not only could it not be stolen, it could only be played by the person holding the key. She would later give in and open it up to whatever noises they wanted to hear, but for now she took a subtle delight in inflicting the silly old tunes on these kids. It was just a way of making her presence felt to Frankie's friends, who could not have been more obvious in viewing her only as a food-serving robot.

It was early in the evening and the party would go on all night, just like last year. Somehow Jerri did not seem quite up for it. She wore no costume this year, just a frumpy, generic Halloween sweatshirt and jeans. The year that had passed since last Halloween had not been a happy one for her, which was something she concealed with precision. There was no particular reason for her feelings, other than "getting old," or "being stupid," or other harsh self-criticisms she allowed to rampage through her head. She resolved to host the party seated at her kitchen table, monitoring events with her visiting sisters. They had coffee with various liqueurs. If a kid entered the kitchen he needed a good reason, because, "The party is out there. What do you want? Go on out there and have your party."

The visiting ladies gently questioned her as to whether anything was wrong, and she gave the obligatory answer of no. Later she opened up a bit and said,

"Maybe it's my nest emptying out. I don't know. Frankie is going away to the Air Force in eighteen months, but he is basically independent now. I rarely see him. And, I guess I just haven't put together anything special I like to do on my own. I don't know what I'm going to do when he's gone. We wanted more kids, of course. But after Frankie it never happened again. Something about Raul. I don't know. He wouldn't tell me what the doctor said. Anyway, for God's sake don't let out to anyone that I said that. It doesn't leave this room, got it? But, anyway, we would have had more kids, but Raul couldn't."

She went on to confide that Raul was always working, and always on confidential consultant matters that he won't talk about. She was tired of listening to his vague descriptions of what he did. He was always so cagey in his way of speaking about it. She did not even ask him about it anymore, but it was the biggest part of his life, so that made it tough, not being able to share in it. He was supposed to be here in an hour for the party, and he would be bringing a lot of people she didn't know, and they would be yelling and laughing all night.

Frankie showed up just at the threshold of the kitchen. In tribute to a movie monster that was popular that year he was wearing a black sweatshirt with little round Vienna sausage cans glued all over it.

His mother sighed, "Yes?"

"Mama, everybody is voting that we change the music. It's pretty serious. They brought some music we could put on. We just need to do it."

A friend of his chimed in, "Yes, that last song was a real atrocity, Miz Costino. We all really think we should put on something else -- that we brought."

Jerri and her sisters looked at the spindly kid. He had a glass eye stuck to his forehead with putty, and on either side of his nose was glued a plastic nose. The two boys stared earnestly at her until she got up and plodded off to unlock the sound system.

"We sure appreciate it, Mrs. Costino."

"Thank you, Mrs. Costino."

"These sure are tasty cookies, Mrs. Costino."

The tenth graders assembled so far this evening wore Halloween costumes that were pretty terrible, as many of them would admit. A few of the young men wore only Army fatigues with some green and black combat paint on their faces. One poor boy at the bottom of the social pecking order had sacrificed two rolls of toilet paper to make himself "The Mummy." He was derided about it throughout the night.

"Hey, toilet paper mummy. Come here, I need to wipe myself."

"Folks, if anyone needs to, umm ... wipe ... please call for Fred Ipton."

The girls at the party opted for cute, or in some cases, sexy costumes. One young woman was a long time in the bathroom with her friends, debating and squealing over whether her black cat costume was too revealing. The pointed ears and whiskers were staying. The legs were the part she had not decided about. The costume had come with pajama-like pants. These all the girls in the bathroom agreed were "imbecilic." But the alternative of a black bikini bottom and fishnet hose failed to draw a consensus.

After much wrangling, the votes were all for the bikini bottoms and hose, and the detested pajamas were consigned to the trash can. It was a decision which was to incite tensions with other girls yet to arrive, which would only escalate as the night wore on.

The roaring, crashing, falling-down-stairs sound of the year's new trend in music came blasting out of the sound system as the girls made their entrance from the bathroom. Frankie's friends had discovered the cat statues at this point, and he was telling them how his father had found them. He strained to talk through a contemptuous laugh,

"My mother has started calling them Jinx and Midnight! The two tritest, most hokey as hell names anybody could possibly come up with!"

The cat suited girl made her way to the bookcase, and declared sensuously that she loved the statues. She moved in to face the one on the shelf in front of her, presenting her bottom to the suddenly fascinated boys. She played a fingertip across the cat's stoic, stone mouth.

She leaned in close, and said in a breathy voice, "Oooohh ... I love your eyes!"

Some of the more conservatively costumed girls began grousing amongst themselves at this overt display, but they were not audible above the sound system. At a sharp rhythmic turn in the music the cat girl whirled around, and began a swaying dance for the boys. Five of them who had been standing nearby started dancing around her.

A muscle-bound guy from the school's football team proved himself as awkward and maladroit on the dance floor as he was on the field, slamming his shoulder against the bookcase and tipping it back about an inch. As the case tipped forward again, books and cat sculptures got jostled.

"Careful man! Damn!" Frankie said, hoping his mother had not seen that one.

The front door flew open, and a tall figure wrapped from the head down in a black cape strode in toward them. He threw the cape open to reveal he was Raul Costino, with vampire teeth gleaming. He fixed his gaze on the cat suited girl and roared out,

"I have come for your blood, little girl!"

Frankie put his hand to his brow in bottomless embarrassment and moaned, "Oh God no."

The cat girl drew her lungs full of air and released an extended, ear-ripping shriek that went on and on until she was breathless and faking a faint into the arms of the football hero. Carloads of adults poured into the room around Raul, all of them wearing expensive, professionally made Halloween costumes. Gorgeous women took immediately to the floor, crazily dancing to the kids' music.

"Back yard!" Frankie called out to his friends, "Right now! Follow me!"

The high schoolers evacuated out the back door into the dim, chilly yard. Raul's friends took over the party, and showed how it was to be done. Raul opened his spectacular liquor cabinet, and his bellowing laugh set the tone for the night. At one point he made eye contact across the distance with Jerri who sat at the kitchen table playing cards and drinking with her sisters. He would later go in and pointedly remind her how important all of this was for business.

Several hours later, when the raucous gathering had been toned down by the first departures of the night, Raul put on softer music and people drifted into conversational knots.

Howie Madden, his attorney, had settled by the bookcase, intrigued by the cat carvings. Raul launched into an extended brag about how he acquired them, and how they must be worth plenty more than he paid. Howie admitted to being fascinated by them.

"They do have a look of antiquity." he said, "They might almost be Egyptian. You need to have them researched, man. You might need some insurance on them."

Raul said he had no time for that. He had no money in them. But Howie pressed the point. He pulled out his phone and snapped a few pictures of the cats. He said, "I'll poke around on the computer next week when I'm recuperating from my foot surgery. Sure, it'll give me something to do. Listen, you might really have something here, Raul."

Out in the back yard, boom boxes were blaring. In a scene that could have been enacted a century earlier, the teens secretively passed around a flask of whiskey. There were other flasks making the rounds, too; one of vodka and one of tequila. Some of the kids had too much of the mix and had vomited all over Jerri Costino's bonsai trees.

Just then a tipsy, poorly costumed witch who had "just about had enough" of cat suit girl abruptly threw a loud slap to her face. A screaming, hair-tearing tussle ensued. The two ran around to the front yard of the house, followed by their laughing, yelling and crying cohorts. The uproar was audible inside the house, and Jerri bolted up out of her chair in the kitchen.

Raul caught her eye from the living room, and dismissively waved the situation away with one hand. He said, "Let 'em play. Let 'em play."

Frankie took advantage of the distraction to move aggressively, and drunkenly, on a girl he had been pursuing for some time. He took her in his arms and tried to kiss her, but forgot about the Vienna sausage cans protruding from all over his upper torso. They complicated the clinch, to the point that the girl wrestled away and delivered her own roundhouse slap to the side of Frankie's face.

He bellowed out in a breaking voice, "Dad!"

Jerri rose from her chair, and Raul again waved his hand at her, and shook his head no. He resumed his conversation with his lawyer and friends.

Jerri settled back heavily into her seat. She poured herself a rum and Coke, and again thanked her sisters for being there with her. She said,

"There is something else that's bothering me tonight. I didn't mention this to you before, because it's kind of silly. But it is weighing on me … It looks like my cat has run away. Remember Skittle? She took off like a shot one day last week when I opened the front door. It's been a week now, and I haven't seen her since. She's gone. She's just gone. And I miss her. I sure do."

Weeks passed, and Raul was out in the front of the house on a brisk afternoon waxing his Jaguar, something he enjoyed doing for himself. The phone beeped and it was Howie Madden, wanting to come over.

"As long as it has nothing to do with business." Raul said, "I'm taking a day off."

"In fact, it has nothing whatever to do with business. But I think it is something you need to hear about." said Howie.

He pulled into the Costino driveway within minutes, clambered out of his BMW and hobbled over on a cane and a surgically repaired foot. He got right to the point while Raul continued fondling the Jag.

"I don't know if you remember, but I told you I was going to do some research on those statuettes you have in your living room." Howie said, "Well, to say the least, I found out some things. I really hate to tell you this, bud, but they are identical to a pair of carvings that went missing from the Smithsonian Institution not too long ago. That is the bad news ..."

Raul held off on the waxing and looked up at him.

"The good news is they don't exactly seem to be straining themselves over at the Smithsonian to get them back! They have assigned a very low dollar value to these statues, still better than what you paid for them, but not enough that any major effort is being launched to recover them. Also, I got it from a friend at the FBI that this is something at the lowest end of low priority for the Bureau. They seem to be waiting for the items to surface on the black market somewhere. And yes, it is the FBI that handles thefts from the Smithsonian."

"That is all very strange, Howie." said Raul.

"My friend, you have not heard the strange part yet." Howie said.

"Well, do I have to give them up?" Raul asked, "Because I'd rather not, you know. If you see it as something that would pose a risk for the business, then okay. But if I can safely hold on to them, that's what I prefer to do."

The lawyer said, "The only risky thing as I see it now is if you were to sell them. You have no plans to do that, do you? Good. Then they can probably sit forever in your living room with no problem. And if any stink should ever come of it, you just say that you innocently bought them and were not trying to profit on them."

"Good enough." said Raul, and he returned to his chamois and wax.

Howie said, "It is weird, though. Some of the stuff I found on the 'net. There's one database of stolen art that lists six pairs of black stone cat figures similar to yours missing from museums around the world. Apparently there are hundreds of statues just like yours in existence. The thinking is that some ancient religious sect was mass producing them. What's odd is how often they seem to turn up missing or stolen!"

This caught Raul's interest, in a worried way. He asked, "Are there any theories as to why that should be?"

Howie said, "There is a kind of a theory. Mystical cults." He took some papers out of his jacket, "Check this out."

Raul wiped his hands and took up the sheaf of computer print-outs. He read, "The Strangest of Life ... Mindy Linton ... Hmmm ..." Halfway into the page he started smiling and looked up at Madden for a second. After a page and a half of reading he was chuckling out loud and shaking his head.

"Yeesh!" he exclaimed at one point. He handed the papers back to Howie with a "Wow."

"Isn't that great?" Howie said, "Wackiness! If you keep the statues you may want to have them spayed. Anyway, so there are some in law enforcement who hold the view that people with strange belief systems might be stealing these statues from museums. Just something to bear in mind. I really don't think you have to worry about that, or the cops either. I just wanted you to know what I found out."

Raul said, "I appreciate it. I'm kind of sorry to hear there are hundreds of them like mine. But then again, if they were mass producing them, there's no hard evidence that mine are the same ones that got stolen. Right? And I like the bit about the mystical cults, in a way. Adds a kind of a tang." He pitched the chamois into the bucket and said, "I'm keeping them. Let's go inside. How's the foot? What are you drinking?"

Two years later Jerri Costino saw her prediction come true. She did not know what to do with herself after Frankie graduated from high school. It was not that her life lacked for activities; there were plenty, even shady thrills like gambling. Nothing she was doing seemed significant, not in comparison to her days of motherhood, guiding her progeny from babyhood onward. A sense of irrelevancy hung over her. The decision to see a psychiatrist came after an incident in which she saw her inner turmoil manifesting itself in the exterior world.

It happened in the hours before sunrise on a still April night. It had been an unusually tender night with Raul. He had wanted to talk, and for a long time in bed they had held each other, his lips near to her ear. Later, when he was in a deep hibernation, her eyes were still open. She was drifting in and out of sleep, but was mostly conscious. She lay on her back, barely breathing. The room was silent at this predawn hour.

She suddenly felt the mattress depress slightly down by her foot. There was no mistaking it. Something was pressing down on the edge of the mattress near her foot. She went from half dreaming into a state of sharp awareness. She made no movement, and soon discovered that she was unable to move, not even a finger. It was as if her brain was not telling her body to move. Her eyes slid shut, but she remained completely alert.

Sweat formed on her face and body as she felt a depressed spot appear a little higher on the mattress, alongside her knee. Her breathing and heart rate seized up with the sensation, but the sleep paralysis was complete. Even if she had been able to move she might not have done so at this moment. Half of her wanted to lash out in the direction of the pressed down spot. But lying motionless also seemed like a good thing to do. Maybe it would go away, whatever it was.

But it only seemed to move further up the side of the mattress. Progressing slowly, it pressed down on the bed alongside her hips. With that, a whirling panic came over her, and she made an all out attempt to move but could not. Her muscles might as well have been severed.

Many times in years past her little cat had come into the bedroom at night, and walked up the side of the mattress and settled down purring by her pillow. She had a habit of leaving the bedroom door ajar for the cat, and had continued to do so over the two years since it ran away. She held on to the hope that her pet might come back someday, slip through the cat door in the kitchen, and make her way up to the bedroom again. She had felt there was at least a chance that her first pet might come home again. Not so much for the other cats she adopted afterwards. They had all run away almost immediately upon entering the Costino house.

This was no cat stepping through the darkness beside her body. Though she could see nothing, the weight of it seemed closer to that of a baby or toddler. Her shallow breathing and the unreal nature of this experience combined to distort her thinking. As time went on with no respite from the sleep paralysis, her stressed and conflicted mind retreated into fantasy, seizing onto pleasant images from a time when in fact there had been a baby crawling beside her on the bed. Baby imagery and cat imagery merged in a dreamlike way within her mental vision. When long minutes passed with no further movement from the side of the bed, she slipped more and more into a dream world.

Wakefulness crashed back on her yet again with the feeling of tiny puffs of air, barely discernable, on the side of her head. Something was smelling her hair. Upon realizing that, her mind closed down in a faint.

The sound of Raul singing in the shower and brilliant sunlight filling the room brought her back to reality. She sat up with a start. The memory of what she experienced overnight was thoroughly clear in her mind. It was no dream. It had been a delusion of her fully awake mind. She decided she must visit a psychiatrist. She would not tell Raul, who would never understand. She only hoped the doctor would.

She sat on the bed and relived the experience over and over, burning it deep into her memory. Only then did she remember something else to tell the doctor. On two other occasions, when she had been alone in the house, she thought she had heard what sounded like a baby or young child sighing. It had been so fleeting that she had dismissed it as the wind. Now she wondered if it was part of a pattern of mental aberration.

The sound had been so similar to that of a baby. It reminded her of baby Frankie, having a dream in his cradle. It was exactly as she remembered the sound of his small lungs filling with air, and exhaling.

Some months after high school graduation, Frankie was having a final fling of freedom before Air Force basic training. At the same time Raul Costino had decided to take his increasingly depressive wife on a restorative cruise of the Caribbean. They were departing for ten days, and Frankie would be house-sitting in their absence.

He lugged his parents' two steamer trunks out to the waiting limousine.

"You're sure this isn't a cruise around the world?" he asked, and the three of them had a smile, mostly just from the good mood of the moment.

Jerri said, "I had to have some empty space for all the stuff I am bringing back! If you don't want me to bring you anything I will just take an overnight bag!"

Frankie said, "Bring back a few pounds of that fine Caribbean smoke, folks. I'll need it for boot camp."

His parents let the wisecrack drop, and after parting hugs and kisses, they settled into the limo. Frankie waved as they pulled out of the driveway. He turned and jauntily jogged back to the house.

"Come out, come out!" he called. A curvaceous young woman dutifully emerged from the nearby guest bathroom, and he took her in his arms.

"'Only got ten days," he said, between kisses, "So we need to make it count."

He put his hands on her round hips, and gently swiveled her body to and fro. Then he was fumbling with the buttons of her blouse. But she wanted music, and dancing. She pulled away from him and started looking through the selections on the sound system. Its cage door was unlocked and standing open.

Frankie quickly agreed to whatever pop ditties she wanted to hear and got her back in his arms again. The dancing that followed lasted only a few minutes.

With her blouse and his tee shirt together on the glass coffee table, the two lay on their sides, entwined together on the sofa. They stayed like that only briefly, as the side by side position did not accommodate Frankie's aggressiveness. He forcefully pulled her underneath him and sprawled on top of her, his head floating through a flood of his favorite fantasies.

She moved to the music, making arousing sounds for him, and thought ahead about where they might end up going for lunch today. She had some concern about the prospects of making love on this old sofa, which was apparently going to be happening sooner rather than later. Overall she was just pleased to be with this handsome, popular, powerful personality. Although she found herself imagining what it would be like if instead he was another young man she knew, who was not as good looking and charismatic, but was still a very sweet guy.

She played her fingers through his dark hair, and let her gaze wander around the ceiling and the framed art on the walls. He was wrestling with her jeans now, and it struck her that he might break the zipper. She whispered at him to be careful, and he reared up and kissed her passionately on the mouth. When her eyes opened again, her head was tilted in the direction of the bookcase, which stood behind the sofa. She dreamily passed her eyes along its shelves.

He felt her body stiffen suddenly, in a way he was not expecting. She gasped, in a harsh, horrified manner, "Let me up." she said urgently, "Frankie ... Let me up!"

She began punching her small fists against his shoulder blades, and squirming toward the edge of the couch. He turned to his side and released her, and she was out from under him in an instant. Looking past him to the bookcase, she snatched up her blouse from the coffee table and began steadily backing away. He lay there for a few seconds, slightly stunned by this turn of events. To his amazement, she was trembling violently.

"Sweetheart, what in hell is going on? You're covered in goose-bumps!" he said.

She made a superficial attempt at laughter, and said, "Let's go upstairs to your room. Yeah, let's go. Right now."

He walked with her to the staircase at the side of the room, but then stopped and held her close for a moment, calming her. He asked her again what was wrong.

She nodded in the direction of the bookcase, and said softly,

"I saw that cat statue ... looking down at us."

Frankie's instincts were good enough to prevent him from laughing, or saying anything she might take as demeaning. So he said, "The cats' eyes do seem to follow you around the room. It's an optical illusion."

"That's not how it looked." she said, hollowly, "It was looking down at us."

They both gazed across the room at the antique bookcase, where the black stone cat sculptures sat on opposite ends of a shelf. They were sitting in the same place they had been for years, staring straight forward, heads held high.

Frankie just said, "Okay."

He put his arm around her and the two of them walked up the stairs in silence. He thought to himself what a strange kid this one had turned out to be. Various psychological and hormonal conditions came into his mind as explanations. He had no intention of talking with her about it any further. Indeed, the incident would never be mentioned again. As they entered his room and closed the door, his only concern was for how he would ever get her back in the mood.

With his four year hitch in the Air Force just behind him, Frank Costino walked into the living room of the family home late on a summer night and dropped his duffle bag on the floor.

"You're looking great." said his father, opening his arms for a hug.

"'Can't say that I'm feeling great," said Frank as he embraced his dad, "but I guess I'm okay. I have some things to talk to you about before I turn in. Where's Mama?"

"Your Mama hasn't been doing well lately." Raul said, "She couldn't stay up this late. She's just ... asleep. You can talk to her tomorrow at breakfast. Let's have a drink."

The liquor cabinet was as impressive as ever, but otherwise Frank noticed some big changes in the place since he was here on leave two years ago. Some of the oil paintings that had hung on the wall all his life were gone. The caged sound system was gone. The antique bookcase had been replaced with a smaller, cheaper version, and most of the leather bound volumes were gone. The Statuary Cats sat on top of this cheap new bookcase, as bookends for an old set of encyclopedias.

Raul said, "I see you have noticed a few empty spaces in the room. Well, don't look for the piano in the den. It's been sold off, too."

"What happened?" Frank asked.

"Medical bills mostly." said Raul, "Great big hefty ones. Mainly for your mother's varied conditions, but then again I can't say I'm in the shape I once was. And I have retired from some of my more lucrative action. The income just hasn't been there lately. It kind of snuck up on us. I have had to liquidate all kinds of stuff ... Junk! I have junked some junk, that's all."

"You sold the paintings and you kept the cat statues?" Frank exclaimed, looking up at them.

Raul said, "Oh, well, you know, I couldn't very well sell our mascots. Besides, it turns out they are not such big money pieces. You will be glad to know that the house itself remains free and clear. It is ours. And it is worth plenty, Frankie. I will never sell this place. You and your kids will get it when I'm gone."

They drifted into the more homey space of the kitchen and settled down with a bottle of single malt at the table in the breakfast nook. Small talk about the condition of the house filled up the time it took to finish off the first shots. Frank admitted he needed the drink. Then he said, "Dad, my news is not so great, either. Emily's staying in the Air Force. She's going to Europe. It's over between us."

Raul's voice turned angry as he said, "What? Those clods can't break up a married couple like that! I'll make some calls. We'll get her stationed here."

"Dad! She's divorcing me!" Frank said, "She's taking the baby and going to Europe. She's claiming emotional abuse, whatever that is ... It sounds like what she's doing to me!"

Raul was silenced. He ran a few scenarios through his mind, but found none worthy of voicing. Surely his son's situation would not have come to such a point had there been any way of doing it differently. He sipped his whiskey in a wordless funk, and left the talking to Frank.

"The baby was the problem." Frank said, "She didn't want me to be around that child." His voice took on a hard edge. "She said I was not responsible enough or mature enough or something, you know, to be a father. I think she just wanted to be the only one that had any influence on the kid. I was just the sperm donor in all this! These days I am thinking she never had any plans to stay married to me from day one. The whole marriage was a big scam on me from the start!"

"What kind of child support are you going to pay?" Raul asked.

"Apparently nothing!" Frank said, "That's the weird part. My lawyer told me she just wants out. I am just supposed to get lost."

"So, no visitation privileges." Raul said.

"I guess if I want to fly to Italy every weekend." Frank said, staring down into a very tall glass of whiskey. "No, in other words. No visitation privileges."

Raul thought it over, and gradually his face deflated with the realization that there was no good answer here. He swallowed a powerful slug of the pricey booze, threw up his hands, and said, "You know what? I'm really sorry to hear about it, but that's life, isn't it? Life's a joke and then you croak. If you want a sugar coating on it you have come to the wrong old man. You just take the lesson, and the sooner you move on, the stronger you'll be. That's the long and short of it, sweet boy."

Frank began nodding his head in the affirmative as he heard this. He said, "No sense making more of it than it is. You're right again, I guess. It's over and the only thing left is to start something new. And start making some damn money."

"Now you're showing brains." said Raul.

"It is just that it is a very, very fresh wound." Frank said, heavily.

"Well, son … that is why the good Lord above created Scotland." Raul said, and poured another shot, "Do you know how long I have been saving this particular bottle? I bought this bottle back when I … "

A loud, deep thud sounded suddenly in the house, followed immediately by a rumbling, crashing noise like something collapsing. It went on for a few seconds, with both men at the table staring at each other in fearful astonishment as it continued. The silence that followed was almost as scary as the racket. Raul quietly moved his chair back, and stood up. He and Frank cautiously ventured into the living room.

On the floor next to the bookcase lay five volumes of encyclopedias, sprawled in a pile where they had fallen. Several feet away from the books sat the black stone cat that had been holding them in place. It was upright, unbroken, and placidly staring straight ahead. Another volume was lying on its side at the top of the bookcase. Father and son stood dumbfounded for several seconds looking at the scene.

Frank spoke up, "I guess they were ready to tip over for a long time, and they just finally went, huh? I would love to have seen how that cat bounced to land upright like that."

Raul softly muttered, "A million to one shot."

With the passage of ten years, Frank Costino had become Sales Manager for a small but rapidly growing executive airline. His home was in Pennsylvania, but it could be said that he traveled.

The traveling was more or less constant, and his wife of seven years had moved beyond the feelings of being the team player who kept a stiff upper lip, and of being the martyr who made sacrifices for a traveling husband. Now she merely resented the fact that hers was the husband who was never home. The two children were beginning to take the same tack, but they were young yet, and got by with anticipating the great celebrations that came when their Dad finally took some time off from work. The little boy had precociously compared his father to Santa Claus, someone who shows up with a big bag of toys once a year.

It came during one of those special times of Daddy being home. A telephone call interrupted the festivities in a way like never before. Frank took the call and heard the rasping, aging voice of Howie Madden, his father's attorney. It was among the last voices he ever expected to hear, and apprehension came with the mere introduction of the man.

"Frank, I hope things are going well for you, and that you are at a point where you can take some time off from work," Madden said, "I have some tough news. Your father had a heart attack this morning. It was fatal, Frank. He is no longer with us."

When only silence followed, Madden stated the fact again in different words, "He is deceased."

At about this moment Frank's kids began screeching and squealing across the room, and he muted the phone and bellowed at his wife to shut them up. She glared at him, and took the children outside.

Back on the phone, Frank said, "I can't believe this, Mr. Madden. Though it has been a while now since I last talked to him. I figured he was doing okay."

"They are saying it was a massive coronary, Frank." Madden said, "Which is rare these days, with all the safeguards. But it still happens. Apparently it was all over pretty fast. I am sorry to say it was your mother who found him there in the living room. She's asking for you. I have a nurse with her, but you're going to need to get down here soon. Your mother is in a terrible state and you're who she wants to see."

"I'll be on the next plane." Frank said, wearily. A kind of emotional numbness settled over him. He saw immediately how alone he would be in his feelings.

Working for an airline sped the process along, and by sunset Frank was checking his family into a hotel in DC. At this point he had no idea when the funeral would be, but it had been so long since he had spent any time with the wife and kids he brought them along. The whole situation would just have to be worked out as it happened. For now he went by himself in a taxi to see his mother.

The drive through the old Georgetown neighborhood was the same trip back in time it always was when he visited. There was a historic designation to this section, so by law they could not make many changes to it. Phantoms of Frank's youth moved through every yard, park and sidewalk. Memories of his father fell into place among them.

The house was all lit up when he arrived. Several cars were in the driveway. It looked almost like one of the old party nights. Of the people in the house, Howie Madden was the only one he recognized. He escorted Frank directly up to his mother's room.

She was sedated but awake, and spoke not a word as she sat up in her bed and held Frank close. At intervals she would weep, but there was none of the hysteria or prostration he had feared might be the case with her. When she finally spoke, it was devastatingly coherent.

"I never thought it would be like this," she said, "I don't know what I thought the end would be for him, but I never expected it would come like this. From what I saw ... it must have been terrible."

"Howie told me the doctor said it had been a quick passing." Frank said, "They didn't seem to think he had suffered much, or at least not for very long."

"I just know how he looked." Jerri said, "And that I will never forget."

"Mama, I am going to politely get all these people out of the house and then I am calling the hotel and telling Pam that I will be spending the night here with you. In the morning we will talk all about it, and make some plans for the funeral, and ... going forward." Frank said, "You look like you need to sleep. I'll make us a breakfast in the morning and we'll take it from there."

She gladly accepted this, and Frank said he loved her, and kissed her goodnight.

The morning brought phone calls and even a delivery man with flowers, but Frank was determined to take care of his mother first. He recorded a message for the phone saying he would soon be in touch with anyone who left a message, and he put a note on the door asking for privacy. He carried a cup of coffee up to her room. She was dressed, sitting at her writing table. She smiled for him, but her words were pained.

"I don't know if I can stay on in this house. But I don't know if I can stand moving away from it." she said. "It's too big for me. It was too big for the three of us ... This house was our great accomplishment. But it's too big. And now I have the memory of seeing your father downstairs ... like that."

Frank held her in his arms and said there would be plenty of time to decide if she wanted to move, or to where. She seemed preoccupied with the subject, but he finally led her on to other matters. They made their way down to the kitchen and the breakfast nook where Frank had put together a simple meal. It was a bracer for Jerri, and soon afterwards she rose and took him by the arm. She walked him into the living room.

"This is where I found him." she said, as they stood near the old sofa. The furniture had been rearranged since Frank had last been here. The sofa and its glass top coffee table now faced toward a television on a side wall.

"I had just come home from my exercise class, and I saw that he was sitting on the sofa. I saw the back of his head. The TV was on. I called to him, but he never answered. That's when I walked around to see him. He was in his bathrobe and slippers. And ... he looked more horrible than I can say ..." Her voice trailed off, and tears spilled.

"I really don't understand, Mama." Frankie said, softly, "All I heard was that he had a heart attack and it was all over for him in a moment."

Jerri held tight to his arm and said, "He was all drawn up. His arms were all clinched up in front of him like he was set to fend someone off."

She struggled to hold her composure as she went on, "His face was all contorted. His eyes were bulging. His mouth was open, and his lips were all drawn back … he looked like he had been electrocuted."

"Oh God, Mama. I'm so sorry you had to go through that."

"I am still going through it." she said, "I will never get the sight of it out of my mind. And for some reason he had taken the cat statues down from the top of the book case. They were both sitting on the coffee table, right in front of him. Why on earth he would have wanted to examine them that day I can't imagine."

"What? Those things are heavy!" Frank said, "He had no business lifting them."

"I don't know what he was doing. Nobody has moved them in years." Jerri said, "Do you think the exertion set off his heart?"

"I don't know. Maybe. We should get rid of those things." Frank said.

"Oh ... no. Your father loved them," Jerri said. "You remember. He always said he would never sell the cats."

As it happened, Jerri Costino was able to live in the family home another five years. Her health was declining, and for the last two years she had a live-in housekeeper who did some basic nursing. Jerri was relying heavily on the woman, so it came as a bitter blow when she departed her position abruptly one afternoon, leaving behind all that she owned. The maid ran out, literally. As she passed by a neighbor's residence she screamed that the Costino house was "possessed."

The housekeeper never returned, never called, and never claimed her last paycheck. For Jerri the hurtful incident was the final deciding factor that she would move into an assisted living home.

Over the ensuing years at her new residence, she often told her son of her desire to return to the Georgetown house. She was the sole owner of it now, and flatly resisted any suggestions of selling the place. Nor did she want strangers renting it. If it could not be her home again, she wanted Frank and his family to live there. The house was closed, and sat unoccupied, with sheets covering the furniture. Thus it remained, until for Jerri Costino the time came that influenza became pneumonia, and then death.

Still the house was not put up for sale. Frank was so preoccupied with other affairs he did nothing with the property he now owned. Another year passed.

His youngest child graduated from high school and departed for college. It was at that juncture that his second wife suddenly, and with little explanation, presented Frank with divorce papers. She said she had been waiting until the children were on their own, and now she was through with him. She would not talk about it with him except through an attorney. She screened out his telephone calls. She also very nearly zeroed out his finances, essentially taking everything before the proceedings were finalized.

It turned out that inheritances were not community property, so Frank was left with the enormous house full of memories in Washington, D.C. And he still had his airline job, which he could do from there. Within two months he had relocated to the old Costino home in Georgetown.

When he entered the place with his suitcases on that first morning he found everything much as his mother left it. He sneezed from the dust. Fortunately sheets were in place on all the furniture. There would be considerable work ahead for him putting the place in order, but he looked forward to it. He felt it could only be therapeutic.

His mother's writing desk had been brought downstairs before she moved out, and now stood in the living room in place of the book case. The Statuary Cats sat at the rear corners of the desk, oddly enough on top of the sheet. He walked over and looked down at them and was surprised to see not so much as a speck of dust anywhere on them.

During the week of his fiftieth birthday, Frank Costino came to an interesting high point on his emotional roller coaster. He found himself flushed with energy, and filled with a desire to seize the day. He had begun dating, and was now taking dance classes with a terrific new woman. He had the interior of the house painted a new color, not dissimilar to what was there before, but new.

On a glorious April morning he padded barefoot into the living room, in a contented but introspective mood. He wore a silk bathrobe and carried a mug of coffee. Settling in at the writing desk he had to wonder why they had always put furniture in front of the bay window. This view was nothing to conceal with a book case, especially in springtime, with flowers and songbirds and new life in motion everywhere.

He took out a large flowery greeting card he had bought the night before, and carefully considered his words before writing, "No special holiday, and I haven't known you long enough for an anniversary. 'Just wanted you to have some thoughts from me on paper. And it needed to be the best looking paper I could find ..."

He sat back and chewed on the pen and thought about what to say. He gazed out at the front yard for a moment, and then back inside to where the Statuary Cats were facing each other from opposite corners of the desk. Presently he wrote, "You have a bigger effect on me than you know, sweet one. When I am with you I have a feeling like I am sixteen again. I honestly feel like a teenager again, just starting out."

He sipped at his coffee and thought some more. There was lot of space to fill here. He should have gone with a smaller card. As he contemplated his emotions, a fleeting awareness came into his mind that the cat statues had not been facing each other before, but had been facing into the room. The strangeness of that fact began to take on some resonance with him as he considered that no one had been in the house lately but him.

He raised the mug of hot coffee and sipped in a big mouthful as he regarded the statue on his left. Its head rotated to look at him, the way a preying mantis will pivot its head for a look.

Man and cat remained perfectly motionless, as did time, it seemed.

The coffee mug was heavy enough that it slipped down from his mouth. As it drifted lower, the cat's jaws eased open. The corners of its mouth sank downward. Its glassy eyes flared open wide. Frank let his coffee mug hit down with a thump and from the right hand corner the other statue emitted a low, rattling growl.

The cat on his left curled back its lips tightly to show shining black fangs. Breath was softly streaming out. Its feline body shifted from the sitting position, turned and extended a paw toward Frank onto the desktop. The opposite cat inhaled deeply, and growled again.

Watching as both statues gradually came to life before him, Frank went from a state of mental disintegration into full blown shock. Coffee trickled from his lips. He had lost his bladder within seconds of the first movement of the stone figure. Now he was paralyzed, with only his wide eyes shifting frantically back and forth between the hissing, rumbling entities.

The cat on the right brought its growling up into a fell-throated scream. Frank turned reflexively in that direction as the cat on the left settled into a crouch. Frank snapped his head back again to find the creature leaping, slamming into him under his jaw. With one devastating bite the animal took out a massive chunk of flesh from the side of his neck. Blood exploded into the room. He shot to his feet and grabbed the beast by its shoulders but could not dislodge it, even in the struggle of his life.

The other cat landed shrieking onto his right shoulder. It sliced its black claws across the man's face and head. Skin and muscle parted like wax, and the claws raked across the skull itself. Frank made two last stumbling steps backward and collapsed, smashing through the glass top of the coffee table.

It was two months before the contents of the murder house were released by the police. It was months later before attorneys for the next of kin contracted an auction company to dispose of everything. It was agreed that the sale would be handled without revealing the name of the deceased. This was to keep out the sensationalist tabloid media and those odd hangers-on that are fascinated by homicides. Antique dealers and collectors who regularly attended the auctions would be the only ones there, and they would not know they were bidding on items from the estate of Frank Costino.

The ornate liquor service with its many high quality unopened bottles drew a healthy sum. The writing desk had been cleaned and refinished by the estate, lessening its value. But it still found a buyer. Various old books and paintings made their way to new owners.

The gentleman in charge of the proceedings then drew everyone's attention to the pedestal holding Lot #129.

"We now offer this striking pair of black stone cat sculptures. Thirty three inches in height they are. And as those of you who inspected them know, these pieces are flawless, folks. Not so much as a chip out of either of them. We will start off the bidding at two hundred dollars. Let me have two hundred dollars. Two hundred ... now two fifty. Do we have two seventy five? Three hundred dollars."

There was considerable interest from the crowd. Some people felt these were the stand-out items of the sale. Up until the bidding topped eight hundred dollars, there were several hands in the air. Then, as it must be, the serious parties were separated out one by one, until the auctioneer brought the gavel down with finality.

"Twelve hundred! Twelve hundred! Going once, going twice ... Sold for twelve hundred dollars to the happy couple in the second row! ... I am sure they will make a splendid addition to your home."

THE END

KITTENS OF
THE STATUARY CATS

A woman curled over with age clung to the steering wheel of a sprawling old time luxury car. She had come to a total stop in the lane before putting on her turn signal and beginning to enter her driveway. A truck appeared from behind, blasting its horn and swerving around her. Trembling, she got her vehicle safely off the street and sat staring straight ahead.

With every trip these days it became harder to ignore the decline of her driving skills. The larger implications of it hung in her mind as she looked out on a springtime scene of new life in her front yard. A single yellow songbird sat on the edge of her bird bath, looking back at her before it flew away.

She was in far better shape for her age than her twentieth century ancestors would have been, had any of them reached this age. Her life had surely been richer than that of anyone in her family tree. There were many consolations she could take and review. But they were only consolations. Sitting here in this antique car she heard her own voice in her mind, saying,

"No more driving … No more driving …"

She climbed slowly out and made her way to the front entrance of the brick house, embracing a bag of groceries with both arms as she went. By the time she negotiated the lock and opened the heavy wooden door she was truly tired out. She stood inside the foyer and rested for a moment, leaning on the knob with the door still standing open. Something caught her notice then, and she glanced over toward the living room.

There, reclining together like twin sphinxes, two extremely large black cats were looking up at her from the throw rug. Had it been two fifty pound tarantulas lying there making eye contact with her the impact could hardly have been greater. She froze in place, though the heavy bag of groceries slipped a little.

She felt oncoming terror building inside her, not yet fully realized. The hypnotic sensation of looking into another world also took hold. They appeared to be cats, but for their size and the glassy, empty look of their eyes. So motionless was this identical pair that she wondered for a second if they were inanimate objects. She was struck by their almost perfect resemblance to the pair of black cat sculptures she and her late husband had owned for so many years. But the sculptures were in a sitting position, not reclining as these were.

One of them crinkled its nose slightly, ending any doubt they were alive. They continued to stare her down, and she began to waver. Her breaths now came out as little whines. Soon the groceries slipped and crashed to the hardwood floor.

The cats' attention shifted to the bag at her feet, and the trickle of green fluid from a broken jar of pickles that was slowly snaking out in their direction. The creatures rose to their feet as a pair. One of them stepped toward her. It stopped and turned to gaze out the open front door. Casually, the two of them ambled past her out of the house. She put all her weight into slamming the door after them, bruising herself as she shoved it closed and locked it.

Lightheaded and gasping, she lurched into the living room and collapsed into the recliner. As she struggled to regain normal breathing she was dealt another blow. She saw that the cat statues she and her husband had bought at an estate sale so many years ago were no longer sitting atop the cabinet at the side of the room. Everything else in the room was just as it had been for years, but the Statuary Cats were gone.

Her heart rate and tortured breathing would not be calmed. She sat hyperventilating in the overstuffed chair, her eyes fixed on the empty space where the cat figures had always stood. She felt the solid world of life disintegrating and phantoms of unreality imposing themselves. Her voice in her mind spoke of

"Angels of Death … Angels of Death …"

Outside the draped rooms of her darkened home the sun shown at full dazzling strength on a rural Virginia countryside. Pine forests and pastures shared the terrain with the occasional houses, corn fields and gardens. Colossal clouds rolled in as the April weather went into another of its changes. Cooler, moister air was moving through the trees in advance of an incoming front.

The woods held a winding network of horse trails even in its deepest parts. A salt lick turned up here and there, along with hoof prints and other evidence of horses. A pair of mongrel dogs ambled together down a shady stretch of the paths.

They were mostly retriever and mostly terrier, respectively. Their difference in size was great enough that their ranking was understood, and they never fought. They roamed together to have an extra pair of eyes and ears on duty. Both had homes and names, and people who were wondering where they were. Both dogs were having a great time, out for an afternoon hunt in the delightful cool winds rushing through these woods.

The larger and younger of the two dogs was a stocky red haired retriever mix. He had just detected an infinitesimal rustle in the brush a short distance off the trail. Breaking away he took a couple of pounces in the tall weeds. There was a rabbit, and the chase was on. They zigzagged through the underbrush for a distance, at a speed the other dog had trouble matching. The cottontail took off on a straight shot toward a creek, which he spanned in one desperate jump. The red dog splashed through, slowing him down a bit. He lurched up the bank and charged forward through the vines and brambles, snuffling frantically at the ground as he went.

He picked up the rabbit scent soon enough, but just as quickly forgot all about it. Another animal's odor had entered his brain. It had him standing locked in place as he sniffed it in and absorbed the information it gave him.

There was a creature upwind nearby that fed on meat. Not canned dog food meat. This was an eater of fresh meat and blood. The scent was unmistakable. This animal was fully mature and in excellent health. It was also female, and heavily pregnant. He looked about with urgency but could see nothing in the dense thicket. The scent was as strong to him as it was troubling. It seemed to be all around him now. Rarely had a scent engaged his instincts so powerfully. His brain was suddenly saturated with an internal command to run! Run! Run!

He scrambled out of the vegetation and up onto a higher section of the trails, where he saw it, facing him. A black motionless figure was seated in the center of the trail in the one shaft of cloud-grayed sunlight that fell there. Her eyes were blanks, like great round water drops beaded up on a black wax cat face. There was no direction to these eyes, but he could sense that she was staring at him intently.

Presently a sound emanated from the cat. No human would perceive it, but it was very clear to him. It was transfixing, a combination of two very dissimilar noises: an ultra low-pitched rumble, and a kind of wavering whine. It seemed to merge with the sound of the creaking tree boughs that interlocked above the trail as they swayed in the building wind. He also heard a distant roll of thunder, as well as the whimpers of his companion, the terrier, who was now watching from the woods.

The red dog's head cocked to one side. The sounds coming from the strange animal were unlike any he had ever heard. They seemed to be rising in intensity. And then, they stopped.

His instincts had given him one chance to flee. Now there would be no other warning but for the briefest glimpse of a black shape in mid air above him. A second cat dropping out of the tree branches slammed down onto his back. Its claws plunged into his shoulders and flanks.

The retriever tore away, yelping through the brush with a cat more than half his size holding on tight on top of him. His attempts to bite the creature failed and its claws ripped at him grievously. In an instant his eyes were clawed out, just as the cat's fangs sank deep into the back of his neck.

A prolonged shriek, sharp pitched and human-sounding rang through the woods. In the back yard of a farm house a quarter mile away, a three year old girl looked up from her coloring book, and her mother, watching over her from the screened porch, glanced in the direction of the woods. Her father turned away from waxing his car to face the direction of the sound. On the state road running along the far edge of the woods, a highway patrol motorcycle officer on watch for speeders also heard the scream. And so did a young woman out riding a gray mare on a lakeside trail just beyond the woods.

Carla was alone with her horse, debating whether she should ride in the direction of the shriek and try to render assistance. She decided it was probably not someone being attacked, but more likely a riding injury. It might even be one of her friends. If anything looked suspicious she would just turn around and beat hooves out of there. She urged the mare down the path into the pine forest, onto trails she knew from childhood.

Three quarters of a mile away, in a deep thicket off the trail, the red retriever convulsed and expired from his mauling. The animal that killed him slowly released jaw pressure on the dog's throat, flipped the carcass over and slashed open its soft belly. Grunting and growling, the cat began gorging himself.

His mate approached with delicate steps and sniffed softly at the kill. She took a few mincing bites out of the soft tissues of its face, and then stood by, apparently not hungry. She made a short mewling call to her mate, turned and went gingerly back the way she had come. Soon he was trailing along behind her. From a distance the terrier stood watching and trembling. Finally he shot away, dashing at his top speed through the woods for home. Some minutes later Carla spotted him from her saddle, racing out of the woods into an open field and crying as if he were scalded. It was strange, she thought, but not a conclusive sign of danger.

The forest was silent, cool, and darkening in the late afternoon. No injured person was responding to Carla's shouts as she rode along. She knew where she was; there was no chance of getting lost. But thoughts of impending dusk, possibly accompanied by rain, stayed in her mind. She would not go much further. An injured rider they would likely have a phone anyway. The trail made an S shape before straightening out. She would ride as far as the straightaway and then turn back if no one was there. Her horse was gentle, due to age. She preferred a more energetic mount, but occasionally went out with this old girl just to maintain the long time bond between them.

As they entered the second curve of the S, the mare stopped short. Carla immediately saw what she was looking at. Amazingly, at the side of the trail ahead was a piece of sculpture. Standing almost waist high, it was the form of a seated cat carved from black stone. The bizarre object sat facing her, as if staring at her.

Nothing could have been more unexpected or surreal to come upon out here. This was no lawn ornament. It was detailed and realistic, and Carla was amused to find that her mare was hesitating to go any closer to it.

The horse flatly could not be induced to approach the cat figure. She only balked, whinnied, and shuffled in place. Carla dismounted and began patting her neck and talking in a soothing tone. She gave her an apple to chew on and held the reins tight in hand as she walked over to inspect the statue. The mare was nervous, being made to go nearer.

The thing was astonishingly beautiful to Carla, who still could not fathom its presence here. She looked at the soft earth around the cat for signs of human foot prints and, oddly enough, found none. The statue seemed to have a light glaze over most of its surface, though under the mouth and down the chest there was something else, as if a dark stain had been spilled there.

The cat statue was placed in front of a tall patch of weeds, behind which was a great sprawl of rocks and boulders. Carla remembered being here before. There were overhangs of rock and little mini-caves, as she had called them, when she was playing here as a girl. It looked as if the cat was standing guard over the area. Carla knelt down, smiling, and at that moment an unearthly noise rose up from somewhere out in the rocky patch.

It was a vocalization, deep enough in pitch to have come from a man. It was a freakish, rolling cry. At the sound of it Carla's horse shied backward and reared, almost jerking the reins from her hand. There was no holding her back now, and Carla's instincts were just quick enough that she was able to propel herself onto the back of the animal as it turned and bolted away.

It had been some years since Carla had been on a runaway horse, and this time was no less scary than the other. Trees were zipping by on either side, and big bumpy roots extended onto the path creating a trip hazard. The trail curved crazily, but somehow the panicked mare was staying on it. Carla tried everything she knew to slow her down, but to no avail. It was getting dark, and if the horse lost the trail and ran off into the woods there could be a devastating wipe out.

There was no bit in the horse's mouth, and pulling on the reins was not working. It was astonishing how much life was left in the animal! Instincts told Carla to simply lean forward and ride it out, and this was what worked in the end. The exhausted horse slowed down and stopped, only after clearing the woods and coming out by open pasture. Carla dismounted and began walking her the rest of the way home. She dug into her pocket for her phone and made a call to a girlfriend.

"Listen, it's me. You have to help me out with something tomorrow morning. Early tomorrow morning! You're going to have to get up early. I mean like five o'clock. Because we have to get something I found out of the woods. I want to get it out before somebody else does. Well, it is a piece of … art. It's a sculpture. Yes, sitting on the side of the trail! I don't know ... I don't know! It's just sitting there. A little statue of a cat! It was too heavy for me to bring out by myself, and anyway Lucy got spooked somehow and ran away. I am totally, thoroughly serious here. I will pay you, if that's what it takes, but you have to be on a good horse at my front gate by five thirty in the morning. Okay. I absolutely mean it, yes … Especially if it is stolen! We will be the ones who recover it! … We are going to wrap it up in blankets and drag it out between our horses. So have a saddle with a horn. All right then. Five thirty. Yes … Bye."

Carla passed that night with her body in a warm, fluffy bed and her mind out on the chilly, empty trail in the pine forest. When a light rain made a spattering sound on her window panes, she imagined the black stone cat sitting out there in the drizzle, water beading on his round face. As dreaming came over her, she heard the low, throaty cry that had spooked her horse. The dream kept it separated from her, in compartments in her mind. But it was still there, calling and calling.

When five thirty came Carla was dressed, coffeed up, and mounted on a powerful three year old gelding named Purpose. Her friend Jackie Ann was nowhere to be seen, but after a few minutes she came into view in the distance, riding her white stallion. Carla rode out to meet her and said,

"We're going to get this done and put the statue in my barn, and then you can go back to bed. We'll figure out what I owe you later."

"It's going to be a lot," said Jackie Ann, "It's still pitch black out here!"

"It is not," Carla said, "The sun is about to break over those hills. When we get to where we're going there'll be plenty of light."

"It also feels and smells a lot like rain, you know it?" said her friend, "There's a front moving in. I am not looking forward to getting half drowned for the sake of your … statue of a cat."

"I brought along an extra hat." Carla said, "If you are that worried about it let's go and get it over with."

She nudged the flanks of her ride, and both girls' horses went galloping down the dirt path that was barely illuminated by the first glow of sunrise. The smell of hay, manure, and rain filled the country air.

After several minutes at full speed they arrived at the edge of the forest with Carla feeling exhilarated, and her friend wary. Jackie looked deep into the gloomy woods and released a groan,

"How far in there do you think it is?" she asked.

Carla said, "Hard to estimate. I will know when we get there. I know exactly where it is."

She led the way down a trail that forked and branched off more than a few times. Mostly they made their way in silence, measuring the strain this was putting on their friendship. Jackie then announced the first full drop of rain.

Things got worse when they rounded a bend and it became obvious that Carla had arrived at her magic spot, but there was no statue sitting there. She jumped off the horse, silently fuming, and tied the reins to a tree limb. Both horses seemed skittish.

"Where's the piece of artwork?" Jackie asked.

Carla examined the spot where it had been sitting the day before. There were some odd depressions in the loamy soil, but no human footprints. With some air of irritation and disgust, she stepped off the trail through the tall weeds and looked around. Hands on hips she scanned the rock strewn area and suddenly called to Jackie,

"Tie up your horse."

With the horses secured to the same tree branch, Jackie hurried toward her friend who was just visible through the brush, gesturing for her to come on. As she drew near, she could see what Carla found.

Some thirty feet away on a flat gray boulder they sat, the seven of them. There were two large, prominent cat statues, nearly three feet high in their seated position. In front of them in a curved row sat five tiny replicas of the larger two. None of these was more than eight inches tall. All seven were positioned facing the girls. Winds were rising and the raindrops were becoming larger and harder to ignore. From a far distance a rumble of thunder moved in. The early morning sunlight was muted gray. The cats were jet black, apart from their silvery, twinkling eyes.

"Have you ever seen anything weirder than that?" Carla asked, grinning wildly. She answered herself, "I never have … Come on."

She strode forward and began stepping from one rock to the next, some of them wobbling under her weight. Jackie Ann followed more cautiously. She could not help looking around in case whoever put these things here might be out and about.

The girls stepped up to the front of the flat sandstone boulder, which was now fully speckled by rain. Carla knelt down to be at eye level with one of the two big cats. Never before had such a sensation come over her. They were mesmerizing.

"Don't you love them?" she asked.

"Okay, what's next?" Jackie said, "It's raining!"

Carla motioned with her thumb back at the horses and said,

"Go bring those blankets. I don't know how we are going to get all of them out of here in one trip. There was only one yesterday!"

Jackie took off, retracing her steps across the rocks. Rain was falling hard now. But as she was about halfway to the horses it started pounding down as a gray wall. Jackie screamed and the horses began rearing and crying. She dashed around the mass of tall grass to discover that her stallion had worked itself loose and bolted. She could just see him receding into the distance up the trail. Carla's ride was bucking and whirling, also at the brink of breaking free. She stumbled back through the mud and weeds and waved her arms, screaming for Carla to come in.

Seeing that there was trouble with the horses, or at least with Jackie, Carla stood up and started in. She paused in the heavy downpour, thinking she ought to try to carry a statue back with her. Returning to them, she was stopped short by what she saw from the big cat on the left. As the rain slammed down, a red stream was running off of him onto the rock. It looked for all the world like a packet of red dye was under the statue, leeching out in the rainwater.

Jackie's high pitched shriek penetrated the wind, rain, and thunder, and Carla set out across the rocks to rejoin her. Jackie had Carla's gelding by the reins and was in an all out struggle to control him. A bolt of lightning hit somewhere in the woods, along with an ear-breaking blast of thunder.

The two young women clambered up on the horse and it took off with them at full gallop, back up the trail the way they had come. For the second time in as many days Carla was on a panicked horse, on the same trail, hurtling through the woods away from the black stone cat. This time the horse's hooves were slipping in wet mud in a most horrifying way, and her friend Jackie Ann was behind her, shrieking and weeping and squeezing the breath out of her. This ride marked the end of their friendship. By the time they made it out of the forest, Carla was only grateful it had not ended their lives.

Rain dominated that day. But by the following morning the weather had cleared entirely, and the area was returned to the full beauty of a rural spring. At a farmhouse next to the woods, in a yard full of wet grass and children's toys, a three year old girl was being sent outside to play alone. She showed no enthusiasm for it.

Her mother, Sandra Eustace, knelt down next to her for a chat.

"You know you usually get to have friends come over, but not every day. Some days, well, there is just nobody around. Nobody home. It can still be a good day. Look at how pretty it is out today."

Little Sandi took a look at the prettiness of the day but still wore an expression of soulfulness such as is only possible at that age. She raised a chubby hand and pointed to the scene of the yard and the woods, but had nothing to say. Her mother sighed and held her for a quick hug.

"Pumpkin, I have work to do, and you are going to have to play out here. You have your baby. You can have a tea party with your baby."

Sandi looked down at the doll in her arms. Its head could be rotated to display three different expressions. She turned it to the tearful one.

Her mother said, "We can call Carla later on, if you're a good girl, and see if she will take you for a pony ride." That seemed to catch her interest. Her mother continued,

"Or maybe Carla would like to go on a picnic in the park ..." by which she meant Shenandoah National Park, which almost bordered the Eustace property. Sandi was still not smiling, and her mother said,

"I know you miss playing with Reddy."

Sandi said, "Reddy's still lost in the woods."

"I know, honey. Maybe he will find his way home some day. If not, we'll get you a new dog. How about that?" said Ms. Eustace.

The child thought deeply on it, then brightened a bit and said,

"Mama, what if Reddy is in his house? He could be asleep in his house! Can I check it?"

Her mother said, "I think if Reddy came home he would be right here with us, not asleep in the dog house. But you can go look. Then I want you to play with your baby out here until it's lunch time. All right?"

This was acceptable to her, and she hastened away to the dog house at the side of their home. Her mother returned to her tasks indoors. Sandi carefully placed her doll on the seat of her tricycle, and then squatted down by the burlap covered entrance of the homemade dog house. She drew back the cloth and put her head inside.

One big cat was reclining across the back wall, with kittens climbing all around. The other was seated next to her. He stood up, eased his mouth open and released a faint hiss.

"Kitties!" Sandi delightedly cried. She began counting them, and then said, "I'll get you some milk! Just wait right here! Stay right here, I will be right back!"

She trotted away to the screen door at the back of the house, made her way in, and called out to her mother that she needed a glass of milk but that she could get it herself. She pulled open the refrigerator door, jammed a chair in to hold it, and climbed up to grab the handle of the plastic milk jug. She was pouring it into a 32 ounce tumbler when her mother came in from the other room,

"Sandi! You don't drink that much milk in a week! What are you doing?"

"I'm thirsty for some milk, Mama!" she said, "I'll finish it all, I promise!"

"No, you will pour back about half of that right now. Or rather I will." said Ms. Eustace, "I thought you were so wild about grape juice. Now you want milk?"

"Yes ma'am." Sandi said, "I like milk the best, from now on."

Slightly baffled, her mother handed off the plastic tumbler to Sandi, with still plenty of milk in it at only half full. The child politely said "Thank You," and carried it outside.

At the dog house she poured it into the dog's bowl and carefully carried it in under the burlap. "Okay!" she said, "I got milk for everybody." She sat down cross-legged on the ground and held out the bowl.

A guttural growl filled the dog house. Both cats took to their feet with their progeny positioned behind them, sitting silent and motionless by the rear wall. One of the two creatures circled behind Sandi while the other approached from the front.

"Here you go!" she said.

The cat behind her sniffed her hair for a moment, then sniffed the side of her neck. He bared his black fangs then, and a low frequency rumbling sound rose up from deep within him. His mate had settled into a crouch in front of Sandi. The blank, glassy balls of her eyes were trained straight ahead.

"Don't you like milk?" she asked, "I thought all cats liked it!" She pushed the bowl closer to the cat in front of her, which made a short, sharp hissing noise that took the girl by surprise.

The newborns at the back of the dog house suddenly broke their silence and began whining and crying and play fighting with each other. The big animal in front of Sandi leaned forward and touched her muzzle down onto the milk. She drew back sharply and emitted a rasping sound. This drew a response from the male, who moved around to settle next to her. Within seconds the two of them had drained the milk from the bowl.

"Wowee! You sure were two thirsty kitties!" Sandi cried out.

The male drew himself up into a seated position. He turned his head to make a slight snarl at the kittens, which fell silent again as each one of them assumed a similar seated posture. The female took her seat next to her mate.

They were staring straight ahead, and as Sandi sat watching them, she began to take notice of how long they had been sitting completely motionless. She stretched out her baby-like hand and made contact with the cat. It was like touching granite. Gently she pushed it, and it bobbled to and fro like a bowling pin. In wonder she sat in the dog house with them a minute more. Softly she said to herself,

"Magic kitties!"

The following morning passed routinely at the Eustace farmhouse, except that after breakfast little Sandi wanted a tall glass of milk to take with her outside. Her mother knew something was up and watched her little girl closely from her office window. For some time Sandi just sat at the picnic table playing tea party with her doll and taking an occasional tiny sip of the milk. When she felt she had kept up appearances long enough, she dashed away to the dog house with it. Ms. Eustace merely shook her head and returned to her computer.

Later that morning a vehicle approached the house, announced by the sound of gravel crunching in the driveway and Sandi running toward the back door yelling,

"The super trooper is here, Mama!"

A gleaming highway patrol motorcycle and its officer came into view at the side of the house. He took careful note that Mr. Eustace's car was not present, and then he shut off the engine, which was quieter than the old twentieth century gasoline kind.

The top part of his face was obscured by the dark windshield of his helmet, but his mouth was exposed and formed a radiant smile for Sandi. He made a little wave of wiggling fingers at her, and she self consciously played with the bow on her jumpsuit before waving back. In the house Ms. Eustace had jammed a blouse on over her tee shirt and was working a brush through her hair. She made her way out the back door and over to the motorcycle at a casual pace.

They made no greeting, other than strained smiles.

Sandra Eustace said, "I'm glad you didn't come to the door. He came back in town this weekend. He could be dropping by any time."

"Well, I shall certainly wish him top of the morning if I see him." said Trooper Barnard, "Do I not get a kiss?"

"Not now." she said, wearily. "Today is probably not a good time. And the whole week is not looking good, Tom. He goes out of town Friday. I'm not sure for how long."

"Friday, eh? A whole week of not a good time," said the trooper, seeming deflated. His eyes were still concealed. "That is tough titty, for sure. To tell you the truth, I was thinking you two would surely be divorced by now, you know it? What are you waiting on?"

"I don't believe I ever used the word divorce." she said, "All I ever said to you was that we were separated. I never made any predictions of which way it would go. Did I ever? Even once?"

She shook her head, and he shook his.

She said, "I will know something definite this month. Now, that is all I can tell you. And I am making no predictions, Tom. Mostly this is all up to him."

He acknowledged that he understood. His mouth regained its tight smile. She could not see his eyes. He reached back and opened the compartment on the side of the bike. There was a bag of carry-out fried chicken which he carefully lifted out.

He called over to Sandi, "Hey you! Doodle bug!" He hoisted the bag up for her to see, and she dropped her doll flat and came running across the yard.

He said, "This is your favorite kind, isn't it?"

"Oh yes! Thank you, super trooper!" she cried, grabbing hold of the bag.

"Well, you and your Mama enjoy it." he said, "I can't stay for lunch this time. I have to go. But you be a good girl and look after your Mama. And … I'll be seeing you."

He gave Sandi a salute, which she returned before breaking away and running off with the bag. Her mother started to call out to her as she went, but stopped and just let her go. She turned back to Officer Barnard, and reached out and lifted the shaded visor on his helmet. His eyes were steady and appealing and his smile was no longer forced. He was a little younger than her. She had a full array of mixed feelings about him, all of which she was prepared to permanently bury as she reconciled with her husband. He reached out and placed his gloved hand on her waist, and gave her a squeeze and a gentle pat.

Sandi rolled in under the burlap cover of the dog house, and cried out, "Wait 'til you see this!"

Startled, the two massive black creatures bolted to their feet with eyes flaring. The female, covered in climbing kittens, thrust up a powerful arm into the air. Her upraised paw flexed four black claws, like obsidian scalpels. Sandi pulled the foil bag and the space was at once filled with the smell of hot fried chicken. All tension dropped instantly from the cats.

Little Sandi lifted a chicken leg from the bag and held it toward the face of the mother cat. She took two quick sniffs, and her jaws slid open and eased closed on the drumstick, shearing through the bone and taking most of it in a single bite.

Sandi looked at the stub of bone in her fingers and laughed ecstatically.

She produced a batter-fried breast from the bag. Both cats were looking at it and sniffing it, but the male lunged forward. Sandi could feel the breath rushing out of his mouth onto her hand as his black interlocking fangs clamped down on the piece. He yanked it away from her and then began a growling game of keep-away with his mate, who wanted some of it. With fluid motions more like that of aquatic life, they dipped and coiled and circled about in the confines of the doghouse, grumbling and rumbling at each other while their tiny offspring whined and mewled.

Sandi had been fascinated by the tiny kittens ever since she found them, but had not yet had an opportunity to examine one. Now she reached out and picked one up and was overjoyed by the squirming little fellow. It had eyes like the glass beads of the costume jewelry necklace Mama had given her. When it opened its mouth to cry, she saw it had rows of pointed teeth like that of the rubber shark toy in her bathtub. Only the shark's teeth were painted white, while the kitten's were as jet black as the rest of him.

Sandi talked baby talk to the kitten, held it close and kissed it, and then the two heads of the big cats moved in.

They looked in close at their kitten in Sandi's hands. Then they looked at Sandi and back to the kitten again. They sniffed at the kitten, and one of them started sniffing Sandi's hand and arm, up to her shoulder.

Sandi said, "If you are still hungry I do believe we have some more chicken left."

She gently placed the kitten on the ground and took up the bag again. As she lifted out another greasy fried piece, her mother's voice pierced the air from a distance,

"Sandra Ellen! Where have you gone!?"

Sandi froze, and the cat creatures also paused and listened intently. The kittens seemed to instinctively follow their parents' lead, falling silent.

Ms. Eustace bleated out, "Sandi!"

She set the chicken breast on the ground in front of them and said, "I better go."

Sandi emerged from the dog house with the bag in her hand to see her mother still standing with Trooper Barnard in the driveway. But Mama had her hands on her hips in a greatly theatrical stance of displeasure that was clearly meant for the child.

"What are you doing young lady!?" Ms. Eustace cried.

"I was just having some chicken, Mama!" said Sandi.

"Not in that dirty doghouse you're not!" her mother exclaimed, "You know better than that! Get right into the house, right now!"

Looking back to Barnard, she softly said, "Driving me nuts, as usual. I better go."

He pointed at her jauntily, and raised his hand up to his head in a telephoning gesture. She nodded, smiling, and he brought the motorcycle engine to life. They parted then, and Ms. Eustace went indoors to Sandi.

"I can't believe you were eating in that dog house, Sandi! Mama's not very happy about that," she said, as she opened the chicken bag, "What! Only three pieces left?"

"I was very, very hungry today, Mama." Sandi said, straight-faced.

Naptime followed immediately for Sandi, her mother again shrugging off a situation that was suspicious, at best. The child was given to fantasy flights and was an all-round handful of energy at this stage. Sandra tried not to let herself get worked up over trivialities. Sandi was a good girl for the most part, and these days her mother had plenty of other matters on her mind.

Barely an hour had gone by when the gravel in the driveway told of the approach of another vehicle. This one sounded more like four wheels. Sandi's nap ended at the sound, and her voice sang out from her room that Daddy was here. Ms. Eustace emitted a leaden sigh, and was about to tell her to stay in bed, but gave up on the idea. She rose from her computer and sauntered out the back door.

Mr. Justin Eustace sat in his sedan at almost the same spot where Barnard had been parked. He did not begin to get out of the car until he saw her leave the screened porch.

To her he seemed to be just noticeably older every time she saw him these days. The climb out of the vehicle was taking just that much longer than it ought to. They made no greeting, and as they spoke it appeared that they were continuing a conversation from only moments before, although he had not been here since yesterday morning.

"Need to pick up that unit out of the shed, and a couple of other things," he said, not looking at her but squinting out to the woods. His head was hairless on top, but his face was whiskery. That was standard for him; by early afternoon he looked like he needed a shave.

She said, "You can't come inside right now. I'm not ready."

"How are you not ready?" he said, with the slightest edge in his tone of voice.

"I don't have to explain it," she snapped, "I'm not ready for you to be in the house right now."

At this point in the past a fight would have ensued between them, but he didn't pursue it. They would have just bickered and wrangled and it all would have just come down to something about her legal rights, which did include a bit about having him stay out of the house, as he understood it. He changed the subject,

"Reddy never came back, eh?"

"Nope," she said, "She's taking it hard. She keeps wanting to play in his doghouse. The neighbor kids are all on vacation somewhere and Reddy is gone and she is all alone here with me."

"Driving you nuts." he said, "… A little bit."

They had their first eye contact and a faltering smile. The screen door opened and banged closed behind Sandi, and she came bounding out to them, all smiles.

Her father crouched down and caught her for a hug.

"Hello sweet pea."

"Hello Daddy."

"I hear you have been playing all by yourself here lately," he said. She thought about it and nodded, and he said, "How'd you like to go see a show with your old Daddy this week?"

She was not sure what that meant, but figured it was something good, and so she hugged his neck.

She asked, "Can Mama go too?"

"Well … I would hope so, yes. I think Mama would have a good time if she came along," he said, "So we will do that one night this weekend, all right?" He looked to his wife and was surprised that she nodded her consent.

He stood and took Sandi up in his arms and said, "So! Have ya been keeping busy? Yeah? What's been going on?"

"I found some magic kitties."

"Magic kitties!" he said with delight.

"And I have had lots of tea parties with the babies. And we are saying prayers for Reddy to find his way home. And the Super Trooper came by."

Ms. Eustace added, "One of her fantasy friends."

She took Sandi from her dad and said, "Did you make your bed after your nap?"

"Yes ma'am."

"Did you make it up right, or did you just throw the comforter over the pillow?"

Sandi thought about it and then said, "I should go check."

Her mother sat her down, and her chubby legs went motoring off to the house. Mr. and Ms. Eustace smiled and briefly chatted more about the girl, who stood out as the one subject on which they saw eye to eye.

He talked a bit about his work, designing consumer products and gadgetry. It was something she had once taken an interest in. Things were going well with it these days. They spoke of the piece he had been building in his workshop in the shed. She thought it might have potential, she said. Their eyes had met, and a civil conversation about the gizmo got underway. The content of their talk was secondary to the respectful tone they achieved. That was significant. The old bond between them could not have had a moment of more certain reassertion had they clasped their hands on each others forearms.

He wanted to get back with her, and thought that maybe he should leave now before he screwed up somehow and spoiled this rare, fleeting mood of acceptance that had arisen between them. They were going to see a show this week with Sandi. That would be something to build on. He decided to aim a little higher then.

He said, "One of my old coffee pot designs apparently made a boatload of money for Bestene Housewares. Remember that bunch? They're having some kind of awards dinner next week, and it seems as though they are going to give me something. I don't know. A plaque or something, I guess. But maybe it will be some money. Anyway, it's a meal, and some applause, and I was wondering if you would like to … be my date."

She regarded him slightly askance, but felt some appreciation for the chance he was taking. She stood there thinking about it until he said,

"I figured, since you were there for all of the work ... Maybe you even helped, I don't remember. But, so, anyway … It is Monday night. Eight o'clock, Monday night."

She smiled, intrigued, and said, "Maybe, if Carla can baby-sit. I'll let you know."

The screen door eased open and they saw Sandi slip out and gently close it behind her. She moseyed along the side of the house quietly, as though not wanting to be noticed. She seemed to be carrying something. When her mother saw she was heading directly toward the doghouse, she said,

"All right. That's it. That is going to be all of that, whatever it is ... Sandi! What are you doing?"

When she saw that the girl was carrying a large glass of milk, she strode over to her, followed by Mr. Eustace.

"I know you are not drinking all this milk, Sandi!" her mother said sternly, "What do you have in that doghouse?"

Sandi shuffled and squirmed, and finally whispered, "Some cats."

"Cats!? You're feeding stray cats?"

"Yes ma'am."

Ms. Eustace walked directly to the doghouse, knelt down, yanked back the burlap cover, and leaned in for a look. Seven black stone cat sculptures gazed back at her with shining eyes. They sat in a row, with two large ones on either end and five little ones in between them. Sandra knelt there in disbelief for some time before summoning her husband with an urgent wave of her hand. He squatted down and peered inside.

After the passing of a long silence, Sandi's small quavering voice said,

"They're magic."

Her father finally spoke up, "Sandi, honey, where did you find these things?"

She thought and thought, and said, "In there."

Her mother said, "They were in here when you found them? You didn't bring them in? No, I guess not. You wouldn't be able to lift those big ones."

Mr. Eustace reached in and took hold of one of the statues.

"No, she would never be able to budge this," he said, as he hauled it out.

Sandi said, "I had a tea party with them!"

"Sandi, tell me the truth. Do you know how these things got in here? Did you see who put them here?"

The little girl innocently shook her head, while her father worked at moving the pieces out of the doghouse. He suggested they take them inside and examine them more closely. With some difficulty he lifted up first one then the other of the heavy cats while Ms. Eustace gathered up the little statuettes in her arms.

They carried them in and arranged them in a row on an antique steamer trunk in the den. Mr. Eustace took a magnifying glass from the writing desk and looked closely at the enigmatic feline faces.

"Damn! These have to be worth money! They're not junk, anyway. I am figuring we have somebody's stolen artworks here." he said grimly, "Why they would hide them where they did is beyond me. It has me worried. I mean for the two of you, being all alone out here like this. These sculptures were clearly stashed on our property by an intruder. And it seems like the act of an unbalanced mind."

Ms. Eustace said, "But you would think a big dog house like that would be the last place on earth an intruder would want to go!"

"It is beyond bizarre," said her husband, "So, what happens when they come back and find the dog house empty? They could be hiding out around here anywhere. There are plenty of barns and stables, and then all of Shenandoah National Park right down the street! I don't like it one bit, Sandra."

The two of them sat on a sofa opposite the sculptures. Sandi had been sent to play in her room. It became very quiet. An eerie sensation came over the estranged couple, staring at the figures staring back at them. Mr. Eustace said,

"Look, I have to be at a meeting in about an hour. I'm going to have to go now. My advice to you is to get the police over here."

"I'll do that. I'll have one over as soon as you leave."

"All right then," he said. They shook hands in parting, and he smiled and said,

"I wasn't supposed to be in the house to begin with."

Seeing that it was late in the afternoon, Sandra chose to wait until morning to call Officer Barnard, in the event he might prove to be hard to get rid of after dark. When she did get a call through to him it was surprising how quickly his motorcycle appeared in the driveway. He must not have been far away.

After hearing the initial oddball facts of the matter, Barnard was in the den squatting down in front of the steamer trunk, eye to eye with the powerful image of the cat. He steadily shook his head in amazement. She gave him a camera, and its flash went off again and again in the face of the statue, lighting up its highly reflective eyes.

"I'm glad you called me, but the local cops would be the ones to know if anything is stolen around here." he said, "Still, I can find out easy enough. Oh sure, I can handle the case for you. I can get into any law enforcement computer those guys can. This does top the list for weirdness, I will say that. To tell the truth, hon, this might cap the weird list for the year."

"I sat here half the night looking at them," she said. "Forgetting for a minute how weird they are … I am wondering if there is any way of maybe, you know, getting any money out of this. I could use a little payday at present. So, what I am thinking is, if it turns out they are not reported as stolen, they would be mine to sell, right?"

He laughed. "You would want to investigate the situation a bit more before you go to auction, sweet pie. These things have got to be stolen! But come to think of it, there might be a reward you could claim."

"Hmm. That sounds kind of small," she said.

"Or they might not be worth anything at all! You don't know anything about them!" said Barnard, "Have you checked their undersides for markings?"

He took up one of the heavy statues and carefully turned it over. He was hit with a momentary jolt of surprise, and then his snide chuckle cracked out, and became a big belly laugh. The cat statue had testicles. Ms Eustace looked on in astonishment. She reached out and passed her fingertip across them. He gently replaced the statue on the trunk and picked up the other one.

Female.

The laughing faded out, replaced by a mild stun. This was only compounded when, one by one, Barnard upended the tiny kitten figurines and found each of them to be anatomically correct. Not that the kittens lacked any of the great detail of the larger two. In all five, the tiny etchings of fur in the stone followed the contour of the body. The nostrils and the intricate structures inside the ears were perfect. And the eyes of the kittens were like miniatures of their parents. Details included swirling fissures, micro thin whorls in the glassy stone that spiraled back into the head. The eyes of the big cats had them, and the eyes of the little cats had them, just in a smaller pattern.

Officer Barnard finally said, "I will go on the computer first thing when I get back and look into this. I hope I can help you. There is some kind of story behind them, whether they're stolen or not."

"I just hope I can swing some money out of them, Tom!" she said, "I hate to sound so pitiful, but I have to grab my pennies where I can find them these days."

She positioned herself behind him, and said, "It's not every day something so great looking drops into my back yard." She started kneading her fingernails into his shoulders, and said, "But it does happen." Then, to spell things out for him, she said, "Sandi is playing at the neighbor's house."

He left off staring at the statues and whirled around, grabbing her and wrestling her laughing and screeching onto the sofa. Apart from a sun dress it turned out she had very little on, while he was layered into his complicated patrolman's uniform. It was a loud, chaotic frolic on a creaking, too-small sofa. They never looked back toward the statues. But even if they had, they would not have noticed the change in the position of the feline heads. It was only the slightest tilt, to observe them more directly.

The remainder of the weekend passed uneventfully at the Eustace home. It was uneventful, except for Sandi being forbidden, loudly and repeatedly, from playing with the cat statues. Uneventful, apart from Ms. Eustace leaving her bed during both nights to walk down the carpeted hall to the den to stand before the old trunk with the stone animals on it. It was almost a compulsion, rousing her out of her sleep to go down there. She quickly looked in on Sandi, but then it was on to the cats. For what reason she did not ask herself. She just went and stood for a few minutes, looking down on their motionless forms reflected in the dim lights from the kitchen. It was not a rational thing to do, exactly. But she did not question herself about it.

Monday afternoon she began getting ready to go out with her husband to his awards dinner that night. Sandi's idol, the neighborhood girl Carla, was to baby-sit. She began laying out her clothes and jewelry far ahead of time, as it was a rare event anymore that had her wearing her fine things and making an effort to look her very best. She wanted to take her time. Only the shower was rushed, as she had learned to keep her three-year-old always within earshot.

No sooner had she stepped out of the shower and began toweling off than Sandi was knocking at the bathroom door, announcing another visit from the "super trooper." Ms. Eustace looked at her own irritated expression in the steamy mirror. She emerged in a bathrobe, her slip draped across one arm, to find him already in the house. He was in full uniform again, leaning against the kitchen sink. Sandi was sent to play in her room.

"We need to talk," he said.

"I told you I was going out tonight! I cannot believe you would show up now!" she said, "Where were you all weekend when I was waiting to hear from you?"

"Apart from an extra shift I worked, I was reading all weekend," he said, "… on the internet. About your Statuary Cats."

"Well, fine. Great. You found something on them."

"That's right. Go on, get dressed. I've seen you in your drawers before" he said.

When she objected again to his presence, he raised his voice and said, "They're stolen."

That seemed to bring her down. He went on, "They're stolen and they're not stolen. It has to do with the statute of limitations. They disappeared from the Smithsonian Institution over forty years ago. That is, if these are the same Statuary Cats that are listed on the stolen art database. And they certainly look exactly the same. Where they have been between the Smithsonian Institution and your doghouse is the mystery. And so is the presence of these ... kittens. There were only the two big ones when they went missing."

He eased open the swinging doors that connected the kitchen to the den, leaned in and regarded the stone artifacts on the trunk.

Sandra said, "So whoever had them all these years carved some little kittens to go with them. That's nice."

"Perfect miniatures of the larger two," Barnard observed.

"So if the statute of limitations is up and nobody else is claiming them, then ownership goes to whoever has hold of them." Ms. Eustace said as she got into her slip.

"There could be some exclusion on that due to it being the federal government that owned them," said Tom. "I haven't researched that part of it yet. Most likely you're right. They are yours to sell. But, there is something else I wanted you to know..."

She stepped away and returned with a vintage evening gown, and began struggling into it. It was more than a little tight on her. She had never worn anything like this for him. It was as if she was becoming a different person before his eyes. She said,

"Go on, I'm listening."

Barnard said, "The investigators had a theory back when the statues disappeared that a bunch of people with, umm, 'strange belief systems' may have carried out the theft. There was this book that had come out years before. It was all about the Statuary Cats ... these two, right here! And it connected the statues to a murder case that happened back in 1967. The murder really happened. That much is historical fact."

"Tom, please don't say stuff like that! ... Somebody got bludgeoned with one of the statues back in the twentieth century? Is that what you're telling me?"

He said, "Honey, this is where the strange belief system comes into it. This book, called The Strangest of Life, was pushing a theory that the Statuary Cats are not really stone statues at all."

Pulling on a silk stocking, she slowed to a stop in her dressing and sat listening to him. He actually seemed somewhat haunted by this eerie story out of the past.

"The author, Linton, said that they are alive. They are living specimens of an animal order that is unknown to science. She said they are living creatures that can control their body chemistry to the point that they can turn themselves solid like stone, and back again at will. The book was amazing. It describes the brain of the creature 'ossifying' its body in layers. Layer after layer like an onion it solidifies from the outside in, and then can reverse the process whenever it chooses to. And that could be decades later! She says there are hundreds of them in existence around the world in homes and museums, where they are not being recognized as living creatures! The ossifiers shape themselves to look like other animals, usually cats. And the worst part of it is how dangerous she says they are. When they de-ossify, they live as predatory carnivores."

"Well, Tom, that is definitely a strange belief system," said Ms Eustace, "But why would you be so worked up about it?"

"Maybe because I just now finished reading the book," he said, "Yeah, the whole thing. It was scanned into the database, complete with photos. I tell you, I can understand how some people might go off about it. There were police photos of murder victims in there, and I mean they looked like they had been torn up by barracudas. See, nobody got bludgeoned with a cat statue. This author Linton was saying that the statues came to life and mauled a person to death."

Only now did she take notice of how haggard he was looking today. In place of his usual healthy glow, there were dark circles under his eyes as if he had not been sleeping. His brow was knitted as he spoke, and he had not shaved today. He stared down at the statues and then out into space as he went on,

"There was more than one person killed. Linton says it has been going on for centuries, for eons, really. The ossifiers predate mankind. They are a fluke of evolution. They have the survival strategy of concealing the fact that they are alive at all!"

"Linton says."

"Yeah," he said, "… To me it was fascinating. Kept me awake. You'll have to read it sometime. Anyway, they think this Linton book might have inspired someone to steal the statues from the Smithsonian. Who knows? It was a long time ago. I am going to do some more checking. Maybe we will find out who had them and who dumped them on your property, and maybe we won't."

"Good enough," she said, "Thanks to you and the statute of limitations I will start looking for an auction house for those things tomorrow morning! I do appreciate you doing all that research for me, dear. You probably better go home and get some sleep. You look a little ragged."

"I might get a nap, but not much more. We have a guy out sick and I'm working his graveyard shift tonight. I'll sleep tomorrow," he said, "Have fun with your old man."

He saluted, and went on his way. As he was riding out on his bike down the driveway he swerved into the yard to allow Carla to pass on her way in. She drove an old style ragtop convertible, so the two of them made eye contact in passing. She did not care for the wolfish way he looked at her, but resolved not to mention it to Ms. Eustace.

In the back yard, Sandi greeted the young woman as a returning hero, and Sandra thanked her for coming on short notice to baby-sit.

"We may be late getting in. If so, it's all right, we're married," she said, "The guest room is all yours, as is the refrigerator. It's just like last time!"

They pinned down Sandi's absolute bedtime as being in one hour. It was spelled out clearly for the little girl, so there would be no misunderstanding. Her mother said,

"She has had her dinner and her bath. She has fed her goldfish. It is not to be fed again! Not one more grain, Sandi! She can color or play checkers on her computer before bed. No more eating. And she is not to play with the statuary pieces in the den!"

The baby-sitter was paid in advance and Ms Eustace departed. There was some sunlight left, so Carla played a bit of dodge ball and tag in the back yard with Sandi, in hopes that all the running around would have her sleeping well. Then they went inside and Sandi was given a small scoop of ice cream before bedtime, if she promised to brush her teeth. This was an utter violation of the stated house rules, and a complete conspiracy between her and Carla, which made it the greatest ice cream Sandi had ever known.

The little girl stood on a chair by her friend at the kitchen sink and together they carefully washed the bowl and spoon and caught up on various news. Sandi said,

"Reddy never did come home."

"I heard about that, honey. I sure am sorry."

"Yep. I think he is all gone," Sandi solemnly said.

"I guess we'll just have to get by with the goldfish and our friends in the neighborhood until we can get you a new dog to play with," said Carla.

Sandi looked up suddenly, and said, "Oh, I have something new to show you!"

She hopped down from her chair and led Carla to the swinging doors of the den.

"You have to cover your eyes now!" Sandi said, and the baby-sitter went along with it.

Pushing open one of the doors for the grand unveiling, she cried out,

"Okay, open your eyes!"

The young woman uncovered her eyes, and there they were, in front of her again. One of them seemed to be training an intense gaze directly at her midsection. She took in a short, sharp gasp. Sandi clapped her hands delightedly, and yelled out,

"These are my sweet kitties!"

The little tyke felt some of her enthusiasm ebb away as Carla just stood there, blank faced, and drained of color. Sandi said,

"Don't you like them?"

"Sandi, where did you get these?" Carla asked, urgently.

"They're mine. I found them in Reddy's doghouse."

It was no use trying to pry any information out of the child. All she wanted to say was that they were magic, and she had tea parties with them. She had no idea where they came from, and Carla began to wonder what her parents might know. The Eustaces were not horse people. It was unlikely they would have been out on the trails. She knelt in front of the steamer trunk and leaned in close, and then closer. She could almost see her face reflected in the eye of one of the big cats. For the first time she gave them a proper inspection, something she was never able to do before in the pine forest.

She removed a stone kitten from Sandi's hands and said,

"It's about time for brushing teeth and off to bed."

Sandi protested only a little, and then went along. Soon enough she was in her footed pajamas, with the stuffed animal of the night selected, ready for her bedtime story. Fortunately, she went out like a light after a few pages from the storybook, and Carla was able to slip out and fix herself a drink.

With rum and Coke in hand she returned to the den and stood before the captivating sight. She had found a flashlight and settled in to pass its beam all over the figures for an inspection of their detail. These statues conveyed more sense of presence than any art objects she had ever seen. Resolving to learn more about them from Ms Eustace in the morning, she drifted into the living room to watch television.

In all of a world-wide feed of channels, there was nothing on. But it took her a while to determine that. When she was ready to call it a night she made her way to the guest bedroom just down from Sandi's room. After changing into a baggy tee shirt and gym shorts, she slipped under the sheet and comforter.

The silence of the rural night was complete. There were no crickets tonight, no wind, and no traffic on the road outside. Miniscule noises were amplified. And so when a moth flew against the screen of her window, Carla heard it. At one point before she drifted off she heard the sound of a pine cone falling somewhere in the woods.

Darkness would have been absolute were it not for various small nightlights that were plugged in here and there in the house. The faintest shaft of illumination from one of these penetrated into the guest room from the hall. The door was left cracked open a few inches so Carla could listen for Sandi in the night.

Later she did hear Sandi stirring, opening her door and padding down the hall. She called out to the little girl but got no response. The thought of getting up did not appeal to her, so she lay there a bit longer and soon heard the refrigerator door open and close. Sandi's unmistakable footsteps returned in the hallway, and the child's bedroom door closed. Carla let it go, and snuggled into the bedding. By the time she was beginning an interesting dream, Sandi was padding through the hallway again.

Carla sighed, and kept alert for the sound of the kid returning to her room. The toilet flushed, and Sandi was soon closing her door again. Time passed and Carla discovered, to her great irritation, that she was now unable to get back to sleep. The bed was quite comfortable. The room was dark and quiet. Sandi was apparently down for the night. But no sleep was forthcoming for Carla. Time dragged, and all she could do was lie very, very still with her eyes closed. She was fully awake, though.

She began hearing faint sounds of the night once again. Some were unidentifiable. Then there came a puzzling trace of a noise. It sounded similar to the creaking of one of the hinges on this guest room door. But it was not the full sound, more like the single catch of a creaking hinge. It went,

"tat."

She decided this was from a breeze that was too faint for her to feel, but strong enough to move the door a few inches. Had the door opened any more there would have been more sound. Full silence resumed in the room, and Carla began drifting off. Then, as clear as any sound of her life, she heard someone exhale.

It was shock to her last nerve, and her every muscle clinched up where she lay. It could not have been more distinct had it been someone's mouth next to her ear. But it was just one outflow of air, short in duration. And it was shallow, the way little Sandi would sound if she made a quick sigh. Lying there, she was torn between the urge to call Sandi's name and an irrational fear of making any sound. For now she was silent.

It could not be Sandi in this room. She opened her eyes, without making any other movement, and saw that the door was not open quite wide enough for the child to have entered. Her eyes had adjusted fully to the faint light, and she could make out shapes and shadows in the room. She was lying on her side, facing toward the door.

No other sound followed.

Carla tried to put it out of her mind. Maybe it was just a fluke noise from outside. Still, it had sounded mere inches away.

Then came a vision so disintegrating that Carla felt a sudden wave of nausea. Directly across from her breasts, two egg-sized black blobs appeared on the edge of the mattress, about two feet apart, pushing down on it. In between them, a black shape was slowly rearing up.

The petrified young woman could barely think. There was a lamp on the bed stand above her head. If she reached for it she could turn it on, but to make any movement seemed out of the question. She should pretend to be asleep. But this was unacceptable too. The decision was upon her, here and now. She dashed her hand to the lamp and flipped the toggle switch.

Revealed at the edge of the bed was the ghastly black head of an animal. Its clawed paws dug into the sheet. It opened its mouth, baring bullet-sized fangs. Gurgling, growling, it then threw open its jaws and screamed at her.

In a single motion Carla's free hand closed on the comforter and she whipped the heavy blanket across the cat. It lunged upward with power like that of a strong man, but the comforter remained over it. Carla propelled herself off the bed and out the door. She stood up and pulled it shut behind her. She found herself quaking and beginning to sob. Then in an instant something hit solidly against the door from inside, and a nightmarish black paw shot out under the door between her feet. It flipped over, reached up and began raking its hooked claws across the flimsy pressed-wood door.

She backed away in a horrified daze, looking down at the paw digging into the bottom of the door, as was visible in the glow of the night light. Unearthly yowling cries emanated from within. She spun around and lunged toward Sandi's room and threw open the door.

The little girl looked up smiling from her bed. Five mewling kittens were crawling all over her, climbing up her shoulders, rolling off of her body. Only at that hellish moment did Carla make the connection between what was happening and the statues down the hall. Her mind blazing, she stepped into the room, reached down and snatched Sandi out of the bed.

The child began crying as her baby-sitter carried her down the dim hallway with the steady racket of the shredding wood echoing behind them. The darkened living room was ahead. As Carla reached out for the light switch, a low rumbling sound struck her from the front.

It sounded almost human, but clearly was not. She turned on the light, and in the living room not ten feet before her sat a black cat as big as the first one, hunched up on the top of Mr. Eustace's recliner. For several long, harrowing seconds it stared at them with its shiny, empty eyes. Then its lips slowly curled back, and a hateful hiss shot out through its teeth. It reached out with its clawed paws and began raking them across the top of the recliner, shredding the material and the foam padding inside.

Little Sandi was gaping at the animal, convulsing in fear. Carla was functioning on instinct and adrenalin. She moved forward with slow, measured steps into the living room.

The animal was in a tight crouch. At any second it might spring on them. Carla reached out to the large goldfish bowl on top of a cabinet. Her fingers curled around its rim, and she snapped her arm forward, hurling it for a solid hit that knocked the creature from its perch.

Screams human and non-human pealed through the house as the young woman sprinted with the child across the living room and into the kitchen. There the cat caught up with her, and seized her left ankle in its claws. It turned its head and chomped its compact jaws on her Achilles tendon, severing it with one savage bite.

Carla threw Sandi wailing onto the countertop and began fighting for her life against the animal as blood surged from the wound. She kicked and wrestled but the creature could not be dislodged from her leg. She tried using her weight advantage against it, and stepped down hard on its hindquarters with her good leg. This released it and sent it off into a squealing retreat.

She hoped she had broken its bones, or inflicted some internal damage on the fiendish thing. Instead, after a pause of mere seconds, it looked as fit as it did before, and screamed at her defiantly.

Carla overhanded a wooden stool at the beast, making it dodge to one side. Next she threw a cookie jar, a cutting board, a jar of olives, a frying pan, and a coffee maker. It retreated further after this barrage. Carla slumped to one knee. There had been too much blood loss. She pressed a roll of paper towels against her gushing ankle. Little Sandi had apparently fainted and lay quietly on the counter.

She looked up to see the cat standing facing her with its front paws in the puddle of blood on the white tile floor. There was a human-like expression of contempt on its feline face. It was as if it were thinking, "I am irritated that I must go to the trouble of killing you to feed."

The creature settled into a crouch. Carla saw what was coming but was too late responding. It propelled itself from the floor and slammed into her with an impact that knocked her over. The real struggle then began. It was on top of her, its paws around her head pulling her face towards its snapping jaws. She jammed the side of her hand against its throat and was barely holding it off as she punched repeatedly at the side of its head. She threw it off and it sprang right back onto her, again and again. The advantage was not with Carla, who was weakening.

Fighting was not working. Her mind whirled and she hit on a new tack. Wrestling toward the refrigerator, she yanked it open, shoved the cat in amongst crashing food containers and slammed the door closed with all her weight against it. Cacophonous fury rampaged inside the refrigerator, but the door stayed shut. Carla pushed her bloodied body against it, and sobbed brokenly.

Suddenly the first wave of lightheadedness came over her. Drifting, drifting, until she angrily forced herself out of it. She fumbled in a nearby cabinet and found a roll of duct tape and more paper towels, from which she made a crude tourniquet for her ankle. Spine chilling cries of rage came from the refrigerator, but the door did not budge.

She wondered if the creature inside might not have any leverage to open it, or just did not know how. Maybe it was momentarily baffled. Whatever the case, she had to take the girl and escape from this house right now. She climbed up on her good leg and pulled Sandi's unconscious form up onto her shoulder. At that moment she heard the clawing sound from the far side of the house growing in intensity. The thin wood panels of the guest room door were crackling. At that same time she heard frenzied clawing inside the refrigerator and saw movement in the plastic stripping around the door.

She jammed her hip against the refrigerator one more time, and lurched out onto the screened porch, slamming the heavy back door behind her. It was then that she looked down in horror at the sight of a cat door, cut in at the bottom. Incredibly, they had a cat door. Carla threw herself out of the screen porch and went limping to her car with Sandi over her shoulder. Her keys were in her purse in the guest room, so she wasn't going anywhere. But there was an emergency phone in that car.

A sound of scurrying came from behind her, and she looked back to see a black shape charge up and hit against the screening of the porch. It grumbled, and there came the sound of claws slashing at the flimsy screen.

Carla reached her convertible sedan, dropped Sandi into the back seat and began frantically pulling up the top. During a sudden storm once she had almost bent the frame, so she took care not to do that. It latched into place and she dove in and shut the door. Trembling and still bleeding profusely, she turned on the interior light and started searching the compartments for the little streamlined phone. At last, it turned up.

Carla composed herself enough to talk to the 911 operator. She was under attack, she said. Calmly and correctly she gave the address of the Eustace farm. She was outside hiding in her car, and in need of medical attention. There was a three year old girl with her. The operator assured her that help was on the way. With a sudden thump, a monstrous cat shape appeared on the car's hood, and Carla screamed and dropped the phone.

The black form of the cat stood out in the moon's glow as it peered into the lighted interior of the sedan. Carla turned on the car's headlights, which distracted the creature for a few seconds. She hit the horn repeatedly. This first startled then annoyed the cat.

It rose up and brought its paws down on the windshield, which withstood the impact well enough. It was then that Carla saw drops of blood spatter on the glass. It was her blood, which fell from the arms and body of the cat when it came down on the glass. Its paws were soaked in her blood as well, and left ruddy paw prints. The cat leaned forward, eased open its jaws, and snarled at her image through the windshield. Dark droplets spattered out from its mouth.

The phone had fallen between the seats, but Carla was able to extract it. She thought to call back to the police, but instead hit the button for Sandra Eustace.

"You have to come home right now!" she cried, "We are being attacked! There are some kind of … wild animals here, and they are attacking us! I am badly hurt and I'm hiding in my car with Sandi! I can't talk, just come on!"

Ms. Eustace verified that she had called the police. Carla cried that they needed help immediately. Ms. Eustace said she was on her way and would call for more help. They ended the phone call, just as the second big cat leapt up onto the car.

The two creatures on the hood greeted each other briefly, and then set to work examining the puzzle box of the automobile. They sniffed around the lower edges of the windshield, and Carla turned on the wipers and sprayed the glass cleaner. This had them recoiling in bewilderment and fury. Then, to her despair, she saw one of them leap over the windshield to settle on the fabric top of the convertible.

A sunken place appeared in the fabric above her head. The weight of the cat creature was substantial. Carla was hyperventilating in fear. At that moment Sandi roused herself in the backseat and called out for her Mama.

Carla drew up her fist and punched at the roof. A cry was heard. The cat must have jumped straight up because the depressed area disappeared for a couple of seconds and then slammed down at her again. The second cat then added its weight to the roof. Carla wept, and Sandi screamed for her mother. Carla tried calming the child, but then decided it was best to just keep fighting. She punched up at the fabric top as hard as she could, again and again. The cats no longer jumped. Instead, the first pass of slashing claws appeared in the car's rag top.

Little Sandi was now shrieking her heart out. Carla struggled on, pounding away at the car top, and honking the horn. Four neat slashes from four knife-like claws came inching their way along. Carla desperately looked around for anything that might help. She took up a long sharp pencil and jabbed it as hard as she could at the most weighted-down spot. There was a scream, and one of the cats leapt back onto the hood of the car. The slashing stopped. But then it resumed, and the cat on the hood walked up the windshield back to the roof.

Carla had a metal nail file in one hand and the pencil in the other and was jabbing and poking them like ice picks up at the creatures. Sandi lay on her stomach and buried her face in her hands. The slashing of the roof continued, and then a black clawed paw shot down through one of the gaps. It probed and swiped the air within the interior of the car. Carla stabbed at it as best she could. Fangs bit into the ribbons of the ripped roof, and Carla remembered the old saying that any place a cat can put its head into a cat can get into. She furiously flailed away with her daggers at the spot where the creatures were getting through.

A piercing wail broke through the air, rising above the screaming of the girls and the car's blaring horn. Carla saw the blue strobe lights of a highway patrol motorcycle speeding up the road and turning into the Eustace driveway. It was slinging gravel as it sped inbound toward them. In the few fleeting seconds that she watched it approach she did not notice the cats had bolted from the top of the car.

Trooper Barnard let his bike fall over as he sprinted to the sedan, gun in hand. He shouted out Sandi's name, and she rose up and pounded her hands on the window.

He holstered the gun and took the two of them in his arms. Through racking sobs Carla was just barely able to get the message out to him of what they had been through. He was appalled at the amount of blood in the front floor, and radioed in the urgent need for the ambulance. It appeared on the road as they were speaking, along with a large contingent of local police, and shortly thereafter, the Eustaces.

Floodlights from the five police cruisers swept across the Eustace acreage while Sandi was reunited with her parents and the paramedics dressed Carla's horribly mauled leg. She asked not to have to lie down on the gurney but to be allowed to sit upright in the ambulance. She kept calling out for the cops to have their guns drawn, and to be careful, but to search every inch of the place for the cats.

"Giant black cats. That is what we are looking for." Trooper Barnard told some of them, "You will know them when you see them."

Greatly baffled, ten local police officers moved out with flashlights into the front and back yards. Barnard and Justin Eustace searched the garden and the shed.

"They look exactly like the stone cats in your house, Mr. Eustace," said the patrolman. "In fact, that is exactly what they are."

"You seem to be awfully knowledgeable about things around here." Eustace said, "I can guarantee you I am going to be up to speed on all of it before the night is out."

At the ambulance Sandi went to sleep in her mother's arms. She was then slipped under the sheets of the gurney, where she would be transported to the hospital for examination along with Carla. They had not yet stabilized Carla's leg, and the ambulance sat in the driveway with its rotating emergency lights sweeping out across the property.

Mr. Eustace caught sight of a distant sparkle in his flashlight. He was stunned to see that it was one of the tiny statuary kittens, sitting in the tall grass. He bent down and picked it up, examining it closely in the beam. He called out to Barnard, and seeing his wife, yelled for her too. Some of the officers ran over from the backyard.

"Look at this thing." Eustace said, as they converged around him, "These were dumped on our property! We have been trying to locate the rightful owners!"

"Here's another one!" said Barnard, plucking a small black figure from the weeds, "This is where we need to be searching. Now, there were five of these little ones ..."

The other cops huddled around to get a glimpse of the find. A flood of lights was trained on the two stone kittens as Barnard and Eustace held them up side by side.

"They're kind of cute ... In a way," said an officer.

"We'll need to get a photo," someone said.

"We will still have to search the entire property," said a captain.

"Get a box to put them in." another voice muttered.

Mr. Eustace suddenly blurted out, "Hey! Is it melting or what?!"

"Mine too!" Barnard said, "Look!"

The people in the small group gasped as the kittens' heads began moving, and looking around. Their tiny eyes blinked in the flashlight glare. None of those assembled could say anything, not even to call the other officers. They only stared, transfixed.

Complete silence reigned for fifteen seconds. In that time the kittens turned their heads to look directly at each other, and a faint murmuring sound came from them, or from somewhere. The little heads turned simultaneously to face front again. Their lips parted and together their mouths opened. As if synchronized, their jaws ratcheted open wide and snapped shut at the same instant, like bolt cutters onto the index fingers of the men who were holding them. The two men's fingertips dropped off together, falling just audibly into the grass.

The riot of screaming which followed was unlike any heard at this spot since the Civil War. Purest hell broke out, with men running and flashlight beams crossing everywhere.

The kittens were released.

From the ambulance Carla pulled herself forward to look. Three patrol cars moved their spotlights in the direction of the uproar and were sweeping them to and fro in a tight pattern. One by one the lights stopped moving, as they fell on two pairs of intensively reflective eyes looking back. They were looking back over their shoulders, not so much at the humans, but at the tiny black shapes slipping toward them in the grass. Carla could see the three other kittens standing there. All five of them were now with their parents. The seven cats looked back at the searchlights for a long moment, and then proceeded on in a stately, unhurried pace towards the edge of the property. They passed under a plank fence meant for holding horses, and vanished into the black night.

Carla knew the terrain they were walking. She knew it from childhood. Beyond that plank fence was the pumpkin patch of the neighboring farm, and beyond that was their corn field. There would be a barb wire fence, and beyond it was wide open land, presently fallow. At the far side of that field would be another old plank fence, and then the misty pine forest began. It would roll on for two or three miles of privately owned woodlands. And then, without a fence or barrier or marker of any kind, it would merge and become one with the two hundred thousand acres of Shenandoah National Park.

THE END

THE JINGLE

The demise of civilization followed within months of the decision by Fresh World Beverage International to introduce a new brand of soft drink. The company had acquired a pink citrus product from a slumping competitor and opted to retain the formula but change its name and lackluster image. New York's giant Sanders Shelly Advertising got the business, and set a course of targeting the family market by way of children aged ten to fourteen. The newly repackaged soda, now called "Ahoy!" was launched globally in a colossal promotion that began during the World Cup Soccer Finals.

Ahoy! entered a world largely at peace. A visitor from the 20th century might have found the spirit of the people to be the most remarkable aspect of this era, not so much the technological advance.

It was in no way utopia, but rather human society in a freer, more enlightened condition than had ever been before. The people of this age knew fabulous floating city states at sea, and intercontinental bullet trains. But what was this compared to the radiance of a dignified society? There was a lack of fanaticism. No longer lurching spastically between ideological extremes, some real progress had been achieved.

When that first athlete ran onto the field for the World Cup Finals, pumping his fists into the air, the explosive uproar of the stadium crowd told of a sense of victory that transcended the event at hand. The televised image of that first athlete, exultantly running a wide arc onto the field, eloquently defined a mood that was catching on in the world.

After the teams had been introduced that day they were taking positions for the national anthems when the first broadcast of the Ahoy! commercial went out to a televised audience of four billion.

Twenty days after the ad campaign began the first complaints were received at Fresh World Beverage. The feedback accelerated, coming in at a rate the company could not ignore. But it was only after a full thirty-five days that the commercial was pulled. Six weeks after Game One of the World Cup, governments all over the world were declaring states of emergency, and martial law.

In the fortified basement of the White House, the President of the United States convened another in a series of emergency meetings with his cabinet and military command. It was Day 12 of the crisis.

The President's elbows rested on the great round table of his Situation Room as he looked dismally down at the dispatch that had been placed in front of him. A mood of angry silence prevailed in the chamber, emanating directly from the Chief Executive.

The soft whirring of printers in another room made the only sound, so the President's voice carried when he spoke,

"I am advised that with the return of the Kroatan to Jacksonville, the entirety of the sea-going submarine fleet is now ... unaffected," he said, "Well, that's something." He slowly crumpled up the dispatch and slung it over his shoulder. A nearby Marine stood down from parade rest, picked up the wad and placed it in a waste paper basket.

Sergeant Poteet stood closest to the President of the three Marines in the room. He had been on the White House duty roster at the time the crisis was recognized, and was the only one of that group fit to stay on when the building was restaffed with unaffected Marines on the second day. Poteet was made a sergeant at that time. The President sometimes chose him to relay instructions to the other troops. It would have been a scene from his childhood fantasies, were it not for the surrounding circumstances.

Not all members of the Cabinet and Joint Chiefs of Staff were present; many seats were vacant around the table. The Secretary of Labor would not be back, having had the psychiatric episode here on day two which prompted President Bayard to station soldiers inside the Situation Room. The President seemed to feel that all those he needed were here now, and without looking up, he spoke again, "Is it still true that communication with your people is the most immediate problem for you all?"

The Secretary of the Interior answered for the group, "Lines of communication are up and functioning perfectly, Mr. President. The trouble is finding somebody on the other end able to communicate with us. People aren't showing up for work. The ones who do often are not worth a damn. It is less of a communications breakdown, than a collapse of discipline and professionalism, due to ... the problem."

The President looked up and across the table at the Chairman of the Joint Chiefs. The sight of the elderly general brought a fleeting smile to Bayard, as the old fellow was so shrunken with age he did not much fill out his heavily decorated uniform.

"General Tedworth? ..."

"Sir, we had better be glad this didn't go down during wartime," said the Chairman, "I tell you what, if it had been a war, any little war, happenin' on top of this ... we could damn well hang it up."

The President just looked at him, no longer smiling. At length, he said, "The situations at Nellis and Bragg, General?"

The General coughed loudly and flipped through the papers in front of him. "Ah, Mr. President, the rioting at Nellis is pretty much over with. The, uhh, fire down at Fort Bragg was declared contained this afternoon, as you will recall. I am informed now, however, that there has been a new flare up and that it has returned to a status of ... out of control."

"That's wonderful." said President Bayard, shaking his head, "Just outstanding. We are in emergency conditions. Emergency means the guys are supposed to try harder to hold it in the lane, General, not chuck their discipline altogether!"

"Yessah!" snapped the geriatric general, "That is a fact sah!"

"I want the message delivered that people get shot for screwing up in an emergency!" the President declared, looking with red eyes from one top officer to the next, "I want that word passed, and now. And then have somebody shot, to show you mean it. We have fallen as far downstairs as we are going to!"

He fell back in his chair, staring straight up at the ceiling. To Poteet, it looked for just a second as if he had died. But he recovered and sat up, as the Chairman said calmly,

"What it's going to take is some relief, Mr. President. Some relief for the men's minds. I think you know very well we have no inherent morale problem. As soon as we get a resolution of this crisis, we will be back on the stable footing we were on before."

"It is understood, Mr. Chairman," the President said, "And since our joint Army and National Guard street patrols are working so well, with no incidents big enough to make my desk, I think you will all agree that we have no more pressing business right now than to hear from our Surgeon General, and her colleague, who will brief us on the progress of their research. Surgeon General Lancaster ..."

She was a tall, physically powerful figure. Her appearance was all the more arresting at this moment as she drew herself up to begin her presentation. Looking at her, Sergeant Poteet thought to himself, better you than me. She thanked the President, and got right to the business at hand.

"I said that I had some progress to report to you today, from our research labs. I want first to stress that this is only a glimmer of hope. We are informing you now, due to the gravity of our situation," she said, and then gestured to the wan, weary looking woman at her side, "Doctor Van Cleave of the American College of Psychiatry will cover the details with you in a moment. Let me just say for now, we have a therapeutic exercise that has shown some preliminary benefit in some of our affected test subjects. My personal feeling is that this technique will not prove to be the answer, but more like a step along the road."

Some audible groans broke out in the room at this.

She went on, "All of us in the research effort agree that our best hope is still that the condition will ultimately resolve itself, and just fade away with time ..."

"But that's not happening yet." said the President, flatly.

"It's getting worse, not better!" exclaimed an admiral.

Dr. Lancaster nervously sipped from her water glass and said, "You would give a pulled muscle time to heal, no? Well, the brain is infinitely more complex than that, as we all understand. I think we are making progress ..." Grumbles were rising around the table.

Dr. Lancaster spoke louder, "Look, it was only forty-seven days ago that the commercial was first aired! For thirty-five solid days it was mashed into the consciousness of the world. Our task force was only set up eleven days ago. Who knows how much sooner we might have started work, but for our failure to believe people, when they said ... they couldn't get the sound of the thing out of their heads."

She quieted them with that. The President nodded sadly. He had already acknowledged his slow response to the crisis. The Surgeon General continued, "I am proud of our progress in this short time. We dismissed our original hypothesis of mass hysteria after just two days. No, it is a genuine chronic mental illness. We're calling it functional rather than organic, but we may yet find some structural change in a subject's brain. All that is absolutely clear about this syndrome is that it is caused by repeated exposure to a certain pattern of sounds. Its primary symptom is the inability of the mind to purge itself of a repeating cycle of that pattern of sounds."

It was with the deepest anguish that she said these words to this distinguished assembly, all of whom were affected. Aside from Dr. Van Cleave and herself, the three Marines would be the only ones in this room right now whose cerebral cortices were not being increasingly taken up by an endless repetition of that commercial jingle.

She noticed the Secretary of the Interior, the left corner of his mouth twitching slightly every thirty seconds or so. He had it bad.

She tried to squelch the emotion rising in her. Somehow she retained her composure, and calmly fielded a question from the Secretary of Defense.

"Have you worked out why some people are affected and others are not?" he asked.

"I am sorry, no." she said, "That is one crucial aspect of this that we have not yet cracked. We know that some people heard the jingle more than a hundred times without giving it another thought. Others began obsessively cycling it after three or four exposures. Some of our subjects claim it is in their minds in a thundering loudness. Others say they can barely hear it, but, as with all the rest, repeating like a loop tape. A large percentage of the population apparently does not hear it during their sleeping hours. But, as you know, the majority of the affected have no relief during sleep."

They knew it very well, she thought to herself, as that is how it is with all of them. She went on,

"You all received my memo this morning with the revised estimate of the percentage of affected citizens of this country. It is at 85%, still well below the stats we have for Europe, South America, and Africa. We are on par with the Asian and Indian numbers ..." Seeing the slumping postures of those assembled, she suddenly thought it might have been better if she had not brought up that part of it.

Surgeon General Lancaster drank deeply from her ice water, and continued, "I mentioned a moment ago the individual variation in perceived loudness of the phenomenon. That brings us to Dr. Van Cleave's presentation. The therapy developed in her lab is the first to show an improvement in symptoms by causing a temporary lowering of the volume of the ... auditory cycle."

She gestured to Dr. Van Cleave, who offered a smile and a nod to the group. She began in the same qualified vein as the Surgeon General,

"Ladies and gentlemen, our work is in its most embryonic stage, but at the first sign of progress, I wanted you to hear about it. The therapeutic exercise is something that could be delivered to the public over the airwaves. Even if the results are modest, there could be considerable psychological benefit to the populace in seeing that we are doing something ... which is to say, that you are doing something."

"I find that very interesting, ma'am." said the President.

"Yes sir. Well, you will have to make the decision as to whether you want to take it to the people," Van Cleave said, "It could have quite the opposite effect if they view it as something inadequate. It is not a magic answer, as the Surgeon General made clear. If it is seen as progress, it may engender hope in the people. And that may buy us a little time to come up with the next step in treatment."

This went down well with the officials, and they nodded to one another. Van Cleave lowered a large flat video screen from the ceiling behind her.

"If I could have the lights lowered a bit, please."

Sergeant Poteet stepped briskly to the dimmer switch.

"Now then," Dr. Van Cleave began, "Let us get right to it." She touched a button on a remote control, and a gasp went up in the room as the screen was filled with a multicolored cartoon image of a nautical scene. A little square-rigged sailing ship with a cartoon sea captain bobbed on a wavy blue ocean. Pink and blue rowboats with round headed cartoon girls and boys floated at its side. It was the first time any of the officials had seen the commercial since it was taken off the air, and they regarded the cutesy graphics with dark consternation.

"This scene is from three seconds into the ad, immediately following the musical device I call the filigree, which opens and closes the commercial," Van Cleave said, "The filigree is probably going to prove crucial to our problem, ladies and gentlemen. It literally ties the syndrome together in the mind, with the end leading right into the beginning again. Most of our test subjects show measurable physical reaction during the passage of the filigree."

"That is fascinating, Doctor," the President said, droplets of sweat swelling on his face as he sat facing the mindless picture. "But, ahh, when do we get on to the exercise, that is going to be of help?"

"The exercise is underway, Mr. President." said Dr. Van Cleave, "We are facing our problem. The first step in purging it from our lives has begun. We are confronting it. I am going to walk through the script of the jingle with you, and show you still scenes of the animation that went with it. We are going to demystify this monstrosity and rob it of its power. The syndrome is an obsessive compulsive reaction at its core. It has to be. We are going to dissect it, isolate its parts, and make it go away!"

With a resolute scowl on her face, Dr. Van Cleave hit the remote, and the video screen was taken over by a close-up shot of the smiling doodle of the sea captain's face.

"The sea captain sings in a rough, baritone voice, 'Ahoy! Ahoy! Ahoy! I'm callin' er'ry girl an' boy!'," Dr. Van Cleave advanced the picture again. Cartoon kids in rowboats. "The girls and boys respond, immediately, with a two second burst of 'Why? Why?' The first why is delivered by a chorus of girls, and the next by boys. In rapid follow-up, the sea captain's voice sings, 'Tahhh make ye thinky o' the pinky drink!' Chorus of all voices then burst out, 'Ahoy! Ahoy! Ahoy!' ... This takes us eleven seconds into the ad."

President Bayard looked away. He rested his forehead against the palm of his hand, and softly sighed, "Ooooohh."

Van Cleave said, "I realize one of the symptoms associated with the syndrome is nausea. If anyone is in distress at any time please just raise your hand. We have corpsmen standing by in the passageway. Otherwise, it is best that we continue on through the review, without interruption."

The picture changed. The President looked up, and there they were. Five identical cartoon sailors dancing the hornpipe on the deck of the ship. To Bayard they were reminiscent of early 20th century cartoon images, while the other characters were shaded to make them look more three-dimensional. He was grateful that the pictures were not moving, and more so that the ghastly soundtrack was not being run.

Van Cleave's voice was taking on a nervous edge, as she looked from one sad face to the next and went on with the script, "The sailor's chorus goes, 'Ooooohhh we wanta pinkeee dreeeeeeenk ... Oooooooooohh how we wanta pinkeee dreeeeeeeeeeenk ...'"

Alarming groans arose from the group. The Secretary of Transportation got to his feet and left the room.

The cartoon captain returned to the video screen in a dancing pose, and balancing a pink soda pop bottle on his little finger. Dr. Van Cleave grimly announced, "The sea captain sings, 'Glory be, I'm all at sea, an' I see what I enjoy!' A giant pink bottle of the product floats by the ship and he sings, 'Avast! A drink of pink for me!' Whereupon all the voices sing in unison, 'Ahoy! Ahoy! Ahoy!' And then, again, 'Ahoy! Ahoy! Ahoy!' After a close-up of the bottle and the closing musical filigree ... the commercial ... ends."

"Mmph." Someone grunted as if he had been punched. The Situation Room fell silent for the next two minutes.

Van Cleave finally spoke up. "We usually review the commercial two or three times per session with our test subjects. But if you want we could wait a while ..."

Panicky-sounding mutters came from the group, and the President raised his hand and said firmly, "We are going to hold off for just a while on any more of … that."

The Surgeon General said, "Well, let me ask, does anyone feel any better?"

A few scattered nods and yeses were discernable, and the Vice President enthusiastically affirmed it.

Van Cleave said, "I am telling you, sir, if we go to the people with this on television, a lot of them are going to experience their first ray of hope since this thing started. That will be a confidence-builder."

President Bayard thought about it and nodded.

"I can see that. We will give it a try. You and the Surgeon General remain here after we adjourn and we'll work out the details."

"And the next step in treatment will be forthcoming," Lancaster said, "As you know, we have the creators of the ... jingle, the Purdeys, in custody now at Quantico. Our work with them continues."

"Yes, that's right," said the President, darkly. He cracked his knuckles, and added, "I will be having some words with them when you are finished ... Now then! Any further items of immediate need before we take a short break?"

It so happened that the Secretary of Defense wanted to pose one last question to psychiatrist Van Cleave.

"Ma'am, I just wondered if, in your research, you have come up with any theory as to how this all came about?" he asked.

Van Cleave said, "We aren't releasing an official theory on the origin of the syndrome at this time, as you know. But if you want a personal view, off the record, I will tell you this. All that we know about obsessive thoughts, and the phenomenon of having music stuck in the mind, has not helped us a bit in treating this affliction. This illness is unique. I am coming to think that had any one or two notes, noises, or voices on that soundtrack been different from what they are, we would not be in this crisis. It is my own view, and I cannot prove it yet, but I think what has happened here is that out of the quadrillions of googols of possible combinations of auditory stimuli, the Purdeys managed to record one, maybe the only possible one, which the human brain cannot dislodge from its circuitry. No, I don't think they knew what they were bringing into the world. I am coming to believe that what has happened is simply a cosmic fluke of the universe of neurology, the unlikelihood of which ... is utterly incalculable."

Late that evening, Poteet entered the small sitting room down the hall from the Presidential living quarters that had been set up with cots and made into a berthing space for his three man detail. Pell and Anderson looked up from the comic books they were reading as he closed the antique walnut door behind him.

"I was having a little chat with the President in the hall. He gave us these." said Poteet, and tossed them each a dark cigar with the Presidential Seal on the band, "Oh, and we are staff sergeants now."

"Staff sergeants!?" Pell cried out.

"That's what the man said." Poteet muttered, "I decided not to argue with him about it. We are to keep on doing what we're doing, day shift security detail, and hopefully not death squad. And ... we're staff sergeants."

It took Pell a moment, but then he asked, "What do you mean about death squad?"

"Nothing, Pell. Don't worry about it." Poteet said.

Anderson said, "You know what he means, Pell! Haven't you been picking up on all those little cracks the ol' man has been making all week, about people needing to be shot for failing their country in its hour of crisis, and life and death duty?"

Poteet said, "He's screaming mad about those two Cabinet Secretaries that left the grounds without permission. They're gonna get arrested. And quite possibly shot."

"And the thing is, it would be a legal order!" Anderson exclaimed, "The Constitution is suspended. Congress and the Supreme Court are suspended. Bayard's a damn emperor for as long as this lasts!"

Pell said, "Yeah, but he wouldn't likely shoot somebody without a pretty good reason."

"Just see to it that you're on line on time and don't do anything to draw attention to yourself." Poteet said, "He likes us, but this place is well staffed with unaffected soldiers, and we are as disposable as paper cups. Believe it ... And hell yes he would have a guy shot, if he thought it would make an example for others."

Poteet paused and said, "I'm not really so worried about any of us getting shot. It's just that I didn't join the Marine Corps to snuff the Secretary of Transportation."

The men fell silent and Poteet added, "Sorry, boys. I don't mean to bring you down. I'm pretty upset about the fact that I can't seem to get my girlfriend on the phone."

"She's unaffected, right?" Pell asked.

"Yes, yes. I have called her mother's place in the country, where she's supposed to be. I've called her apartment, my apartment, the phones just ring and ring. Sometimes there is no ring at all. I think the telephone system is breaking down."

Anderson said, "I got a call through to my brother today."

"Tell him about what your brother said, Mike!" Pell said, "It's the brother who does ham radio!"

Anderson said, "He's upset enough as it is, Pell! Just shut up about it."

Pell did as he was told. Soon enough, Poteet said, "Okay, I'm not really up for any more rumors, but if it's the brother with the ham radio, I guess that's different."

Anderson shook his head with disgust, and said, "The whole world's going down the torlit, Bill. Everybody's got the jingle. Everybody's frayin' out. People are killing each other, killing themselves. If it's hellish, it's happening, right now, all over the world. I don't want to go into all the stuff he said."

Poteet said, "All right, look, I don't know how it's all going to play out, but we are sticking to our duties as long as we have a heartbeat, just like in wartime. This is wartime. If you are going to be working with me, I want to hear that you are with me on that. All right!?"

"That's right!" Pell said.

"That's it." said Anderson. Then he looked around and said, "Hey, we got six hours before we're back on again. Let's smoke these things and have a beer."

They slid open one of the room's expansive windows, and moved some chairs and a cot. The Havanas were fired up, and the three men blew rich smoke out into the humid summer night. The view of Washington was unusually dark this evening.

Anderson said, "The thing is, even if Lancaster and all of 'em get the neurological situation rectified, how long is it going to take to put the world back like it was?"

All was quiet. The night air had none of the usual traffic sounds. Sirens, one after another, wailed away in the far distance.

The next day in the Situation Room the three Marines stood by while President Bayard listened to glowing reports from his Chief of Staff on the public's reaction to the video they televised the night before. The move was a brilliant success. The news networks that still operated spoke of how the country was filled with hope over the new therapeutic exercise. They ran video of crowded auditoriums, with close-ups of teary-eyed people watching the broadcast. Heartfelt testimonials of support for the Bayard administration were offered up by regular citizens. But the gaunt, stone-faced president only listened impassively, and at times seemed not to be listening at all. He only nodded his assent for more air time for the Van Cleave programs.

Bayard whispered over to his Vice President at one point, who in turn replied, "You're going in person? Wouldn't you rather talk to them over a video conference?"

The President shook his head, stood up, and said, "The Vice President will carry the ball here for a few hours, ladies and gents." He then gestured to an aide and said, "Have Marine One readied for Quantico." He left in the company of his Secret Service men.

There was no one these days with enough of a sense of security to ask President Bayard if he felt all right. When the massive presidential helicopter was fully loaded with the equipment and personnel that always accompanied him, no one said anything when the President remained outside for several minutes, staring up into the whirling rotors. Staff sergeants Poteet and Anderson, tapped to carry military communications gear for the trip, sat looking down at him through their window. He made the impression of a Biblical figure, gazing upward, with the wind blast shaking his longish, graying hair.

Bayard was in a state of somber, introspective awe. He was mildly dazed by the fact that the pounding, penetrating noise of the helicopter rotors did not in the slightest way diminish the tinkly, jingly, bell pinging, singsong refrain that was cycling on and on in his head. The rotor noise had something of an opposite effect; it made him aware of the extent to which this phenomenon had invaded him.

There was something like a bubble in his mind. He could feel it now, so distinctly. It was doing a very slow rotation, the way the room around a drunken man will slowly revolve. Only the jingle existed within the bubble, cycling and cycling and coming together with itself. Outside of the bubble -- there was also the jingle, but in an overlap with the identity and thought processes of President Bayard. He walked forward, mechanically, up the ramp into the aircraft.

He passed a directive to the pilot to take it low and slow on this flight that he might observe conditions on the ground. Aviation in America had come to a standstill; there was no danger in low altitude travel.

The giant military chopper passed over urban neighborhoods of Washington, D.C., on a southwesterly course. Here and there cars would appear to be parked at crazy angles in the middle of a street. National Guard personnel carriers rolled along. Very little vehicular traffic overall, instead clusters of people milled about in intersections and other open areas.

An aide to the President felt compelled to lean over and speak in his ear, "The National Guard consistently tells us that outright riot scenes are rare. It is a godsend that only a very tiny percentage of the affected have violent manifestations. Most of them are quite the opposite ... They're almost sedated." The aide had forgotten himself in saying this, and had momentarily forgotten that the President was one of these sedated, affected ones. The aide melted back into his seat, and the President just kept silently looking down at the world.

Coming in over Quantico, Bayard was disconcerted to see large numbers of men clustered casually on the grounds. It was not possible to estimate their numbers, but it looked like the entire Command was out meandering in the sunshine.

A very proper honor guard of unaffected troops stood by the helicopter pad, along with the Commanding Officer of the base and his staff. Upon disembarking, President Bayard was yelling over the rotor noise, "What is the story with all those idle men on the grounds, General?"

"Limited duty for them, sir!" the base commander shouted back, "They have the problem, sir! I keep them on base, and as active as I can, sir!"

Bayard screamed, "This is damned unacceptable!"

The C.O. said, "Yes sir! It is!"

They strode off toward a row of simple black sedans. Bayard climbed in back of one with a saluting Marine holding the door open. He vented steam toward the General as they rode across the base, "I have the condition myself, sir! I am still functioning! I am not wandering the White House in a bathrobe and bedroom slippers!"

The C.O. said, "The limited duty for affected personnel was my decision, Mr. President."

Boiling inside, Bayard just stared out the window for a minute, muscles visibly clenching. Then he looked over at the base commandant and said, "... I take it you are not one of the affected. You don't have this."

"That's right." said the General.

The President said, "... All right. For now, just take me where I'm going ... Take me to them."

The convoy of black Fords worked its way into the interior of the base, finally arriving at the high security stockade. The President clambered out before the car came to a complete stop.

Deep within this Marine jailhouse, the air had a sharp odor of disinfectant cleaner and the voices of inmates and guards echoed down cement-walled passageways. The President would not have to venture into an actual cellblock, however. Mr. and Mrs. Purdey had been brought out to an exercise room for their meeting with him.

Armed Marines snapped to attention as he strode between them through the door. On the far side of the room, between two more armed MP's, a young couple sat dolefully huddled together at a table. The barbells and exercise equipment had been removed for this occasion. Only a large red canvas punching bag remained, hanging from a chain.

The base commandant along with the chief of the stockade and two Secret Service agents trailed into the room behind the President. He stopped and told them bluntly to wait outside. They dutifully did so as he walked on toward the seated prisoners. Mr. Purdey's eyes popped wide open, and he called out in a glad voice, "President Bayard!"

The President stared at his rabbit-like face as he drew near. Then he looked to the MP's and said, "Dismissed. Wait outside." The guards were hesitant to leave but had no choice but to follow the order. As they departed, Mr. Purdey said excitedly, "They didn't tell us who was coming to visit today! We thought it might be a relative, or maybe a lawyer. Well, anyway, I am Wesley Purdey, and this is my wife Heidi."

"We are sure glad to see you, sir," said Heidi Purdey, "We voted for you both times!"

Wesley Purdey said, "Definitely pleased to see you. Surprised but pleased. The thing is, we really are being held here in violation of our rights. We were down at our beach house last week, and we get suddenly bundled off by troopers, ultimately to here, without so much as a toothbrush. So, we would ask that you take a hand and see if we can't get this matter resolved."

Bayard's immensely bloodshot eyes went back and forth between them, this pleasant couple in stockade dungarees. He raised a shaky hand, and pointed to Wesley. "You ... You came up with the music. And you ... you wrote the ... the <u>words</u>!"

The Purdeys looked to one another and lost their smiles. Heidi spoke up firmly, "Now, listen. We have been over and over this with your 'Research Team' folks. We don't know ..."

"You have been over and over it?" Bayard interjected, "I have been over and over it. Over and over it, over and over! ... You are going to undo what you have done! Did you know that!?"

"We don't know what to tell you!" she screamed at him.

"You'll think of it!" Bayard yelled back, "You are going to work it out! ... Why did you choose those particular words!?"

She slumped forward on the card table, and said, "Like we told your people a thousand times, it was just the wording and music that came to us when we sat down to work ... Do you know how many commercial jingles we have produced in our careers? It's what we do. This one, I can tell you, was no different in terms of how we approached it."

Wesley sought to lower the volume and intensity of the situation, and said in a gentler tone, "There were some, ah, very subtle differences in how this one was produced. The ad was to appeal to children, but we thought a certain variety of sound devices would make it engaging to all ages. We were experimenting with sounds and timing, just as any musician does. We threw in reverb on certain words. We utilized some newly developed musical instruments, as well as some ancient ones from my collection. We built a multilayered track of musical devices that played just under the lead tune, creating an interesting effect. It's something I call a musical thicket."

The President did not look remotely pacified, and Wesley leaned forward and spoke to him in a voice of confidentiality,

"I know all about the problem that people are having, but it just can't be from the jingle itself. No. No. You know what I think? I think Fresh World put something in the formula. Some kind of mind control drug."

"That's not what I think," the President said, "That was the first thing we checked. Know what I think? You want to know what I am thinking?" He looked over their heads, paused for a second, and went, "Glory be, I'm all at sea! An' I see what I enjoy! Avast!! A drink of pink for me!! ..."

Bayard glowered down at them. To Heidi he looked just like the Halloween mask of him that was sold every year. The President Bayard mask, come lividly to life.

Taking a cue from Wesley, she spoke in a calm, earnest manner, "Sir, I ask that you first try to appreciate how we are feeling about all this. After all, up until the third week of the ad campaign, my husband and I thought we had brought about the single most successful commercial jingle in advertising history."

Suddenly unsure of what she hoped to achieve with the statement, she quickly added, "Mr. President, my husband and I are certainly committed to doing everything in our power to resolve this situation to your satisfaction. We are going to work day and night with the researchers until we have the answer."

Bayard bellowed out, "And you will have the answer pretty damn quick! Or I am going to have you shot! You and your husband, side by side, for a firing squad of eager volunteers!"

A few minutes later, the door opened and President Bayard was out and striding down the passageway. He called the base C.O. over to his side and snarled, "You get with Research, and you tell them you are to be notified at once when the moment comes that those two are not needed anymore. Within that hour, your orders are that they are to be shot. Is that understood?"

"Yes sir!" shouted the C.O., straining to keep up.

"Good God I want 'em shot!" Bayard exclaimed as he blew past Anderson and Poteet. Then he shrieked out, in a hair-raising falsetto,

"I wannem shaaaat!!!"

Later that evening back at the White House staff sergeant Poteet succeeded in getting both a ring and an answer at the home of his girlfriend's mother.

"Elise!" he shouted.

"Billy!" she cried back, "Where are you?"

"I'm still here at this damn stinkin' White House, hon. It's no leaves, no liberties, no going off of the grounds, and for how long I do not know. I wish I did, believe me. But how are you? I haven't been able to get a call through until now!"

Elise said, "I'm okay. Mother had been taking the phone off the hook without telling me. We've been getting crank calls. There's only the one phone now, here in the bedroom."

"Are you sure you're all right?" Poteet asked, "You sound ... different. Is anything wrong?"

"I'll be all right." she said, but there was a definite emotional catch in her voice now. When Poteet did not respond right away, she began to sob softly.

"Elise!" he said, "Pull yourself together, baby. We can't talk long. Tell me what's going on."

"Ohh, Mother has been taking in affected people! There's half a dozen of them downstairs! And ... they're just so weird, and scary."

"Who are they? Why in God's name is she taking people in?"

"Because she's old and people take advantage of her!" Elise said, "It started out with one old man she said she knew, and that just seemed to open the gate. It's her house. I can't really say anything about it. Although I have. We have argued terribly about this, and she is in total denial that these poor people might pose a problem. My brother has left us. It's just Mother and me. And the boarders."

"Unbelievable." Poteet said, his head in his hands, "I am going to come up with something, honey. I'm getting you out of there."

"In a way, I don't want to leave Mother." she said, "I don't know if she would leave with me. The boarders haven't done anything, exactly. They're just unnerving. I came out of the bathroom one night, and there was one of them standing at the top of the stairs, humming that jingle, and looking completely zapped. They may be totally harmless, like Mother says. And, we have a good lock for the bedroom door."

"All right, Elise, listen up" Poteet said, "I will try to call you this same time tomorrow, but I cannot make any guarantees as to when we will talk again. It may be a while! If that is the case, I am going to count on you to be level-headed and take care of yourself until I can get back to you."

Through sniffles and sobs, she promised him she would.

Poteet went on, "Now, look, you might need to get out of that place at some point. Do you think you could find your way to my parents' farm in North Carolina? Remember? It's a place to go, if need be. And look here, if the phones go out, and you have to relocate, I want you to write out for me where you are going. Write me a note and wrap it in a plastic bag and put it under the concrete elf in your mama's flower bed. You got that?"

"Under the elf. Yes." she said.

"'Cause I don't want us getting dislocated...if things get bad." Poteet said.

Elise said, "I'm so glad you got through this time!"

"Glad we didn't get cut off." Poteet said, "Well, listen, I think I had better steal a few seconds more, and ask you one other thing. Whenever we can get together next ... will you marry me?"

"Yes! Yes!" Elise cried.

"Good." said Poteet, "The future is going to be tough, and challenging, no matter how things play out. We're going to need each other."

"I love you," she said in a shaky voice.

"I love you, too, precious. You be strong for me, and I'll talk to you soon as I can."

He hung up, thinking, "And only God and Bayard know when that might be." He turned out the light in the ornate little office he had been allowed to use for privacy during his call.

Stepping out into the plush hallway, upstairs at the White House West Wing, Poteet had to pause to get his bearings. He had already gotten himself lost here once. It didn't help that his mind was so preoccupied. He ambled along, turning at what he hoped was the right intersection of corridors.

Glumly, he strolled down a very lengthy, empty passageway, only to be suddenly struck by the sight of an odd figure stepping out from a room at the far end. The light was not good, and the man could only be seen as a gray silhouette. But there was a distinct strangeness to his movements, as if he were intoxicated. Now the man began to make his way down the hall toward Poteet, and it became clear that whoever this was he was operating with a considerably diminished capacity.

Poteet quietly cursed to himself. This was the only hallway that was not stacked up with military security, and he had to share it with this boozer. Now he was going to have to deal with the guy, whoever he was. Poteet figured that, given his luck, it would turn out to he the Secretary of the Navy.

The man was not staggering, exactly, but there was a slow deliberation in his gait that would not do for anyone who wasn't walking on ice. Poteet called out,

"Good evening, sir!"

There was no reply from the fellow down the hall.

Or was there? The man made a whispering sound, or perhaps it was only labored breathing. With each overhead lamp that the two men passed under, Poteet could see a little more detail. Judging by the uniform, it was one of the White House domestic servants. Poteet let out a disgusted groan as he watched the chap lift his arms in front of him, as if he were feeling his way through fog.

The distance between them closed to the point that he could see the man clearly. Poteet froze. The man continued trudging forward, with an expression on his face of such bottomless delirium that Poteet could only stare, and draw in a gasp of shock.

He kept coming. His face was reminiscent of the exaggerated madmen of old silent movies. His lips seemed to be forming the words, away, away, away. But then he took a deep breath, and it came out clearly, as, "Ahoy ... Ahoy ... Ahoy ..." He closed in on the stunned Marine, who only reacted when the outstretched hands came in to grip the flesh of his face. Poteet grabbed for the man's forearms, but he was surprisingly strong, and could not be immediately dislodged.

A struggle ensued in the corridor, although Poteet was so transfixed by the eeriness of the deranged man he was not fighting him all out. That changed when he felt one of the man's fingernails scrape his left eye. Poteet gave him a knee to the crotch and followed through with the hardest right cross he could deliver.

The encounter ended there, with the butler out cold on the carpet, and staff sergeant Poteet lurching down the hall with one hand gently covering his stinging eye.

Poteet's scratched cornea was treated personally by the Surgeon General of the United States. With a black patch in place, he was at his president's side for the next morning's round of meetings. Although the business covered was riveting, Poteet's thoughts were all for his beloved fiancée, so far away in the countryside, in a house of strange strangers.

Within three days the Bayard government went from treading water to swallowing water. The Attorney General dispensed with the double-talk in the Situation Room and stated directly that the Lancaster/Van Cleave therapies were not working. A horrendous spike in murder and suicide rates intensified the loss of hope, as people began to employ death to save family and friends from impending psychological meltdown. Police forces were turning on themselves, adding to the growing chaos. The Attorney General did not hold back in delivering his vision of expanding madness. His ringing phrase was,

"The jingle reigns supreme over the human mind!"

President Bayard, never looking more haggard, said only that he would continue with the recommendations of the Surgeon General and her research team.

While blood ran in the streets, there was concern expressed that President Bayard had not made a live television address in quite some time. And since he had also made no public appearances since the crisis began, rumors were now spreading that all his communications to the public were prerecorded. This he would put to rest tonight, he said, with a speech broadcast live. It would be the defining speech of his presidency, he said. But to Poteet it seemed that presidential speeches had been described in just those words fairly regularly for most of his life.

The day shift was relieved at 6 P.M. by the overnight Marines. Not being allowed to leave the White House, they returned to their quarters to watch Japanese cartoons on an old TV set.

It was during a lull in the on-screen action that Anderson spoke up, "I had a few words with some of the brass today after lunch. I've been debating whether to tell you guys about it."

"It's that good, eh?" asked Pell.

Poteet said, "I can't think of anything you've ever hesitated to tell us before."

Anderson said, "This isn't going to boost your morale, but, it's like this. I was asking them about the next rotation of troops coming in, the ones who are going to relieve us. And, well, it's the funniest thing. There aren't any."

"Maybe not for the time being, but they eventually have to relieve us." Pell said.

"Not for the duration of the crisis." said Anderson, "It appears there is a severe shortage of non-jingling servicemen. The President and his people think we are doing just fine, and so here we are. The lieutenant suggested thanking God that we are here, instead of some of the places we could be stationed."

Poteet said, "We can request emergency leave for humanitarian reasons. I need to get to my fiancée, and real bad."

Anderson said, "Yes, you can request emergency leave, and you can get turned down for emergency leave. Our personal emergencies are not their foremost priorities."

"We will see about that," Poteet said with anger.

Anderson said, "Okay, Bill, try for it. But I am telling you they don't want us roaming the streets of Washington, and they damn sure don't want us out in rural Virginia somewhere! They just can't afford to lose any unaffecteds like us."

Poteet said, "Uh huh, well, even guys in shooting wars get some leave now and then. I will sure take this to Bayard himself if I have to."

His comrades wished him all the best with it. Pell wanted a change of subject, and popped in an episode of an especially ribald comedy show about girls with big chests who worked on the bullet train. Poteet had often found it funny in the past. For this screening though, no one was laughing.

Poteet's mood had soured. He could not stop thinking how the program had the feel of a relic. This could possibly be among the last of all TV shows, as he had known them. Watching it left him feeling increasingly rankled; even in his bunk at night watching the tube, he had no escape from feeling the finality with which the familiar world had been snatched away.

He was about to yell for them to turn the stupid thing off, when Pell said, "Hey! Bayard's speech is about to come on!"

"Aw, well, by all means, let us see it!" Poteet said, "Let's see the defining speech of his presidency! We need that big hoist in morale."

Pell changed the channel to a news station and said, "I hope he doesn't have any microphones hidden in here, Bill."

A woozy-looking TV newsman spoke to fill time until the top of the hour. Pell commented on what a lot of pointless jabber he was spouting, to which Poteet shot back, "Have you heard any of Bayard's speeches recently?"

The Presidential Seal filled the screen as the appointed moment drew near. The newsman's voice dropped an octave as he announced, "Ladies and gentlemen, live from the Oval Office at the White House in Washington, D.C., the President of the United States." And there was Bayard, solemnly staring out at the world. As he parted his lips to speak, a nervous tic suddenly pulled his mouth to one side.

Another more violent tic followed, this one cocking his head to the side. He spoke, "My f-fellow Americans, Thomas Paine once wrote, 'These are the times that try men's souls.' I th-think each of us can relate to that quotation today ..." At the word each, his voice cracked like that of a growing boy.

"Nope," Poteet said, standing up, "Not gonna sit through it. You boys let me know if he says anything worth hearing. I'm going down to the soda machine. Either of you want anything?"

Anderson said, "Yeah, bring me back an Ahoy, will ya?" He looked up from the TV, to meet Poteet's one steely eye. Anderson smiled evilly, and said, "I'm hankerin' for one o' them cool, refreshing pinky drinkies." He laughed obnoxiously, and for Poteet, the time was not quite right for sailing through the air and pounding him into the historical wallpaper. For now, his eye hurt, his energy was flat, and he was thirsty. He departed for the vending machine.

The downstairs rec room was jammed with off-duty personnel and the drink machine was sold out. Poteet drifted on. There was another machine down a couple more flights of fire stairs. It was in the proximity of the Situation Rooms, so he might be turned away, not being in uniform.

He emerged into the basement corridor, and made his way unopposed to the nook with the vending machines. Not only unopposed, he was totally alone. Not as much traffic down here, he thought, as he made his selection. He stepped back into the hallway and sat down on the cool tile floor. Here was a quiet place to think.

Moments later somebody slammed down on the opening bar of the fire door at the end of the hall, and with a reverberating boom, it flew open. Two uniformed Marine sentries came hustling down the hall toward Poteet. At first he thought he must be in trouble, then one of them saw him and called out his name. The other said,

"Let's ask him!"

"You don't have a phone on you by chance, do you, Poteet?" asked the first Marine, a kid named Dubois with whom he was acquainted.

"A phone?" he asked, "No. What's going on?"

"All right ... We got a situation here," Dubois said nervously, "All I have is this radio to the duty officer, and he is not helping us. We need to get a call up to the Secret Service."

Poteet said, "Wait a minute. What have you got that the duty officer won't handle?"

The Marine said, shakily, "It's Tedworth. The General. He's gone alone into the Situation Room ..."

"Okay. So?" Poteet asked.

"Well, it was to be secured until their meeting tomorrow," Dubois said, "And, anyway, it sounds like he's in there playing the disc of ... that commercial."

Poteet gasped. "The Ahoy commercial?" he said, "He's running it? With sound, and everything?"

The two sentries looked wide-eyed at one another, then at Poteet, and nodded their heads. Dubois said, "You know they have one of the last existing copies of it in there. Anyway, the duty officer says that the Chairman of the Joint Chiefs can go wherever and do whatever he damn well pleases. But that can't be right, you know it? The man is affected. And nobody is supposed to be exposed to that thing anymore. I am thinking we need to go over the duty officer's head."

Poteet thought for a moment, then took charge. He walked down to the fire door, pushed down on the thumb latch, gently eased it open, and looked inside. The hallway had several recessed doorways on either side. The third door on the right was the central Situation Room, but if anybody was in there, no lights were on.

Poteet said, "I don't hear anything being played."
At that moment, a snatch of sound like a high pitched, high speed xylophone echoed through the hall followed by a thunderous baritone singing, "Ahoy! Ahoy! Ahoy! I'm callin' er'ry girl and boy! ..."

Dubois cried out, "Wow! He has really upped the volume!"

Poteet pressed a finger on the shoulder of the other sentry, and said, "You, get upstairs and get to the Secret Service. Dubois, stay right here with that radio."

Poteet stepped softly and stealthily down the hall, not that anyone could have heard him over the blasting audio. As he reached the Situation Room, he found the door was standing open. It was dark inside, except for shifting colored lights on the left-hand wall, from the wide screen video that hung at the far right, presently out of his view. He pressed his palms over his ears, and stepped inside.

The stooped and slouching figure of the aged general stood out in a black silhouette against the broad, gleaming screen he was facing. He was in his full dress uniform, with cover and epaulettes, not entirely unlike the giant cartoon sea captain who loomed before him, roaring out in earsplitting decibels, "Avast!! A drink of pink for me!! ..."

The sound of the thing was insidiously mindless. There was an undercurrent of sound that would wah-wah in and out of reach of the herky-jerky kiddy tune that was itself largely dominated in turn by eccentric vocals, reverbing on certain words. The core structure of notes would at times cut out, or not go where it seemed like it ought to go, leaving tiny, evenly-spaced frustrations in the experience. At this volume Poteet noticed things about it that he had missed back when it was on TV every fifteen minutes.

When shortly it ended, Poteet lowered his hands from his ears, and said,

"General Tedworth, sir?" A loud hum filled the room, as the sound system was still at full blast, but with no input.

Tedworth turned and glanced at him, then went back to facing the dark screen. Poteet got a cold feeling in his belly as he saw the remote control in Tedworth's left hand, and quickly deduced he was going to play it again.

Though just in his T-shirt, and cut off jeans, Poteet came to attention, and yelled out, "Staff sergeant Poteet at the General's assistance, sir!"

Tedworth made a partial turn toward the young man, and said, in a faltering voice, "Had to hear it again ... for real ..."

Poteet wasn't sure what scared him most, this man's state of mind, his rank, or the fact that in a very few seconds he would start up that cacophony again and there would be no way to say anything to him.

"... Have to see it one more time." said the General. And then Poteet knew what scared him most. Tedworth's uniform was complete down to its side arm, which hung heavily from his right hand -- his famous gold-plated .45 revolver.

A flying tackle would be one option, but even in this extreme scenario, Poteet found himself intimidated by the fact that this was the Chairman of the Joint Chiefs of Staff. He was also standing just far enough away that the tackle might fail.

"General Tedworth, sir!!"

The General turned and waved him away with the gun, to which Poteet did not immediately respond. But when he stopped waving, and brought the cannon to rest pointed right at him, Poteet hit the deck.

He executed a roll to line himself up with the doorway, then vaulted out into the corridor in two desperate, stumbling leaps. There was a weird, plinking, music box sound as he got to his feet, and then,

"Ahoy!! Ahoy!! Ahoy!!..."

In case he was being pursued Poteet lurched into a recessed doorway down the hall. He peeked out, saw no sign of Tedworth, and made a wild sprint for the fire door. Dubois opened it just enough for him to slip through.

Poteet grabbed the sentry's radio and slammed down the button. "This is staff sergeant Poteet! Come in! Come in!"

The night officer responded, though not right away. Poteet tried to make him understand, "Sir, we have a situation in the Situation Room! It's an emergency!"

The lieutenant j.g. on the other end said that this had better not be more about General Tedworth going down there alone. Poteet said, "Sir, you don't understand. He is in there playing the disc of ... the jingle! And-and he has his side arm in his hand!"

The duty officer only wanted to know what Poteet was doing down in that restricted area when he was not on the duty roster.

Poteet said, "The issue you had better consider, sir, is that General Tedworth is in the Situation Room, maybe in an unbalanced state of mind, and playing that disc very, very loud! Listen!"

He opened the fire door and thrust the radio out at arms length as the commercial's ending chorus resounded down the hallway,

"... Ahoy!! Ahoy!! Ahoy!! ... Ahoy!! Ahoy!! Ahoy!!"

Then, in quick succession -- kaBLAM!!

Late in the afternoon on the following day, very little work had been accomplished by the crisis government based at the White House. Work came to a complete stop at 4 P.M. The President summoned his remaining Cabinet Secretaries, top staffers, and military command to the East Room, and after the briefest words of greeting and thanks, he began calling out names and somberly handing out Presidential Medals of Freedom.

The unscheduled ceremony stretched out into a couple of hours, with President Bayard often lapsing into prolonged conversation after hanging the decoration around the recipient's neck. Out in the Cross Hall, at either side of the great room's main entrance, staff sergeants Pell and Poteet stood at parade rest. As names were called Pell craned his neck around in an effort to get a peek at the action. At length he said, "You mean all these guys are getting medals? I didn't figure there were that many of 'em made!"

Poteet barked out, "Shuddup and face front! No talking! What's the matter with you?" Pell complied instantly, although there was no issue of rank involved.

In the East Room the talking went on, and after the medals were all handed out, the crowd remained on, in what seemed the subdued atmosphere of a failed cocktail party. President Bayard went from the role of boss to host, and circulated, if joylessly, among those in attendance. In truth, he was feeling pretty terrible.

Long weeks of carrying the relentlessly revolving ditty in his head while shouldering the burdens of his office in time of crisis had left the President in a condition far worse than he dared admit to anyone. How wrong the researchers had been! The passage of time had done nothing for this monstrous affliction except entrench it. Now, for the first time, he found himself having trouble hearing what people were saying. He retreated to stand alone by the piano.

Bayard stared down upon the felt hammers as they struck the taut metal strings, and his guests gave him some space. He leaned heavily on the side of the open piano, and then and there, something happened to him.

The three-dimensional, mental bubble he had been sensing for so long ceased its rotation in his head. It had stopped revolving because it was breaking. The experience was not that of a bubble popping, more like an egg yolk rupturing, coming undone, and spilling itself out in all directions. His eyes slid shut.

When they opened again, a different piece was being played on the piano, though he was only just aware of it. The rampaging jingle had expanded into total occupation of his mind.

Pell and Poteet came to attention as President Bayard walked between them out of the East Room. Guests had started to drift out some minutes ago, and the two Marines expected the affair to end altogether before long. Poteet noticed that the President did not take the immediate right for the staircase, but continued down the Cross Hall and turned at the North Portico entrance.

A Secret Service agent appeared from the East Room, and said, "That's funny. He usually lets me know when he's going to the can." He scanned the empty hall. "Did he go upstairs?" he asked Poteet.

"Actually, sir, he stepped out by the North Portico entrance." Poteet said, "Getting some fresh air, I would guess."

He and the agent looked at one another for a second, and Poteet said, "I'll check on him for you, sir." He trotted off to the North entrance.

Bayard was walking away at a brisk pace across the north lawn of the White House, almost to the fountain at its center, when Poteet shoved open the heavy glass door and stepped outside. One of the sentries posted there said, "Is he all right?"

Poteet said, "It's okay. I got it." He crossed the driveway and made his way out between the columns onto the lawn.

He called out, "Mr. President!" But the receding figure did not break his stride. Poteet trotted along, and again yelled, "Mr. President!" Then, he said to himself, "Uh oh..." as he saw Bayard break into a run, and then an all-out sprint.

Poteet barreled off after him.

The President was running in a northeasterly direction, making for the fence. Poteet only hoped there was enough ground to catch up to him before he got there. Bayard was pumping his arms, motoring across the grounds at a clip his pursuer did not think possible.

Poteet took a quick look back, hoping to see that the North Portico sentries were watching him and were now joining the chase. Instead they were properly posted up by the door, out of view and oblivious. And where was the perimeter patrol? He spotted them in the distance, almost at the opposite side of the property. Apart from the guard shack at the northeast gate, he was on his own.

Poteet had not gained any ground on this man more than twice his age, and looking around for help had lost him some. Clearing his mind, he drew on all the adrenalin he could summon, and tore across the lawn as fast as he could make it happen, with his Presidential Medal of Freedom bouncing up and down on his chest.

President Bayard had more than a fifty-foot lead when he reached the ornamental fence, and jumped to grasp the top of it. He vaulted himself over with a minimal struggle. Landing on his feet, running, he crossed the street, sprinting eastbound for New York Avenue.

Poteet veered right on the lawn to keep up with him. Reaching the fence he bruised a testicle going over, and fell down flat on the sidewalk. Resuming the chase with a gritty determination, he passed the northeast gate, and screamed at the Park Service guys,

"Yahh, it's him! Now call the Secret Service!"

Bayard flew up New York Avenue in the middle of the street. Fortunately no cars were coming. No cars were moving anywhere. In fact there were very few people in sight. Those that Poteet encountered looked frightening, almost lobotomized. He said nothing to them and kept running, his chest burning.

A couple of blocks away, the President cut down an alley and bolted left up a side street. He had executed two more such turns before Poteet caught up and tackled him on a sidewalk in front of a row of boarded up businesses. He pinned his shoulders to the pavement, until he was sure he was not going to run any more.

Poteet got to his feet, gasping wildly for breath, as was the President who he left lying there. He slumped against a mailbox and looked down at him. Bayard's eyes were unfixed and rolling. As his breathing stabilized, he began muttering incoherent sounds as he lay there, flat on his back. Poteet looked around and found no one in sight to help him.

The Marine took stock. He did not know what street this was. Only the obelisk of the Washington Monument in the distance gave him some sense of direction after the circuitous chase. He had his side arm in case of trouble. Twilight was setting in.

The only trouble so far was the President, whose mental faculties were gone. He could not form an intelligible word. Periodically, he would stand up and start to casually walk away. On being stopped and made to sit on the curb, he would just stare into space until the next impulse to wander came to him. Poteet considered the difficulties of trying to guide him back home. When a street light came on above them, he decided to stay put until help came. They couldn't be that far from the White House. Surely a search team would be with them soon.

Much later, after a starry nighttime sky was well established, Poteet took stock again with a new attitude. When Bayard stood up from the curb the next time, Poteet remained leaning against the mailbox. His fingertips slid lightly across the cool surface of his Presidential Medal of Freedom, and he watched as the last vestige of the government of the United States of America shuffled off into the darkness. He did not remain long in contemplation before setting out to find a vehicle to hot-wire. He was going to Virginia to find his wife.

On the horizon, red glows from distant fires could be seen, one of which was the final ray of sunset.

The sun would revisit the monuments of Washington.

After the passing of two hundred thousand dusks and dawns, daylight found the great obelisk unmoved, though not unchanged. Darker, and bearing visible cracks, it supported a dense network of vines above the canopy of the old growth forest that grew up to its base.

An immense herd of deer crashing through the depths of the forest drew the attention of a stout woman with long red hair, as she sat on a stump by a dirt road, holding a wailing baby. She looked in the direction of the sound, but when she caught sight of the obelisk, she quickly turned away. She was afraid of it, as were all of her contemporaries. No road ran close enough to it that a person might enter its shadow.

Her rough cloak was deerskin. A strip of dried venison stuck out of the corner of her mouth like a cigar. Many screeching children, naked, long-haired, and dusty, play-fought in the woods before her. A boy of about five years strode up to her, pulled open the front of her garment, and spent a couple of minutes nursing and trying to nurse before she knocked him away.

She remained sitting impassively amid the shrieking urchins until she heard the sound she had been waiting for. The steady clopping of hooves and the rumbling of heavy wooden wheels on wooden axles announced the arrival of the horse cart. She got to her feet and released a long, high-pitched shout, to assemble her offspring.

Two emaciated gray mares dragged the sturdy but ponderous four wheel conveyance down the trail, while muscular young men helped by pushing from the rear.

It came to a stop in front of the waiting mother and children. She approached the bearded driver of the cart, and held up a large turnip for him as though it were a precious gem. He looked at it for some time before snatching it away and tossing it into the wooden box at his side. He sat staring straight ahead as they all climbed aboard.

The path plied by the horse cart was mostly through forest, but small communities of thatched huts stood along the route as did the remnants of fabulous constructions as old as the world itself. Some of these sites were nice to visit, and sleep in, although most were tabooed to a spine-chilling extreme.

It was to one of the good sites of antiquity that the cart riders were traveling today: to the roofless, windowless, gutted shell of the National Cathedral, high atop the area's one hill.

Their needs brought these simple people to this place. Their deepest, innermost needs were understood and articulated here by the priests. Many other horse and ox carts were standing outside these vined stone towers. There was always someone here, and the service was always the same. It was because it was always the same that they kept coming.

The cart riders filed into the open-air center space of the structure, where a crowd had already assembled. On a raised platform at the front of the congregation, ten priests in simple vestments stood in meditation. Adding to the wonder of this place for many was the fact that children often became calm on their own here. The children's needs were also being satisfied within these walls.

The sun came out from behind a cloud, suddenly filling the space with golden light. Seeing a sufficient gathering, the high priest seized the moment and stepped to the front of the platform. Absolute silence fell upon the congregants, as the other nine priests made a long, deep intonation.

The high priest held out his hands, palms up in the sunlight. He looked into the sky, and drew in a deep breath. In a mighty voice that carried throughout the sanctum, he began the timeless canticle:

"Aaaaoooeee!! Aaaaoooeee!! Aaaaoooeee!!..."

THE END

Condemned to Repeat It

The efficiency was precisely arranged, and categorically clean. Freshly applied peel-and-press wallpaper squares lent a floral backdrop to a smiling portrait of John Paul II. An anguished crucified Christ offset it on the opposite wall. New looking throw rugs were neatly positioned on a floor devoid of dust. White linen cloths lay across the arms of a love seat on which Monte and his date were centered.

She remarked that the place didn't give the impression of being a bachelor pad, and Monte gave his faint, fading laugh. Like a ventriloquist's chuckle, it sounded almost identical each time he produced it. That was fairly compulsively, she noticed. It was not too unpleasant, coming from him. She affected a chuckle of her own in response, as she had often done in the brief time they had known one another. Sometimes he also got a little push on the knee, as she wished the laugh would either intensify or cease, though she never said so.

Monte seemed a bit subdued this evening though he could not be sure how he felt. He sat with a chagrined smile on his face, feeling whatever it was, and letting her do most of the talking.

"That's a fascinating sea shell arrangement," Evie said, "stacked up like that. How did you ever find so many that fit together so well?" A single sea-oat, dropped through drilled holes, held the stack together.

In a sudden bout of awkwardness, Monte could not be drawn into conversation. But feeling restless and confined on the couch, he stood and offered his elbow, on which she rested her hand. Then, quite naturally, they began a sort of measured procession around the cramped room, examining Monte's miniatures.

With an air of formality which was almost Elizabethan, and which secretly delighted them, the pair moved from point to point in the room. From the shells and the terrarium with the live mantis, they stepped to the awe-inspiring castle in a bottle, and the palm sized carved teak chess set.

"Absolutely too small for playing!" Evie declared.

"No, it's just the right size!" Monte said, "See? It brings two heads together," and he made an opening move. Forehead to forehead they played along, giggling, until she pulled him away to the next exhibit.

Their promenade went its instinctive way, until the collection of knickknacks was exhausted. They stood facing each other by the sofa, with Evie seeming far more at ease than her friend. He decided he was feeling nervous being alone with this very proper woman whom he barely knew. Deep inside, in a mental language without words, he bitterly denounced himself over it.

She would be perfect for him, he thought. Beyond that, he was indebted to her. Their church could have paved its parking lot this year; instead those resources had gone to hiring him as a special Outreach Worker, due mainly to the advocacy of Evie, coming on the heels of his own Olympian feat of self promotion.

The church needed a boost in membership, and this he had pledged to deliver. He had no ordination, no seminary, and no social service degree. But he was relatively young, exceedingly enthusiastic about the mission of the church and was prepared to go down to that beach and get those bikers excited about the Bible. He was going to get some fresh blood in the pews! At the past four weekly parish admin meetings he had been quite the impressive fellow, if somewhat weak on credentials.

"Well, I guess I should dish up the stew now," he said.

"The stew?" she asked.

"Sure! Can't you smell it? I've had this in all day for you!"

She felt a little embarrassed for not complimenting him on the delicious aroma that filled the apartment. But it was such a mild, unimposing smell, and fit this place so perfectly -- it just hadn't grabbed her. She commented now about how wonderful it smelled. Monte was soon beaming, and breathing in the scent of domestic order that pervaded his home. He gave her hand a quick squeeze, and stepped into his immaculate kitchenette.

Since he was still visible to her, he decided he had better come up with some topic of conversation, lest Evie start talking again about the shooting of the Pope at St. Peter's Square in Rome. The episode was still in the news, though it was now clear that the Holy Father would recover. It was a fresh trauma in the Catholic world. Evie had often spoken in hushed tones of the incident, and the recent attempt on President Reagan's life, as signs of Christ's impending return. To Monte, they were simply horrors he had heard enough of.

"Now, this kind of stew is typical of what I've had most of my life." he said, "For dinner, I mean. We had this a lot where I come from. I really have to learn Southern cooking. 'Think you could teach me about it?"

"Well ... that depends ..." Evie said, "... on how much effort you are prepared to make. Boiling greens can get pretty involved in itself."

"I never would have thought so!"

"You can handle it, Monte!" she cried, and settled back on the sofa, watching him intently as he worked. He had a stocky appearance, as if weightlifting had figured in his past. But the muscular edge had gone, and now he was left a smoothed-over looking person, big for his height, and awkward. He was young, somewhere in his twenties. His dark features suggested a Latin heritage.

His mannerisms always conveyed a sense of drive, she thought. It was the open-ended energy of a recent convert. She had never known a male as enthusiastic about the work of the church, especially not at St. Dominic's, the one lonesome parish in this coastal North Carolina town. She had attended masses there since her infancy. Monte had shown up last month.

He shot a glance at her as he sipped a spoonful of their dinner. She gave her best smile, and from Monte there came the feathery laugh. So faint it was inaudible and didn't move a drop from the spoon. Just at that moment a jolting thing happened to the new man in town. His telephone rang. This was the first time it had done so since he moved in, and it took a moment for him to register the harsh, jangling noise.

"Hello?" he answered.

"Hi. I found a wallet with this phone number in it." said an indistinct male voice as a stiff wind blew in the background.

"...You did."

"Yeah. On a bench in the park downtown."

"Hmm." said Monte.

"It has this number and another one, and I think a car key." said a young man, "It looks like a car key."

"Well, that is odd, I must say. Are you sure you dialed the right number, friend?"

The caller read the number back to him, and Monte looked at Evie with a puzzled smile. "Well, gee, I haven't lost my wallet," he said, "and I am the only one who lives here. Can't imagine why my phone number should be in there. It doesn't have any names or anything, you say?"

"No, it doesn't." the fellow said, "It's kind of weird. It has this little card in it with your number on it, and next to that is written 'The First.' Then there's another number under that, and 'The Last' is written. And there's a car key ..."

"Hmm. How odd."

"And ... a cigarette. But that's all. It's a real handsome wallet. Well, anyway, I thought I would call you first." he said with a laugh.

"Glad you did." Monte said, "That is interesting. Wish I could help you."

"... 'Cause I figure somebody would want this key ... I was hoping I might pick up a few bucks for returning the key." said the caller, "Well, maybe the other number will claim it."

"I hope so!" Monte said, "And look, you are welcome to call me back if you find the owner. I am interested to know what the story is."

Monte concluded the call with "God bless you," and ran that conversation through his mind a couple of times.

"So what did they want?" Evie asked.

He shrugged, and began dropping ice cubes into tea glasses. "Somebody lost a wallet." he said, "I don't know why it had my phone number in it ..."

Monte looked down into his stew as he moved a big wooden spoon around in it. His face took on a look of great seriousness as he watched the vegetables rise, bobble, and submerge. "Evie, I want to get involved in that Save the Children project." he said, "I was late getting into church the other day ... 'only heard some of what you were saying about it. But I think that is something I would really, really like to get involved with."

"Oh, that would be fantastic, Monte! I can't think of anyone I would rather do it with. We could go the two of us, door to door. It'll be fun!" She stood and smoothed her dress, "You know," she said, "we've needed someone like you around here for so long."

"Well ... that's sweet of you to say."

"You're a spirit-filled man, Monte," she said, moving into the kitchen doorway and leaning against it, "This town doesn't have enough people like you."

"Doesn't have enough people at all!" Monte said, smiling.

What a woman, Monte thought. And they could be married by this time next year, he figured. Undoubtedly they could just live here in the apartment, though there was not a lot of room for entertaining. He regarded her face, imagining it aged twenty years, thirty years.

He said nothing until his silence began to make him look uncomfortable. "Well, yes ..." he stammered, "I guess it's God's will that I live here. I keep meeting such sweet people ..."

This exchange was as intimate as their talking had gone this evening. But as Monte put the crock of stew on the table and sat down with Evie, his mind was searching for even milder subjects of conversation. He folded his hands for prayer. Evie immediately did the same, and a solemn grace was offered. It was then the telephone rang again.

"Maybe someone found something with your signature on it this time." Evie said.

"It's probably that same fellow calling back." He picked up the phone, "Hello?"

"Hello!!" cried a voice from the receiver, "Listen to...me ... I can't talk long! ..."

The voice trailed off, and Monte's brow rumpled, as a very sincere-sounding bawl of pain turned into violent coughing.

"Who's there!?" he demanded.

"P-Please don't hang up on me ..." begged a sobbing, breaking voice.

Without going further with the phone call, Monte felt it. A contaminating presence was intruding on his home. Evie jumped up and came closer as he sputtered, "What is going on here?" Then, raising his voice, "Is this that same guy?"

"Yes sir, it's me." the trembling voice confirmed, "Mister, I am in terrible trouble."

"Well, so, what is going on?" Monte shouted.

The young caller wildly gasped, through sobbing and choking, "I-I found that wallet, mister ... and ohh God ... I just-t thought I'd try to return it ... And like I didn't think it'd b-be no problem if I smoked that ... cigarette in there. I was smokin' on it when I was talking to you."

His words were interrupted by a burst of raw coughing, during which Monte and Evie had a brief eye contact. He wasn't sure how much she was hearing, but he wished she would back off a bit.

"I called that other number in there. And s-somebody asked me first thing did I call you ... And then they wanted to know did I smoke that thing." The poor fellow sounded to be weeping openly, "... An' I said yes ... and he said ... then you're dead, and he hung up!"

A torrent of hysterical weeping poured out of the telephone into the silent kitchenette. Evie had her hands over her mouth. Monte, looking from one point in space to the next, ultimately heard himself say, "Pull yourself together here! Calm down!"

"He said I was dead! 'You're dead' he says to me ... and mister, my lungs are on fire!! Ahh God, I feel like my heart is gonna explode!!"

"I'll call an ambulance," Monte said, calmly, "Where are you exactly?"

"I tried that ... I called the number in this phone book. I got a recording saying after eight o'clock to call County General! I called them and they said it would be a half hour before they could get a unit out here! They said call the police." His voice dropped to a low, phlegmatic rumble, "I am downtown, if you call this a town ... There is nobody, I mean nobody, around."

"Well-l, ahh, I'll call the police." Monte said.

"Mister ... you sounded like a decent person, so I called you back." He drew and released a deep breath, "I'm out on parole. By law I am not even supposed to be in North Carolina. An' also ... it was a joint I smoked, not a cigarette. They'd know I'm on something. They'd test me, find it in my blood. Besides, God only knows what else he rolled up in there with that pot. I-I would have called the cops myself, but I would end up back at Raleigh ... And you know what?" he said, as he was completely breaking down, "I just think I would really, really rather take the chance on whatever that fool laced this joint with ... running its course!"

In his cheery yellow kitchenette, Monte listened to the man gnashing out his words, "I will not...go back ... to prison!" The voice was of more than physical pain. Monte sat down and stared straight ahead as it went on.

"I was just thumbing down to Florida, mister ... I was just passing through ... I don't know anybody here ... anyway, it's like a ghost town."

The voice succumbed to wheezing, "I-I don't think I can walk for help brother ... My head is pounding, and I'm seeing ... things..."

"You're what?"

"I'm seeing things!! Bugs! Horrible things! I need someone to take me to the hospital! ... My name is Pete. I-I don't have any money, but my God sir if you will come over here and get me I will pay you back some day!"

Monte stared at the stew pot, reeling inwardly at the turn this night had taken. Briefly he considered what Evie might be thinking of all this. And then his thoughts fell on a larger question -- his phone number, in the wallet.

Soon he became aware of his long silence. He began, "My name is Monte ..."

"Monte, I've got to sit down. I am in ... pain. I'm in the phone booth ... in front of the Shell station on ... Ocean Boulevard. About two blocks from the beach."

"I see." Monte said.

"I can't talk ... anymore, Monte. If you can't come ..."

Monte twitched. "I'll be there as soon as I can." he said, and ended the terrible phone call.

He stood up slowly. "Could you hear what he was saying?" he asked Evie, as he crossed himself.

Wide-eyed, she said, "Some of it."

"Is this incredible?"

"Monte, what are you going to do?"

"Well ... I said I was going out there to get him." he said, with a sudden look of realization on his face.

"Oh heavens, Monte." she said. Then, not liking the old-lady sound of that, she added, "Call the sheriff's office, Monte. You don't know what you're getting into!"

"No. No ... no police." Monte said, pointedly, "We can't do that. I said I wouldn't."

"Why, they will probably call the cops on a guy like that first thing after they treat him in the Emergency Room."

"I said I wouldn't call the cops, Evie."

They spent a moment avoiding each other's eyes, each looking at the other's face as it looked away. Finally, Monte cried out, "My God, he could be dying out there! I have to go!"

Evie said, resignedly, "Then I'll go on home. Monte, please call me as soon as you can. And you'd better wear a heavy coat. There's a ferocious wind out tonight."

She was right about that. Raw and penetrating, the wind slammed into Monte from across the empty ocean. Ironically, it seemed to be pushing him back toward his apartment. For just a moment, it stopped him. A full moon disclosed the image of Evie, walking across the lot to her little Saab. "I'll call you." was the last thing he had said to her.

He climbed into his old-smelling station wagon, slid the slickened key into the ignition, and almost too powerfully it hit him that he did not want to do this. Of all the weird, risky things he might do, running this particular errand would surely be dead last. The car fired up on the first try, even though all week it had been slow starting.

The sound of the tires going down the gravel driveway was intensely distressing tonight. He began a spontaneous rambling talk with himself. He hunched over the wheel and drove on, down an access road to a deserted stretch of highway that cut through black, undefined coastal marshland. Other than the moon, his were the only lights shining. In the car there was no heat. The fuse was gone. No music. The town's radio station signed off at sunset. Over and over he replayed the two phone calls in his mind as he moved along. Maybe there had been some clue in what Pete had said.

The more he analyzed the problem, the more fragmented it seemed to become. Strangely, in the darkness and solitude of the car it was still not easy to think. Through all of his mixed feelings, a solid belief began to emerge that the caller's story was true.

A catlike creature dashed out onto the road and crouched down, its reflective eyes locked in the headlights. Monte slammed on brakes and his tires sent a nerve-shattering shriek through the swamp.

As soon as the car had stopped and its frame pitched forward and dropped back, he applied the accelerator and crept forward again. Pausing to collect himself would be wasted effort. He gathered speed and glued his gaze straight ahead.

His mind worked in pictures, and he was often haunted with pictures. Tonight he saw several possible scenarios for the mystery awaiting him, overwhelming Cinemascope mental images that overlapped crazily onto memories of his own past and present. The miles slid away, and he stopped pondering and focused only on driving through the darkness to the resolution.

Small structures looking like stage props appeared in the distance. Then it seemed they were all around. One story cinderblock buildings in hallucinogenic shades of pink and green. He was in town.

The streets were very poorly lit, but he knew where he was going. The gas station was right on the main drag, one of the streets he knew well. He had to make only one turn, and to find it he kept watch for a billboard that demanded, "See Snake Zoo!"

This town may have been prosperous at one time, but recent years had brought a heavy decline in tourism. It had become a tough beach, with plenty of biker bars in evidence as he drove along. Some were padlocked for the winter, but here and there he saw beer lights.

He made the turn onto the Boulevard and slowed down. His destination was closing in on him, and he wanted to be completely aware of his surroundings. This was the tourist district in summertime. Signs screamed: Shark Jaws-Teeth-Skin! Win Fin Hats! ... Zodiac! Z-0-D-I-A-C! The Past Disclosed! The Future Foretold! ... Goofy Golf!-- GO FOR IT!! But only a wind-blown bag moved on the street.

Lights on aluminum poles wavered in wind blasts on every other corner; vast pools of gloom lay between them. Monte saw that beyond the last light was a deep darkness, which would be the park. To the right of it he saw bait shacks and more tourist traps like those up the street. To the left was a gas station. Directly under the last light stood an old enclosed phone booth. He slowed to a crawl half a block away. There was no one standing in the booth. The man had said he would be sitting down in it. The booth's lower half was obscured by a logo panel.

There was still the possibility of a hoax, he thought to himself as he drew closer. Maybe some student had a crush on Evie, and wanted to ruin his date with her. Maybe it was a wild goose chase, an initiation for newcomers by the local hicks. Monte didn't think so, but now he would know, no matter what.

He pulled the door latch of the car, and with the airlock broken the wind came ripping in like a big animal.

Clambering out in the frigid squall, heavy with ambivalence, he slammed the door, and suppressed a childlike whimper. A part of him bore compassion and sensitivity, but not the part that had made this trip. His caring side would have anguished over the fate of the caller, but would have done so at home. It was another side of him that approached the phone booth now, a side that didn't get out much anymore.

A youthful face, clenched into a hideous death mask, greeted him from the floor of the booth. Monte stared impassively down at it for a moment.

He saw no flinching whatsoever in the rigid, drawn-up form. It wasn't a seizure. And it wasn't a joke. Pete was an authentic murder victim.

Pressure rushed to the top of Monte's stomach. He braced himself with both hands against the booth, but could not tear away from the nightmarish sight. There was no need to check for a pulse. Bared teeth and bulging eyes told of the hellish ride this young person had been set up for tonight.

There might have been a few moments to think, to draw a few breaths. Instead, from somewhere within watching distance, perhaps from one of the darkened sheds or a payphone in the park, a seventh digit was dialed. Mad jangling filled the booth above the dead man. Four ... Five ... Finally Monte's quaking hand reached in to answer.

With the scarred receiver pressed against his face, everything fell into place. He heard a voice from long ago say, "Hello Jack ..." and it was as if there had never been any mystery. A single shock wave bolted through his body, but with it passed all the tension. There came an odd calm, as he heard the gravelly voice ...

"Jack ... I want you to take the little guy away with you. That is, unless the sheriff has been summoned."

"No."

"No Sheriff? ... Hmmm. Well fine, then, he's all yours!" said a man insidiously tickled. "Take him to that cozy home place you've set yourself up in ..." The voice trailed off into breath on the line, which mixed with the wind to make the phone's sound a reptilian hiss.

The caller returned, "I thought surely you'd get to sweat out some police tonight! You had a problem with authority, as I recall it. And loyalty, too. But that's okay. It's so good to talk with you, and be close to you again."

"Is that the only reason you pursued me, to make me sweat out the police?" he asked, stepping carefully into the booth, out of the wind.

"No ..." the caller growled, and Jack realized that he was quite possibly in the field of a rifle scope at this moment. The man at the other end of the phone line had kept himself armed continually in the dark days when they had known one another. Apparently his personality was little changed over the years.

"No, Jack, I want only to make you remember ..." he said in a soft voice that shifted instantly into an explosive rage – "You ran out on us!"

With an air of calm, Jack replied, "Well, you must have done some running too, friend."

Jack's eyes closed, and an image of his pleasant apartment came to him. He heard himself slurring, "So ... are you going to shoot me, then?"

"You deserted on White Day!" was the answer of the poisoner. He repeated these words, lathered in hysteria. Jack just leaned backward, heavily against the door.

In silence he squinted up at the moon's face. Then his eyes flicked back down to the twisted figure at his feet.

White Day, they had called it.

He clapped a clammy hand across his face. He had come so far. He had rebuilt, found Christ, and started his life over. Now in one night it had degenerated to this point. Perhaps his own life was to end tonight as well. Staring widely, he thought, what if it doesn't?

He erupted, with, "What do you want of me?"

Looking frantically from one dark window to the next, he listened to the disembodied voice sigh, "Jack ... I had hoped you'd understand."

Changed again to composed, gentle tones, the voice implored, "Look at him, Jack. That's what you missed." How much older he sounded! The poisoner paused to draw a deep rattling breath.

Jack said nothing, but nodded his head. He knew he was visible to this man.

"I don't know when I might visit again," said the poisoner, "But I may. You know, there are so few of us left!"

"I am not part of 'us.'" said Jack, with fear and firmness.

"Well, Jack, you know, there were some survivors, any of whom would see fit to kill you. I still can ... any time. But I am figuring that you are, in fact, still part of us ... We have had a time of fellowship ..."

As he wondered how much more he could take, a dial tone came over the line.

Trembling, he hung up the phone, and slumped back, now totally drained. His head throbbed as he absorbed the reality of this phone booth. Metal and glass, the aftermath of an abomination three years and three thousand miles removed.

If he lived to do nothing else, he had to get out of this phone booth. Yanking the door open, he stepped out and then pulled the body out by its feet. After a frantic struggle he hoisted the dead weight into balance across his shoulders. Like a horror movie hunchback he lurched away, snapping his head from side to side in search of tormentors in the shadows.

Monte loaded the cadaver into his Cargomaster station wagon. Hurrying back to the driver's seat, he got the engine started and sped away, heading back by a different route to the two lane highway. Once on the road, he kept it well below the speed limit, and came to full, obvious stops at stop signs. It would not do to be stopped by any cops on this trip.

Darkness all around, the pictures of memories flooded back uncontrollably.

There he was, in the white hot midday, amid the throngs of the calamitous faithful. His clothes were sweat-soaked white cotton. His hard, muscular arms were stretched out before him. A very youthful black couple faced him. His hands gripped their shoulders.

What if they had known then that the pictures of their faces at that moment were being sealed into his mind for life? The adolescent boy was stoic, fearless. The girl, who perhaps better understood the reality of the situation, was softly crying. Both pairs of eyes were locked onto his as he shifted his gaze back and forth to meet them. He spoke religious clichés. He did not recall now exactly what he told them, but the rest of the memory was vivid as ever.

A scene with hundreds of young people in chaos unfolded in his mind. The wooden pavilion stood as the center of their universe. Inside there hung a sign with the honored quotation, "Those who do not remember the past are condemned to repeat it." From inside the pavilion the grainy public address system broadcast hysteria, thoroughly saturating the multitudes of this wretched, thrown-together encampment in heavy fanatic blather. A sense of barely controlled pandemonium hung in the air around the little group of three. The self-contained three, standing so resolutely, at least had an image of calm.

Though they were barely teenagers, the boy and girl were in love. Even here that happened. He had been the only one they had told of their feelings, because he was their "real friend." They were two of the few here with no close relatives.

As White Day dawned in this isolated tropical settlement, they had drawn together. Strong and silent, they had a last communal together against a backdrop of frantic screams, wailing hymns, distant shots, fussing babies. In quiet dignity they stood stone still as the loudspeaker nattered, "Oh hurry! Hurry!" Standing so still, they had a small feeling of having rebelled.

The real moment of truth came all too soon, however, as one of Jack's comrades came and stood nearby. Jack was one of the law-enforcers of the settlement, after all. If he wanted to minister to these two, fine. But he would have to hurry.

Getting the message, Jack stepped back, turned and picked up a plastic gallon jug of purple liquid.

"This will be like going to sleep." he told them, and the madman on the PA system echoed his words verbatim. Unshaken by the coincidence, he raised the jug to the girl's twitching mouth. He held her attention while she drank under the intensity of his stare.

Intense with what? If he had known then, he didn't anymore. Certainly it was not any sense of devotion to Jones. Certainly it was not that he believed CIA paratroopers were on the way in to kill everyone, as the loudspeaker declared. If he had any real thoughts or beliefs at that time it was strictly coincidental. His was a static existence then.

It did not change for him until the moment his two young admirers, having swallowed his grape-flavored syrup, began to die in his arms. There was no tranquil fade-out to sleep, but instead gasping, gagging convulsions of cyanide poisoning.

Was he really surprised when they began their death throes? The truth was that he had known this was not a drill, and that they were actually going to drink poison today. And yet, he had not thought that much about it. Even with his own death on the agenda, there he was, going through the motions, unseeing, insensate.

As the young couple fell away from him, obviously beyond pain, he slapped his hands on his head as if under arrest. He staggered back. And then there came a blind spot in his memory sequence. He had either closed his eyes, or as he suspected, his open eyes simply would not register the larger scene around him.

After a second or an eternity, his remembered self whirled back into action, spinning around to face his astonished-looking comrade. With one bounding step he reached this man and put all his strength behind one crushing punch to the solar plexus.

He began an incredible run as an unstoppable force. Another man tried to restrain him and received such a badly smashed face for his trouble that all others began stepping back. He reached a fence, vaulted himself over it, and tumbled out into the jungle. Then, from random points, the gunshots began.

A continuous crisscross of rifle fire escorted him out through the underbrush. Barrage after barrage shredded foliage all around, grazing him a couple of times. He gave up all hope of surviving, but kept running. Vines and saplings slashed him as he crawled and ran serpentine.

Surely they would pursue him out here, he remembered thinking. But gradually, over a period of minutes, the shooting tapered off. He became aware that the shots he continued to hear were not aimed for him. He kept running. It would be a long, long time before he would outdistance the loudspeaker, calling, "Hurry mother! Save your child!"

In a slimy low patch, much later, he slipped and fell flat. He remembered lying on his side, wheezing and wondering if this would turn out to be quicksand. For a long time he remained curled up in the cool, black muck, drawing deeper, steadier breaths. Presently, a weird screeching sound struck him, and he raised his head to behold a jungle bird of dazzling colors. It perched without fear a few feet away, and greeted him again. He had escaped.

Though he had not the slightest notion that he could get out alive, here he was! Rolling over in the mud, still afraid to make any noise, he quietly released a soft, fluttering laugh.

He still had to escape the Guyanese jungle, and that would take him many days. It was dark under the tree cover. The air was dank, and great black moist places stretched out across the humus covered ground. He was surrounded by animal sounds, and animal silences.

How similar it had looked to this place at night, he thought, looking out at the Carolina swamp. He let the car behind him pass, and found a spot to pull over. He left the engine running; it wouldn't do for his car to die now. He shut off the lights and put on the parking brake.

After dragging the dead man out on the roadside, he rummaged through his pockets for the paper with the phone numbers on it. The fateful wallet turned up but turned out to be empty. A key, a battered photograph of a girl on a motorcycle, half a roll of breath mints ... and at the bottom of the last pocket, there was a little slip of paper. The only evidence he could eliminate outright, he tucked into his own pocket.

The man who had died so horribly to punish a stranger, received for his burial only a roll into the frigid swamp water. Prayers for his soul were postponed until safer surroundings could be reached. The station wagon quickly departed.

As he neared the turn-off for home he did not slow down, but sped up, and rolled on down the highway. He decided now that he liked the empty road with darkness all around, and did not wish to part with it just yet. With his half-tank of gas he drove on, and did not pull over to fall asleep until nearly sunrise.

At midday the eighteen-wheelers passed frequently. He sat staring at a smashed moth on the windshield, feeling another truck roar by. Sunlight had taken some of the chill out of the car. For a few minutes he had let the radio play, to help his orientation.

South Carolina was a few miles ahead. On this same highway he could reach Florida and the port city where he had reentered the United States. Leaving the country from there would complete a great spiritual cycle, he thought. But he lingered a bit longer. When he sat up and rubbed his face, he started the old car and drove across the median and back north the way he had come.

Monte stepped into a cold living room. The furnace had gone out again. He snarled obscenities.

In the kitchen he turned on the electric stove, and stood waiting for heat. Then he remembered Evie, and picked up the phone.

"Yes, it's me," he began, "I'm all right. I guess it was all a joke ... He was gone when I got there."

"Why, Monte, I really cannot believe this!" she prattled, "I have been trying to reach you all day and there has been no answer!"

"Oh, Evie ... I had unplugged the telephone." he said, "I managed to pick up some kind of head cold or something out in that wind. I've been sleeping."

"Well, did you hear?" she asked, in a tone he was not prepared for.

"Hear what, Evie?"

"Well about the body!" she exclaimed, "The body that hunter found this morning!"

"What hunter?"

"Monte, I don't know who the hunter was, but they found a dead man in the swamp off of the connector, down real close to your place! The sheriff says he suspects foul play! Why, there's not been anything like this around here in years! Or ever! ... I just don't know what we are coming to, Monte."

"I don't either. I surely don't." he said. Then, softly, and with sadness, he spoke her name, "... Evie."

"What?"

"Evie, I really am ... so sorry about what happened to us last night."

"Well, do you think there was any connection between all that and the body they found today, Monte?" she asked.

"Evie, I can't talk now. I feel sick. Very sick. I have a very bad cold," he said, "I must go now."

"But, Monte ... last night ... you were fine."

He cut the call short, hung up, and unplugged the telephone. He went back to standing over the bright orange spiral, feeling its heat streaming up against his face. He did not realize he was weeping until the tear fell onto the burner. It sputtered and danced, then dried away, leaving a tiny smudge of the substance on which empires are built.

THE END

The Golden Sisterhood

(Lives of the Honeybees)

In an open expanse of tall grass, a cubical metal structure stood elevated on stanchions. In the cool predawn silence its windowless gray form gave no clue to the dynamism of the residents who lived within its walls. At this moment, their internal clocks were sounding off all at once -- and they awoke.

Just inside the entrance to this commune, the first loose ranks of sisters were assembling sleepily to await sunrise and a new workday. Twenty of them stood, shifting from side to side, stretching their legs and waking up. One sister clearly had more energy than the rest. Twice she broke out of formation.

She stepped outside onto the terrace to check conditions. It was still totally dark, but the air was brisk and felt great moving across her body. To burn off some nervous tension she went into a whirling dance for a moment, all alone on the dark terrace. Then, she dashed back inside.

Excitement, coupled with an overriding sense of communal purpose was the highest level of happiness attainable for her, and her sisters. But they were able to enjoy this ultimate state for most of their waking hours.

She returned to her place in the row and snuggled close to the sister nearest by. This sister returned the cuddle. Softly pressing their golden bodies together, the two took in the familial smell, and the sense of belonging of which they would never tire.

Their close contact seemed to catch on, as others in the ranks began drawing closer together. First light would begin a time of mostly solitary manual labor in the often hostile outside world. In these last few moments before day began they could revel in awareness of that most important part of their lives -- the family bond. Their mighty family stretched back into the depths of this building. It included Mother, a few hundred fraternal males, and roughly fifty thousand females, all full-blooded sisters.

Again one sister was the most eager, and for the third time this morning she ventured onto the terrace. This was only her second day on food production duty, the community's most important job. It was all she could do to contain herself until the sun appeared.

From the first day that she had been deemed fit for work this one had been burning up the ladder of available positions. First had been housekeeping. No small matter in this place. The nursery came next, in which she and a skeleton crew of sisters her age were responsible for the care, feeding, cleaning, and transport of multiple thousands of infants and juveniles. She graduated next to the vastly more physically demanding position of construction worker. These had been twenty hour shifts of continuous fabrication of new dorms, nursery spaces, and food storage compartments.

Most recently she had held the highly dangerous and tremendously important post of security sister. The commune was under a constant threat of attack by marauding invaders of all kinds, seeking to raid the food stockpiles. On this very terrace, she and the others of the defense force, armed only with their daggers, had distinguished themselves in combat. Many hundreds of her sisters had perished here that the family might endure.

She had no capacity for reflecting on events of the past, though. Her consciousness contained only a zeal for duty so overwhelming it electrified her entire body. Her stocky, hairy, muscle-bound body was a turbine of vitality in service of Mother, and the fruits of Mother's great fertility. The selflessness of her devotion was both absolute and perfect. Her physical health was likewise perfect. But then, it would have to be; the first sign of illness or abnormality was cause for a sister to be stabbed and thrown off the terrace.

As the first faint trace of sunlight stimulated the three tiny eyespots on top of her head, she stiffened slightly. Another couple of minutes and there would be enough light for her primary vision. The terrace filled with sisters now, all in a quivering agony of anticipation. Finally came the moment of release, and they barreled away from home to start work.

She knocked off the first mile of level straightaway in just over a minute. Then came mountains, and she began guiding by landmarks. It became a convoluted course over jagged terrain, but she had every leg of it committed to memory. Only when she reached the ridge overlooking her work site would she stop.

Arriving there and surveying the scene, she was less than impressed. A gaudy jumble of advertisements sprawled out all around, but she knew most of them to be misleading. The sisters had overworked this territory; it was her feeling that it would soon have to be abandoned. Making the best of it, she moved in.

Everywhere was the garish clutter of signage. All promised paradise if she would only stop and come on into this or that nook. Many of the displays were printed to react under ultraviolet and other bands of light that she could see. In a desperate bid for her attention no extravagance was spared. Almost all of it was wasted, however, as she was looking for one specific configuration. She accepted no substitutes.

Locating a turquoise bell shape with five flanges and ultraviolet-reactive swirls, she stopped at last and went in. Unlike so many of these places, this one turned out to be a well-stocked larder, untapped until now. She would clean the place out, but first things first. There was supposed to be a drink waiting for her in the back.

Sure enough, there it was. A brimming goblet of liquid refreshment, placed just for her at the rear of the nook. It was precisely what she craved: a sugary concoction of stimulants designed for maximum work energy. Greedily, she jabbed in her hairy, hollow tongue. In three strong pulls the drink was gone, and she turned immediately to the task at hand.

The product itself came in the form of round gold colored blobs, stuck on an elevated display stand. In this particular unit there were five stands holding maybe thirty blobs each. One at a time she worked them, raking off the globs with the efficient combination of her multi-hooked forearms and the pincer-like parts of her head. As she accumulated a certain amount, she mixed in a little of the sticky compound she carried with her and compressed the doughy results into containers at her sides. The last two stands got a rush job, because there is only so much sunlight in a day.

She shot away and immediately found another likely stopping place. But upon making her entrance, she was frozen by a sense of danger. The nook was already occupied.

A sister sat within, her face covered in food. It was somebody's sister, but judging by the insidious odor, not one of hers. A stand-off ensued between the two inside the cramped enclosure. They would shift slightly back and forth, or to and fro, but neither was going anywhere and it was only a matter of time before one of them attacked.

She would have to attack this interloping alien. This outsider was into the family's food supply! Good food meant for Mother and Mother's new offspring had been violated by the foul mouth of this malodorous invader. With each millisecond of seeing the creature, and with each microbe of its smell, she became more inflamed. She became a bundle of living hate -- and she attacked.

They seized each other, bit down hard, and slashed away with their hooked arms. The deadly daggers came out, and each managed to avoid a concerted thrust from the other. The alien broke away, rolled to the opening, and in a flash fled the nook.

She regained her footing and stood still for a moment, looking out, and taking stock of herself. One eye was punctured. One limb seemed strangely stiff. But there was nothing to require a work delay. Within the minute she was processing food at a new workstation, her life and death battle forgotten.

The workday ran smoothly from then on and took a major turn for the better around midday. She returned from a food run to find that one of her sisters was diagramming the route to an all new food production territory. A vast new range had been discovered, and the way to reach it was being mapped out for all to see, right now, on the commune's main floor.

The diagramming sister wagged her round body from side to side as she stepped out the pattern. Each step, each posture she took, symbolically charted distance and angle from the sun. The location was triangulated perfectly for the observers, who committed the course to memory. It was clearly a far away place, but they wasted no time leaving to seek it out.

Arriving there with the first wave of her siblings, she found it to be a place of dazzling potential. The old territory was finished now. Here the sisters had found an endless, untouched paradise of labor. The food nooks went on beyond the horizon, forever. Her heart soared at seeing the immensity of productive work that she would have here. It began at once.

The following day was one of vigorous, spirited, unceasing toil at the new work site. Like her many sisters, she maintained a pace that strained her functional limits. Eating was on the run, and slacking was unknown.

In a single-minded frenzy she stripped the food globules from the stands and packed them into the holds at her sides. When the weight hit a certain point, her brain switched modes and she began the three-mile rush for home through heavily wooded mountains.

On her seventh return of the day, as she was being unloaded by a young house-sister, there came a great turning point in her life. The house-sister reacted to it first, stopping her work suddenly and walking away. Then, it hit her. At first it was only a faint chemical smell, but it corkscrewed into her consciousness and changed everything there.

A curious mix of powerful emotions washed through her. A triumphant euphoria was combined with a calming, almost tranquilizing effect. Her perception of the light in the commune seemed to change, and the movement of the sisters around her had taken on a floating, slow-motion effect. Her own movements were similar now, as she followed the crowd assembling at the rear of the floor.

Mother was passing by.

Trailing food pieces behind her, she shoved her way past her sisters and a few larger brothers who had left their naps for the event. Despite an increasingly transfixed brain, she made it all the way to the front row. There, for only the second time in her life, she saw her mother.

Almost twice her size and greatly pregnant, Mother slowly passed in procession. She resolutely took a step forward, and the sisters at the front gave way as those at the rear closed in. A cluster of her progeny five rows deep surrounded her at all times. Her enormous abdomen, which barely cleared the floor, was the center of fixation.

It was deeply gratifying for her to see that Mother was in such good condition. The overall aspect was one of great health and proper function. With the inspection happily completed she lapsed along with her siblings into a stupor of adoration which would last until well after Mother had passed out of view. The chemicals emitted from Mother's body ensured that.

The chemicals alone would not have been enough. If Mother had not been in such good shape, she would have been slain on the spot, and shuttled to the terrace for dumping with the next run of garbage. The nursery was full of potential replacements for Mother.

After the encounter she had a bite to eat and slowly returned to a more normal frame of awareness. But it was not entirely the same after that, and never would be again. The intensity of her commitment had been taken to all new highs.

Though no sex life was fated to the sisters, she whirled in exultation as she bounded out into the fresh air and dazzling daylight. New dimensions of identity had opened up for her, a solar heroine in service to her kind.

As it would turn out, the new invigoration brought on by Mother's visit was well timed. For in the next twenty-four hours, the sisters' home came under attack.

She was returning home from a food run when she came upon the scene. A colossal, shaggy monstrosity was towering over the commune building, its giant forearms resting on the roof. It began shaking the structure, as if to break it open. As she bore in to attack the beast, she saw that every available sister was in action. The giant brute was covered in furious soldiers, fighting it to the death!

The monster was hundreds of times her size, but she hesitated not at all. Dagger poised, she hurled herself into its mid section. The outcome was not what she wanted. Its gargantuan form was covered everywhere by a dense jungle of coarse, black, hairy mat. It was much thicker than her entire body, and was completely impenetrable. She had to disentangle herself from it and fall back, as the fiend banged horrifying blows against the roof of her home! Along with teeming thousands of her agitated sisters, she circled the creature now, searching for a point of attack.

Climbing up its body, she came to rest atop one of its shoulders. There, in full view, was the great monstrous face. Blasts of breath and froth surged forth from the mouth. There were small eyes, barely exposed. But between the eyes and the mouth there were large areas without the protective cover. She sprang to the attack!

Hitting home on a perfect spot, she slammed her stiletto into surprisingly tender flesh. Instantly, six other sisters had followed her lead, then another six. Like an explosive earthquake the creature reared up beneath them, shaking hard. She separated from it, but as she did, a wrenching pain tore through her. She could feel that her body had sustained some deep hemorrhage. Falling onto the terrace, she looked up to see the immense black shape retreating, replaced by the light of the sun. She lay very still and soon discovered that, in fact, she was unable to move.

Time passed, and presently two of her sisters appeared, looking down on her. Their decision was not long in coming. She was gently nudged, bumped, and rolled off the ledge, to spiral down into darkness.

On the cool, damp ground below, her once-powerful legs began to fold, and she had a last moment of consciousness. It came not in agony or terror or rage, but in satisfaction, such as only her kind can know. She had been an exemplary asset to the hive.

THE END

DUMPSTER OF THE MIND

In a cramped and stuffy office a woman sat at a surplus teacher's desk. She might have looked a little like a 1950's schoolteacher were she not dragging deeply on a cigarette. The usually cluttered desktop at present held only her overflowing ashtray, her coffee mug, and front and center a cassette tape recorder, quietly rewinding. Behind her on the wall was a poster with a soothing tidewater scene, a framed degree in psychiatry, and a group photo of the staff of this county mental health clinic.

After listening to the tape for the first time this morning, she discovered that the patient speaking on it was not who he had seemed to be up until now. In her eyes he had been suddenly transformed into a mystery man. Two subsequent playings had left her absolutely unsettled and unsure how to proceed with this client. Her next meeting with him was tomorrow, and she was faced with a total reevaluation of his therapy.

The matter discussed by the patient on the tape first arose in one of their sessions two weeks ago. No sooner had he touched on it than he began backpedaling, not wanting to talk about it. Persistent prying would not open him up about this disturbing experience of his distant past, though all signs pointed to it being something of importance to him, at least at the time it occurred. Last week she had been able to extract a promise from him that he would record the details of the incident for her. The cassette had come through in this morning's mail.

The content of the tape was all the more baffling and dismaying in light of the client in question. She thought she knew him after a year of working with him. He was not one of her compulsive liars. He was not delusional, aside from a period at the beginning of treatment when he had gone through delirium tremens. He was a thirty year old white alcoholic who was approaching a year of abstinence and relative stability. He was not the client who occupied the most of her time, or gave her the most gray hair. If anything, this fellow was distinguished by slow and steady progress in his recovery. For some time he had seemed predictable, not one to manifest a jack-in-the-box.

When the tape rewound, she hit the play button again and her gaze drifted onto the old discolored easy chair where he had spent so many hours. She thought back on times when his mood had been boisterous and cocky, but so often with a sidelong glance to her for reassurance. His voice, filling the room again, had that bluster. But his words would crack here and there, on some aggregate that confidence had not yet smoothed out.

"Okay Fran, you asked me to tell you about this experience of mine, omitting no pertinent details. But I should also say that maybe I made too much of it, when I brought it up that last session. Whatever it may have done to my head at the time, it is not something I think about much anymore. Maybe I should never have mentioned it to you at all, Fran.

This was five years ago. I was living at an apartment complex in south Florida. Quail Landings. The place was built back in the Sixties as young adults' apartments and it was still that when I lived there. I think it was designed to have what was supposed to be a futuristic look. All the buildings were modular, with slanting exterior walls and a round, bulging-out Plexiglas window in every foyer. Very sterile looking. Despite the space age styling, Quail Landings was falling apart when I lived there. My friends and I called it Quail Droppings.

This circle of friends represented the second part of the problem – they made up my boozing society. This was right in the middle of my heaviest drinking days. I make no bones or excuses about how we were; I only want to make it clear that I was not having delusions. Drinking was my life back then, but I have never had a prolonged hallucination in my life ..."

Fran stopped the tape and took a pull on her cigarette, and then her coffee. She hauled out her note book on this chap. Some skin-crawlers had happened during DTs in the early going, but no other such distortions that she was aware of. Still, with today's revelations, the note had to be made –

"Possible visual hallucinations five years past."

She hit Play, and the voice, older than its years, resumed.

"... We were at my place every night, ridiculing TV shows, and getting tanked. The TV was the court jester ... and we were the crowned heads. We liked nothing better than making fun of TV shows and commercials, the stuff that some chump in Los Angeles thought to be worthy entertainment for us.

We were a pretty overbearing bunch, but then we were all young. We all had presentable girlfriends. We made enough money from the suckers at the TV shop where we made up the sales force. And we had these god-awful TV shows to make fun of! We were turning our livers into scrapple, but we felt pretty damned superior.

My personal point of pride was being able to outlast the rest of them in whooping and boozing, retire the night as the beloved host, spend a respectable amount of time servicing girlfriend Beth, and still be able to get up the next morning and sell TVs. Looking back, the thing that kills me is how few of their names I remember. I thought we were all so close. But now, aside from Beth, the woman I might have married, I recall Terry something-or-other, who I thought to be my best friend, and a guy whose name was Claude but who actually liked to be called Cloudy. There were maybe six other regulars in the group, and I can't name one of them. Maybe I've tried to put them out of my mind.

The sad thing is -- we were close, in a way. It wasn't like so many co-worker relationships, where you feign friendship but never lower your guard. We may have been a bunch of sloppy drunks, but there was a deeper bond between us. It just turned out not to be strong enough ...

And that leads me to the dumpster, the final piece of the picture.

Across from the balcony of my apartment was a dumpster. I hated it from the day I moved in. It stank like hell; if the wind was not just right, you could forget going out on the terrace. And it was an eyesore like you cannot imagine. I would have had an unobstructed view of an Everglades marsh, but for that gigantic rusting box.

The damned thing looked absolutely ancient. It had seemingly never been painted, and the door on its side was rusted shut.

On that first fatal morning, I was in my cheapest suit and tie, all ready for work. Beth had already left, and as soon as I carried out a load of garbage I would be leaving, too. Nobody else was about. I even remember the early morning light and the coolness of the air as I trudged across the parking lot. My head was a little tight from the night before, but I was sober.

I went up and chucked the bags over the side. Then I stepped back and stood by the guard rail, looking out over the swamp. I was yawning and waking up.

I heard movement inside the dumpster. Quietly I waited, and heard it again. Thinking it to be raccoons or possums, and for some reason curious to see which it was, I put my foot on the big bracket on the side, grabbed the top ledge, and pulled myself up. I looked in, and ... I was shattered by what I saw. There was some kind of person in there.

I had never seen anything like him, not even in movies. He didn't look like he could be alive. But he was moving. Ever so slowly, he was reaching out an arm toward something in the garbage.

I tried telling myself it was some kind of monkey. Someone had thrown their dying pet spider monkey in the dumpster. But that did not stand up to continued observation. It was bigger, or at least longer, than a monkey. It was plainly not a monkey. And with that, something happened to me. I was covered in gooseflesh and I went into some kind of paralysis, maybe temporary shock. My mind was jammed, but my eyes were locked onto whatever it was.

He was so skeletally thin -- like a marionette. The arm was no thicker than a carrot. The fingers were like hideous little twigs. They reached and closed around an old chicken bone.

The body was dark and shiny, like it had been dipped in dirty motor oil. The thing was lying on his side in the sprawl of plastic bags and debris in the dumpster, literally right in front of me.

The head was particularly disturbing to me as it was so inhuman. It resembled the small, flat head of a tree sloth. Honest to God, I don't see how it could have been human judging by the head.

His mouth was wide and lipless and slightly open. I couldn't make out a nose. On this occasion I did not see eyes on the face, though there were places ... where eyes should have been.

It drew the chicken bone toward its mouth with its dead-looking hand. The feeling of revulsion that came over me broke the hold I was under, and I pushed myself backward, off the dumpster. Stumbling backwards, gasping for fresh air and almost retching, I nearly took a bad fall. But I recovered and ran like a crazy man back to my apartment where I locked the door and collapsed on the sofa.

How long I was there on the couch, shaking and talking to myself, I don't know. For that matter I do not know how many minutes I was hanging on the side of the dumpster.

The telephone rang after a while, and it was my boss wanting to know why I wasn't at work. I was pretty short with him, told him I was sick and wasn't coming in, and I hung up. With my hand still on the phone, I thought to call the apartments' resident manager. Instead I went charging down to talk to her in person.

She is another Quail Landings figure whose name escapes me, but her face I can't forget. Round, freckly, chinless. I stood there in her kitchen trying to explain the situation, with her idiot kids sitting there eating Trix and staring at me.

I told her that there was somebody in the dumpster over by my building. No, not dead, but not too healthy looking. No, not a vagrant or scavenger. Somehow at that moment I could not bring myself to describe exactly what I had seen.

She took on the same look of feigned concern that she wore whenever we complained about anything around there, and asked what I wanted her to do about it. I said, for starters, I want you to come out here and take a look at this thing, and then I want you to decide what to do about it. Because it was none of my affair!

She sweetly explained that she was not about to walk across the complex and go poking through a dumpster, that she had to show two apartments that morning and take her kids to school. I tried to make her understand that this was not just some derelict crashed out in the dumpster. I then really tried to describe what I had seen, and maybe I was raising my voice a little. She started kind of guiding me to the door. She said if I thought it was a big enough deal I should call the police. I told her it looked hellish, like an animated corpse. She hissed at me that I was scaring her kids, and literally pushed me out the door.

I could not believe how worthless she was. Her entire function there was just signing up tenants. We had no service or support, and certainly no security at that damned place.

I could see her point about the cops was a good one, though. I should have called them to begin with. I ran back to the apartment and hit 9-11. The dispatcher came on and I tried to explain my problem. There's a strange looking person lying in my dumpster.

Whoever or whatever it was it was a matter for the police, I said. Finally I got the dispatcher to agree. Officers were on the way, she said. I grabbed a beer and sat on the balcony waiting.

Several people came along, flung their garbage into the dumpster, and walked away. There was never a need to look inside. It may have been years since anyone had inspected the interior, despite the fact that the entire container was a mass of rust, and leaked a continuous black stream.

An hour later I called the dispatcher again, and was told a unit was on the way. An hour after that, I made another call, and was told flatly that my situation was not real high on the list of priorities today, but that a unit was on the way. About an hour after that, a squad car pulls into Quail Landings. And I am smashed drunk out of my skull.

Getting downstairs was ... memorable. Wobbling out to meet that cop was sickening.

A young officer at the wheel never got out of the car. His partner came up to meet me with a definite look of displeasure. He was an older man with a gray mustache and graying hair. He was stocky, though, and I would not have wanted to fight him. He identified me as the caller, and asked what the problem was. It was pretty obvious that he was much more interested in my condition.

I launched into a high-speed rap about what I had seen. My descriptions were vivid. He stood there checking me out and hearing all about the shriveled, subhuman creature in the dumpster. He suddenly let out a heavy sigh, looked out into space and said,

"Well . . . that's all over."

He began scribbling on his clipboard. He was in a hostile temperament, no doubt because of the shape I was in. I figured he might haul me away on some public drunkenness charge. Still, I begged him to go to the dumpster and look it over. He just glared at me.

Finally he ordered me to remain by the car, and he walked out to the dumpster. He tried to get the side door open. I yelled, "It's rusted shut!" But he kept struggling with it, making a big racket, shaking the whole container. He gave up on the door and boosted himself up on the side as I had done. My heart pounded as he looked in.

He got down, came back to where I was standing, looked me in the eye with total loathing, and said,

"Nothing but trash."

I had to stand there, humiliated and sickly drunk, as he scratched interminably on the clipboard. I never got a copy of the report. When it seemed he might be through with me, I blurted out that the little man might be hiding underneath the garbage, but he was definitely in there.

The cop's response was to poke his finger on my chest and say he had better not have to come out here again on account of me, and asked if I understood him.

'Yes sir, understood absolutely.'

The proud public servant went off to greater challenges then, while I carried my stomach back upstairs.

I don't recall much about the rest of that afternoon. Around sundown, friends began showing up, including my girlfriend Beth. I wept on Beth's shoulder in front of everybody. This was a first for our group, and the first time I think I had cried under any circumstances in years. It just happened spontaneously when they all came to see me. I can't say I felt a great deal of support from them. The guys looked bewildered, maybe kind of embarrassed. I got the idea that most of them only came because Beth had rallied them to my side.

A sudden death in the family might produce the kind of atmosphere we had around that table that evening. Nobody said anything except me, the devastated one. I knew I was making less and less sense the more I rattled on.

I soon had enough of all this and grabbed my friend Terry by the arm and said, 'Come on.' I took up the kitchen mop and the two of us marched outside.

The sun had almost set by this time. It was even darker at the dumpster, which was shaded by trees, but I was not dissuaded. I walked up, kicked its rusty side three times, and waited. I thought I heard movement inside. Terry said he heard nothing. I gently pulled myself up and looked in. It was half full of garbage, and as always, reeking like nothing else on earth. I cannot imagine what the tenants were discarding in there, but I had to hold my shirt up to my face.

I jabbed the mop handle into the trash again and again, yelling for the bastard to show himself. Terry suggested that maybe it had gotten out and gone away. I tried again to make him understand what I had seen. Whoever or whatever it was, it barely had the strength to pull a chicken bone to its mouth. It would not be scaling the sides of this container and bounding away. It might have worked its way under some of this trash, but if it was in here this morning, it was in here right now.

I could not reach the full contents from where I stood, so I told Terry we needed to climb in to get at all the garbage. He said that would be a one man job. I clambered over the side without hesitation.

I waded knee deep in bagged and unbagged garbage and thrashed it thoroughly. The onset of darkness added to the madness of the scene, but my emotional state made me persistent. The smell was choking me to the point that I knew I would soon have to give up. I yelled out,

'Who could survive in this toxic mess?'

Terry said he couldn't imagine.

I decided to quit, and I clearly remember holding the mop like a lance at my side as I looked up at the evening stars coming out. I had conquered my fear, or so it seemed. For one brief moment, I felt victorious. Then, I started moving toward Terry, and as I stepped I felt something slash my ankle.

I screamed and vaulted over the side, nearly knocking Terry down as he tried to catch me. I yelled out that it had stabbed me. Feeling down to my inner ankle, my fingers slipped on running blood. Cursing my head off, I hobbled across the parking lot and back upstairs.

Beth was mortified that I had managed to cut myself in that cesspool of bacteria. She wasted no time slamming me for the stupidity of climbing in there. I only ran a hot tub of bath water and started stripping off my clothes. The cut, on closer inspection, proved to be a small thing. Beth said 'Emergency Room, now. Tetanus shot.' But I just shut the bathroom door and sat miserably in the tub.

I sat there long enough for a very hot tub of water to turn very cold. When I came out everyone had gone home but Beth -- and Terry. I pulled Beth into my room and shut the door. Soon we were in bed holding each other.

Beth got me talking, and we talked in a whispering way that was soothing to me. But after we had exhausted the topics of deformed, starving hoboes, UFO people, and supernatural demons, the talk turned to whether or not I might be cracking up. Beth was pretty noncommittal about it.

She slept well that night while I battled nightmares. The flat, unnatural head with its lack of a face reared up at me until daylight. Nightmares pursued me long after I had otherwise blocked this episode from my mind.

Terry was still there the next morning, looking well rested. He and Beth had a nice breakfast, and I believe I had a beer.

Beth told me I should be getting ready for work. Stretching the truth only slightly I told them I needed another day to clear my head. In fact, I was staying home from work to meet the garbage truck when it came.

I stood on the balcony and watched Terry and Beth leave in Terry's car. I was not aware they had arrived together the night before. Beth looked up at me as they pulled out. She did not wave goodbye.

I hardly noticed at the time because my thoughts were focused not on Beth, but entirely on the garbage truck. I think I saw that truck as my deliverance. It would remove the contents of the dumpster. It would haul away the emotional downpour that had not lifted from my head in twenty-four hours. My mind would be clear, and my old lifestyle could resume again ... when it was all hauled away. I stayed posted on the terrace so there would be no chance of missing the truck.

My next goal would be arranging for that dumpster to be replaced with a new one located elsewhere in the complex. The view from my terrace would then be perfect - unspoiled marshland, all Spanish moss and cattails, egrets and Florida foliage.

But then there I was, looking out on that reeking, leaking, metal hulk. It seemed more unnaturally ugly on that morning than ever before. I remember looking at it, and thinking – 'It's in there. Live, dead, or whatever, it's in there right now!'

Hours crawled by, and finally the sanitation department showed up in their bright white truck. I ran to meet them.

The driver had already inserted the truck's lift apparatus into the brackets of the dumpster when I got there. He was all set to hoist it up when I pounded on his door. I told him somebody had been lying around in there not long ago, and he had better check it out. He seemed to share none of my excitement or concern about this, but I was able to get him out of the cab and up on the side for a look. I said it was a little fellow, not even four feet tall, and that he might be hiding himself under the garbage.

I thought I saw the driver's eyes fix on something. He slowly look-ed away from the dumpster, and toward me, with a big zany grin on his face. Then he started laughing! Hanging on the side of the dumpster, he let out a loud, derisive laugh that seemed to go on forever. The other guys on the truck wouldn't look at me. They smoked and stared out at the swamp. The driver kept right on laughing until I decided he must be stoned.

He hopped down eventually, and before climbing back in the cab, he clapped me on the shoulder and said,

"You're all right!"

Then the hydraulic lift boosted the dumpster up, up, over the cab, and shook it out thoroughly into the back of the truck. My sense of relief was powerful. The lift came back down again, and the driver backed up to disengage. With another vaguely disturbing laugh and a wave bye-bye, he wheeled about and left Quail Landings.

It was overcast and cool, and I stood there by the dumpster feeling blissfully alone. I no longer cared about the identity or origins of ... the little fellow. Whatever it had been at one time, it was now dead or dying in a garbage truck on its way to a landfill. Suddenly I was looking forward to the day! To close out the episode, to confirm the dumpster was empty, I hoisted myself up on the side and looked in.

There he was, clinging to a flange of metal near the top, not three feet from my face. Its head was moving, slowly craning around to face me. There were no eyes visible in the sockets ... but there it was, looking at me! A huge Florida cockroach was crawling up its greasy back. Then I saw the mouth ease open. The corners of the mouth rose up, and it grinned.

With that, I came totally undone. I launched into an explosive, uncontrollable screaming fit, shaking the side of the dumpster. I kept it up even after the wretched creature let go of its grip, and dropped like dead weight into the muck at the bottom. He slowly curled up into a tight ball in the corner and lay still.

I fell back and began looking around the apartment buildings. A few curtains had been pulled back, and people were looking at me. Now my cries were for help.

It took a while, but a few tenants stepped outside. I pointed at the dumpster, quaking in my shoes.

Two guys about my age sauntered over and got up on the container. They looked down for a few seconds at the object in the corner. One of them tossed a rock at it. He then gave his verdict -- an old discarded toy, probably plastic.

Two other tenants climbed up. Another rock was thrown. They pronounced it to be a dead dog. Long dead, said one.

I blew up and swore that it was alive. My neighbors just looked at me. One witness said,

'It isn't breathing, bud.'

Another said, 'It's dead now, whatever it was.'

A few of them walked away, and I was still making a scene, crying and cursing. I then noticed the amused look on some of their faces. They were looking at my crotch. It seemed I had lost control of my bladder. They drifted off to their homes, smirking.

If I had been shattered by the first encounter I was now utterly pulverized. I was never a strong person. I'm still not. But at that moment especially, I felt spiritually annihilated.

The extent to which I later put those days behind me and carried on with my life is something I am proud of. Not that I don't still carry scars of the past. I think that the fresh start that I later made came from the way that I concluded this whole episode. But before I came to that point, there was one more monumental bender on tequila yet to go. After the last of my neighbors had left, I ran to my apartment and didn't even kick the door closed. I made straight for the liquor cabinet.

Some time after sundown Terry and Beth showed up. Beth had come to pick up her belongings. We had an immediate fight, but not a very long one. Being stinking drunk may increase the desire to fight, but doesn't do much for the ability. Terry had no trouble at all in flooring me.

The next day was a fiery hangover. I just walked from bed to sofa to bathroom and to bed again. No escape. A few times I stood on the terrace and looked out, contemplating on that putrid monstrosity that had pulled down my whole life in the span of forty-eight hours. I went through that hangover thinking about the little fellow, as I had dubbed him. By the time sundown rolled around again, my full-blown hatred for the little fellow was more than I could contain. My plan of action then came together.

I packed my car with my most important possessions. Then I began wadding up sheets of newspaper and phone book pages and popping them into plastic trash bags. As I filled a bag, I would soak it down nicely inside with lighter fluid. I had enough paper and fluid for eight bags.

With no hesitation I left my apartment for the last time and marched to the dumpster, four bulging bags in each hand.

When I reached the dumpster I kicked it three times hard, and was rewarded by that soft, shuffling sound from inside. In went the bags, in went a little paper torch, and down came the lid of the dumpster. I just walked away, back to my car. I could hear the poofing sound of the bags igniting, but I didn't look back until I reached the car.

Pulling out of Quail Droppings for the last time I saw a column of fire pouring out of the dumpster, bouncing the lid up and down. Anything inside was incinerated, vaporized, and removed from the face of the earth. Twenty minutes later I was on 75 North to Atlanta.

I can't say I never gave it a second thought after that. I may have murdered a human being that night. I don't know. I don't dwell on it anymore. I have to keep looking forward. I almost never think about it now.

It's funny, the one thing that does stick in my mind. That cop, who answered my call that day. I described for him in detail what I had seen, and he just said, "That's all over."

His words could be taken a couple of different ways. All over, as in finished, finalized. Or, all over, as in ... everywhere. All over the place.

I don't know. I don't look inside dumpsters anymore. I pitch my garbage and walk away. And I don't think on the past, either. I have a long life yet to go. I can't be looking back ..."

A silent minute later, the tape ran out.

The walls of the office had closed in on Fran, and the air had turned to smoke. She placed the tape player in a desk drawer and locked it. Seizing the few minutes of freedom before her next session, she stepped outside.

Her convertible sat alone in the clinic's parking area. She could put the top down and do a few fast miles out on the highway to clear her mind. Another option was the meditation garden that she had lobbied for and helped install alongside the clinic. She moved out away from the building and paused in a cool wash of breeze. Her eyes fell on something then that held her attention.

Minutes passed before she took another step, and when she did it was not in the direction of the garden or the car. Walking a straight course with a purposeful pace, she headed to the far corner of the parking lot. Under the shade of weeping willow trees, a battered garbage dumpster stood.

THE END

BRICKWORKER

When he awoke that morning his wife had begun removing the bandages that gripped the top of his head like a python. He sat up in his bunk and helped unravel them until soon they formed a dingy pile on the floor.

"How does it look?" he asked. She frowned a bit, and held up the mirror for him to see himself. His forehead was still slightly discolored from medicine. It was swollen and calloused, and the ridges of scars were somewhat dirty-looking.

"'Really think you should be back at work today?" his wife asked, "It hasn't been two weeks."

Keeping an eye on his mirror image, he forced a little smile, gave her a pop on the butt and breezily said, "We got to make those points."

His nose was broken, more than once. It was folded over and lumpy. But he wasn't concentrating on his nose. He gave the mirror a slow turn from full face to semi-profile. It was exhilarating to see that thickened, toughened flesh above his brow. He put his hand on his forehead and said confidently, "I am ready for work today."

He jumped up from the cot, changed suits, and hurried into the next room for his breakfast. There at his place was the news folder and a container of bright blue gelatin. Slurping away with a special zest today, he scarcely looked at the paper.

"Did you see this item?" asked his wife, "... They're thinking of letting women work the Walls."

He looked appalled. "Well I hope you don't ever get that urge, 'cause it's out! No, I won't have that. They let women do whatever they want these days, and you never hear me complain about it. But, no. Working the Walls is a man's job." With flat finality, he added, "That's all there is to it."

"You just can't stand the thought of sharing your glory with a woman. I never said I wanted the job. You just can't have anyone else at your ... preeminent level! I don't see how you can stand to have any peers at all!" -- It was only what she wanted to say. In actuality, she made no response. It would be like trying to argue with a natural force, which was how men of his occupation were described in the newsfolder -- continuously.

A Brickworker's wife is a special life. That was the unofficial slogan of the spouses these days. It had been the headline to the photograph and paragraph of the two of them in the newsfolder one time last year. Some of his celebrity was hers, if only for occasionally posing for photos with him, and the flag, or a logo. Sometimes she wished she could offer the public more than her smiling face, perhaps a glimpse inside her personal feelings. She assembled her colorful booklets and papers and turned away from him saying,

"I can be at the infirmary around six to pick you up."

"All right then," he said jauntily, "I am going to make enough today to pay off that upholstery downstairs. All of it." He winked at her blurry image. She stopped, startled.

"That's going to take an awful lot of ... work!" she said, "Are you up to it? We can always wait on luxuries like that."

"It's no luxury." he said, "Besides, I can do it. I've been itching to get back to the Walls all week." She offered him a worried look, and departed in silence.

He finished his breakfast, the food product with the same taste as yesterday's. The product always had a tangy, sweetener's taste and a deep, vivid color. It was always the same texture -- gelatinous. He ate the cloudy, tepid substance as he did every morning, because it was there in front of him.

He had to hurry now or he would be late for work. He gave a final glance at the sprawl of statistics and cheerful phraseology that was the newsfolder and grabbed his translucent hat.

Although it was only a couple of blocks to his place of employment, he took his car. These streets were not secure anymore, not even in the early morning. Also, he knew anyone who saw his long, handsome sedan glide by would know right away what his position was. The income of a Brickworker was enviable, and judging by the billboards on this street, the prestige of the profession was supreme.

The first sign, visible from his bedroom window, depicted an elderly man and woman whose faces were transfigured with joy. Their eyes had a teary glisten and the woman's spindly fingers were interlocked and clutched against her chest. Above their heads in gold tinted letters ran the line, "Our Grandson is a Brickworker!"

Midway along the next block, and covering most of the windowless wall of a bread bakery, was the Youth Support billboard, which changed from time to time. For the past few months it had hailed the achievement of one of his colleagues. "Y.S. Stand and Cheer!" it said, amid hundreds of tiny stick figures with upraised arms, "P.N.Festen, Quad State Regional #846 -- MAX REPS THIRD QUARTER!!"

Passing this point, the close mix of apartment buildings and industrial installations began to give way to trees. As he topped a gently rising hill, the view was at once dominated by the Building of Walls, and the gigantic high-rise billboard that had been posted for many years alongside the final approach.

Taller by far than any bakery on earth, the colossal sign showed a three quarter view of a man's head, muscled shoulder and upraised arm. The towering face, with eyes that followed the viewer from any angle, had long been part of his life. He looked like he could be a food advertisement -- so healthy and well-fed. His face had more dimples than any living face he had ever seen, though most were on his forehead. The image rested on a base of three-dimensional letters, which read, "BRICKWORKER PRIDE."

The Brickworker slowed now for a checkpoint, was waved through, and entered the circular driveway at the Building of Walls. Turning the car over to the valet, he proceeded briskly up a massive concrete ramp spattered with pebbles. There, at the entrance, he met his "early morning smilers" - a guard with German shepherds. He knew them well and considering they only met once or twice a month, they had developed a deep mutual regard. With a slight bow of respect, the guard pulled the door open wide for him, as he did each working day.

Once inside, it was a monotonous walk down endless corridors of glazed brick. Everywhere, glazed brick. He had to make numerous turns in these unmarked, windowless halls to arrive at his section, yet he never got lost. The tight halls could barely hold more than two people going in opposite directions, and the ceiling was barely more than six feet high.

Glazed brick on the ceiling, glazed brick on the floor. Sometimes it would bother him unless he walked quickly and kept his gaze fixed straight ahead.

At last a series of doors began alternating on either side of the hall. Metallic and painted gray, they were spaced just far enough apart to clear each other when opening. Counting down unmarked doors to the one that was his, never pondering why they were built to open outwards, he was startled to hear one of them fly open and crash back against the wall. A man in a worksuit stepped out into the corridor, turned very slowly, and faced him.

For a moment they stood that way in silence. Although the lighting was dim, he began to feel that there was something wrong with the fellow down the hall. The man began moving toward him with a staggering gait, passing under a light which showed his face to be streaked in blood. This injured Brickworker pitched forward, slumping against the wall, his co-worker too late to catch his fall.

Kneeling by this fallen comrade, he screamed out, "Get out here! Who let this happen?" In an instant three men in plastic aprons dashed out from the doorway.

"Who let this happen?" he roared again, "Why is he out here alone like this?"

"He ... just wandered away ... somehow ..." muttered an aproned man. His counterparts struggled to lift the unconscious worker.

Staring down into the blanching eyes of this glorified clerk, he muttered, "Inconceivable." Then he reached out and lifted up the name plate pinned to the apron, and read the tiny name that was printed there on plastic tape, so easily peeled off. He looked back into the downcast eyes, and then turned, walking on without a word, counting down to his door.

Inside, across a long, partially lighted room stood another group of three men in similar black suits. They began to tie on aprons as he approached. All smiled and exchanged greetings. "So good to have you back." "So nice to be here." Then he flattened their smiles, relating the episode that had just taken place outside.

"...I couldn't believe it, and I was there in the middle of it," he said.

"They're hiring just about anybody these days," sighed one of his group,

"Please don't ever worry about any of us slacking off like that."

"I never would." he said, looking from one man to the next. He folded his arms across his chest and seemed to strike a pose, gazing off toward the dim ceiling, "I am here today ... to realize enough ... to upholster three rooms of my home."

This more than impressed them. They looked upon him with reverence, as if he were the man on the recruiting poster. In fact, there was a resemblance.

He made his way now to the glazed brick wall at the far end of the room, his group following close behind. They carried clipboards with numerous complex charts and forms to be filled in. Odd terms of jargon appeared in small type on their paperwork

He paused before the wall and viewed it silently. Handrails jutted out from the bricks.

If he truly wanted to make the points he had talked about, it would mean working like never before. He grasped the handrails and began slowly drawing deep breaths, swaying his body forward and back. Stray thoughts came to mind. He imagined the honor that would come of today's work. Then, other images came. He remembered friends who had died young working the Walls.

Such negativity often hit him just before work. But he always overcame this weakness, and it never damaged his performance. Willpower was everything. His thinking had to be focused now. Away with thoughts of failure. Thoughts meant nothing on a Card. Only points counted.

Tight grip on the rails, he leaned back and dashed his head against the brick wall with all his might. The blow dissipated into his skull. He pulled up again, shaking his head quickly. The first one was always the worst, he knew. After the first one or two, numbness would start setting in. He thrust his head against the smooth, unyielding brickwork again, feeling blood this time. The protective surface of his calloused forehead had been shattered.

The trio of men stood in close, watching, counting and recording effort. They provided a live evaluation, while video cameras ran silently from various angles. The words they jotted on the forms were clichés of Brickworker performance assessment: "Robust Stroke" -- "Steadfast" -- "Vigorous" -- "Channeled."

He used his arms to thrust and concentrated entirely on keeping his neck muscles stiff. The top of his head was a sprawl of colliding nerve explosions. His brain did not register it all. Mainly he was aware of the ache in his jaw, and the tiny pinpricks of light dancing before his eyes.

He was getting into the rhythm of it now. It would be impossible to stay conscious without rhythm. Crash, and crash again. He would dash himself against the wall until no awareness remained.

Ahhhh, the money he would make.

THE END